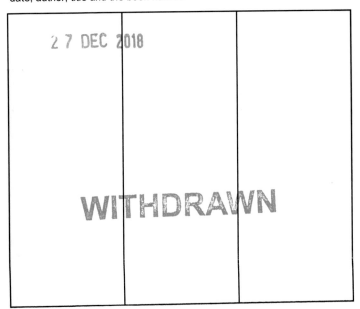

Hidden Instincts

Hidden Instincts

Lisa Renee Jones

Five Star • Waterville, Maine

First Edition
First Printing: November 2004

Set in 11 pt. Plantin by Ramona Watson.

Printed in the United States on permanent paper.

Library of Congress Cataloging-in-Publication Data

Jones, Lisa Renee.
    Hidden instincts / by Lisa Renee Jones.—1st ed.
        p. cm.
    ISBN 1-59414-205-X (hc : alk. paper)
    1. Women lawyers—Fiction.   2. Trials (Rape)—
Fiction.   I. Title.
PS3610.O627H53 2004
    813'.6—dc22   2004043314

To my kids for giving me a reason to
reach for my dreams.

Prologue

A shame to bruise such lovely skin.

Her body lay naked on the bed, her long, blond locks positioned just so around her creamy white shoulders. A bright red mark on her left shoulder caught his attention, frustrating him. He gently positioned a lock of her silky blond hair so it wouldn't show.

Wanting her to look perfect. Stepping back, he surveyed his work. A slow smile turned up the corners of his mouth. Unable to resist, he moved again and ran his gloved finger down her ivory cheek. Pale and still, she was like a china doll displayed for his viewing.

Beautiful.

Calmness was settling inside him now. His job was done. The power his success yielded was surreal, yet so alive it delivered a boost of elation.

She had been a real high. Every step of the way had been a battle of wills. No cries for mercy, no whimpering. As if she sensed the outcome before it happened. As if she knew he didn't believe in mercy. The fight had been invigorating, making him hotter and hotter with every twist and turn of her soft little body. Taking her had been so sweet, so perfect, he'd drawn it out. Slowly he had explored, touching her, moving inside her, soaking in the pure high of owning her.

But in the end, she hadn't been as perfect as he had first expected. She had been a disappointment. Because she had given up. He yanked his hand away from her face, disgust coiling inside, remembering the low churn of anger when she had stilled beneath him. It had turned to rage, pushing him higher and higher, forcing him to squeeze the breath out of that delicate little neck.

The calm followed—so bittersweet in the aftermath.

He had hoped she would be different. But she wasn't. For that he had made her punishment long and painful. Besides, she wasn't the one he really wanted. He knew he was settling. But one day, he would have who he really wanted. She would be his. Balling his fists at his sides, he clenched his teeth. It angered him the way she had left him, going to Washington as if he wasn't important. He'd had no choice, no option, but to try to find a replacement.

Because she was his light, and without her, he was dark.

He let his eyes slowly close. *Come to me, Lindsey.*

Chapter One

Lindsey Paxton had to play nice with the very man who was screwing up her life.

The elevator doors opened on the twentieth floor, his floor, and she stepped out into the corridor. A long hallway greeted her, giving her the unnerving feeling that she was in an Alice in Wonderland clip. As she searched each of the heavy oak doors for the proper address, the hallway seemed to get thinner and smaller. Nervousness was very out of character for her, yet the wrenching in her gut refused to be ignored.

At the very end of the hall, she found his apartment number, and forced herself to take a deep, calming breath. She hadn't realized how apprehensive she was about meeting Mark Reeves, her father's ex-partner, until she was actually standing in front of his door.

Life as she knew it was going to be impacted by whether she could convince him to take control over her father's law firm. She needed him to run the firm so she didn't have to.

Mark had her in a compromising position, and she hated it. She could only pray he was willing to be reasonable. Lindsey reached for the doorbell and gave it a quick jab. Waiting for a response, the seconds seemed to go by like minutes. Feeling impatient, she punched the button again. Seconds ticked by, and still no answer. It would be just her luck to have traveled halfway across the country, and manage to show up at his door when he wasn't home.

She needed him to be here.

Intent on knocking, wrist in position, the door flew open. To her distress, she stumbled forward, her hand reaching for support, and landing on a very hard, very masculine chest. She looked up in shock to find a man, one she presumed to be Mark Reeves, staring down at her. A devilish smile slid onto his full lips as his eyes rolled down to the placement of Lindsey's hand. Embarrassment swept over her as she followed his gaze. Yanking her hand away, she took a step backwards as if she had been slapped.

"I, I'm sorry," she heard herself stammer in a voice that didn't resemble her own.

Mark leaned a shoulder against the door jamb and crossed one booted foot over the other before clasping his arms in front of his T-shirt-clad chest. The casualness of his attire did nothing to lessen his good looks. If anything it enhanced them. He looked like a young James Dean, standing there, oh, so cocky, and masculine.

He was, in her book, a handsome, real life version of the *Devil*.

Had he not abandoned her father's law firm, she would be back in Washington where she belonged. Instead, she was here, in Manhattan, desperate to find a way to get back home.

Mark gave her an assessing gaze. "Did you think holding the buzzer down would assure my attention?" His voice had a lazy quality, but it hinted at amusement. And his eyes were far too alert as they slipped down her body, and seemed to take in each and every detail.

She had carefully dressed in a fitted white, long-sleeved suit. One that was feminine, but not overly revealing. The skirt fell several inches above the knee. It hadn't felt short when she put it on, but the way he looked at her made her reconsider. Her jacket had a zipper straight up the middle, which she left open just enough to be feminine. His eyes assessed the area as if she revealed more than she concealed.

She had the distinct impression he was trying to unnerve her, and she wasn't about to let him think he'd succeeded. Despite the heavy weight of his stare, she managed a cool reply. "I didn't hold the buzzer down. When you didn't respond, I thought it was broken."

He narrowed his eyes at her. "Did you ever consider I might not be home?"

"Actually, no." She waved a hand his direction. "I see you *are* indeed at home."

Looking at his light brown hair, a bit too long for the attorney he was, she assumed he was into nonconformity. "Normal" and "compliant" were not words that would be used to describe Mark Reeves.

His lips lifted in a slight smile. "You're persistent, I'll give you that. I wasn't going to answer the door."

"I don't give up easily." She took a breath. "Not when something is important. I really need to talk to you."

Mark stood watching her for a long moment, seeming to contemplate every crevice of her face and body. She had to will herself not to fidget. She felt naked under his intense scrutiny. He was far more attractive than she had expected. Not that she hadn't seen plenty of good-looking men. There was just something about Mark that really demanded her attention.

After several moments, he said, "Your pictures don't do you justice." His tone was suggestive.

"What?" she asked surprised. "Pictures? You know who I am?"

The amusement in his eyes seemed to brighten. "Do you think I could work for your father for five years and not

11

know about his amazing Lindsey Paxton?"

Lindsey's frown deepened. His tone was a bit sarcastic, and she didn't like it one bit. "I had no idea. He and I . . ." Lindsey stopped short. She mentally shook herself for even starting to explain her relationship with her father. She stiffened her spine. "It doesn't matter," she said, steel in her tone. "I need to speak to you. Can I come inside for a few minutes?"

"I'll save you the trouble of coming in. You can tell your father no." His tone held icy decisiveness, and his eyes were growing cold.

Not a good start. His feelings towards her father were still raw. She needed to get past the front door if she was going to plead her case. Arrogant, controlling men like this one—lord only knew she had worked with plenty of them— had to be handled with care. This was not the time to tell him why she was here. Inside his home where she had more sure ground was the place to lay it on the line.

As of yet Mark hadn't moved from the spot where he was comfortably perched. He either wasn't planning to invite her in or he was going to make her ask. She gave him a direct look that said she was not leaving until she said her piece.

"Mr. Reeves," she started to speak, her tone sharp enough to match his, pausing for effect, which he took advantage of to interrupt.

His tone softened. "Mark is fine." He smiled. A sexy, compelling smile that only served to enhance his strange shift of mood. "I hear 'Mr. Reeves' enough in the courtroom."

Her lips pursed. She found this man far too appealing for her own good. Especially since he was the enemy for all practical purposes. Why, then, was she drawn to him?

"Fine." She paused for a split second. "Mark," she said with sharp enunciation. "My father wouldn't approve of me being here at all. I'm here for my own reasons."

Their eyes locked in an unblinking stare. Curiosity flashed in his deep, dark eyes but quickly disappeared and was replaced by an expressionless mask. "Well then, I guess I should invite you in." There was a taunting edge to his voice. "For some reason I find hearing your reason for visiting an entertaining idea." His lips settled into a mocking smirk.

She bit her bottom lip to quell the sharp response that begged to slip from her mouth. Mark stepped to the inside of the door, and in an exaggerated, gallant wave, motioned for her to enter. She picked up her briefcase and entered the apartment. Lindsey followed Mark down several steps into a sunken living area. Inspecting the room, she hoped for some insight into Mark's character.

The entire front of the living room was filled with curtain-free, ceiling-to-floor windows, allowing for a brilliant view of the towering Manhattan skyline. Lindsey walked to the sleek, contemporary, black leather couch facing the view and sat down.

The apartment screamed money and luxury, and a pampered lifestyle. Not that she faulted him for his choices. There was a time when she had chosen the very same things. Walking away from partnership rights in her father's law firm had been a good decision. No, she didn't have the money she had before, but she had her self worth.

Something she prized far more than material items.

Mark walked to the glossy black bar to her right. "Would you like a drink?"

"No, no thank you." She didn't look at him. Her focus was on the city. "Spectacular view," she commented, unable to help herself. It was hard not to miss a city that beck-oned the senses and stirred the soul.

How had she forgotten the lure of New York?

She could feel his eyes on her. Knew he studied her. "Thanks," he said. "It helps me think."

Lindsey turned and watched him pour himself a whiskey. It was her first opportunity to assess him. He carried him-self in a commanding fashion, moving with confidence. Rounding the bar, he moved in her direction, drink in hand. His jeans fit his strong, muscular legs like a glove while a white T-shirt hugged his well-defined waist and broad shoulders. A light stubble on his square jaw matched his slightly too long, sandy brown hair, giving him a rebel edge. The woman in her couldn't help but notice how his defiant air and good looks made for one hell of a sexy man.

Mark sat down in a large, leather chair across from Lindsey, leaning back in a relaxed fashion. He took a slug of his drink, and then pinned her in a stare. "So, why are you here, Lindsey?"

She sighed, trying to expel tension so it wouldn't be evi-dent in her voice. "You're aware my father has cancer, I as-sume?"

His voice held no emotion, no sign of remorse. "Yes, I know."

"You're the person he was grooming to take over the firm." It was not a question but rather a statement of fact. They both knew it to be true. He was hired to take over the role she had resigned from.

He tilted his head a bit. "Was. Was the person." He paused, and then added, "Actually, he settled for me when you left. You were always his first choice."

She cleared her throat, drawing her spine up stiffly. "I understand what it's like to bump heads with my father.

Your falling-out is understandable."

"So kind of you to understand." His voice was laced with sarcasm.

Lindsey inspected his face for a clue to his mood. His aristocratic bone structure gave him an unapproachable air. She intentionally softened her voice. "I know my father can be difficult." Just talking about her father tended to make her tense, and she hoped it didn't show.

He leaned forward, resting his elbows on his knees, his glass dangling from one hand. "A falling-out is an understatement, Lindsey. Edward is a very difficult man."

Her defensive mechanism flared. Why she felt protective of her father, she couldn't say. "I understand you are as well."

Mark's eyebrows lifted. "What exactly does that mean?"

She smirked ever so slightly. "You have a reputation." In the courtroom he was known as a cobra with a deadly bite if crossed. In his personal life, rumor had it he was an extremely private person who rarely let anyone get close to him.

"From the mouth of your father, no doubt." His voice was colored with acid-like disdain.

"Oh please. I've hardly spoken to my father over the last few years. Your reputation extends far beyond him." And popular vote was correct; he was without a doubt a worthy opponent she would enjoy taking on in the courtroom. Of course, she would never step into a courtroom again, so that would never happen.

He looked at her a long moment. She had no doubt he knew he had a reputation; in fact, he was probably proud of it. "It must extend quite the distance," he said. "Don't you live in Washington?"

"I was in Washington and hope to go back soon." Thus

her visit to him. "I'm on a leave of absence from work due to my father's illness."

"FBI, right?" he asked calling up his memory.

"Right."

"Weren't you here local for a while? In some special crimes unit?"

Lindsey didn't immediately respond. Her eyes drifted to the ground as her mind flashed back to some of the horrific crimes she had investigated. She had gotten out of practicing law to avoid the turbulence and bureaucracy of the legal system. In the process, she had gone from bad to worse. Her criminal law background had made her first pick for criminal investigation, and in a city like New York, that had meant she was in big demand. When the opportunity to transfer to a counter-terrorism division had come about, she had jumped at it.

"Lindsey?"

Lindsey mentally shook herself, desperate to snap out of her own dark thoughts. As she refocused on Mark she realized he was staring at her. Something in his eyes made her stomach flutter. There was a sizzling awareness between them. Something she didn't understand. It laced the air, hidden behind their conversation. She pushed the feeling aside, and said, "Yes, sorry. FBI, then and now. Only now I deal with counter-terrorism. No blood, no bodies, no red tape." She wished she could yank the words back, but they were out before she could stop them. Her feelings about her career were none of his business.

"I take it you saw a lot of violent crime?"

"In the local office, all the time. Local officials called us in as back-up. In this city that was a regular thing."

He studied her a moment, as if he wanted to ask more. Instead he said, "Tell me about this reputation I have."

She raised a brow and shot him a knowing look, thankful for the change of subject. "Your way or the highway." Inwardly she smiled, because despite her disapproving tone, she actually respected his success and the methods he used. He wasn't dishonest or devious, just ruthlessly competitive. He won fair and square, no foul play.

Mark's lips turned up with a confident smile. "I like to win, if that is what you mean. I have little tolerance for obstacles."

"And my father was an obstacle," she stated in a toneless voice. Even as she said the words, they didn't make sense. What obstacle would her father offer that would bother Mark? Her father could be impossible at times, not listening to new thoughts and methods. Mark could have easily gotten tired of walking around his idiosyncrasies.

Lindsey crossed her long legs and watched as Mark's eyes shifted and followed the path from her hem to her shoes, and then back up again. She should have been insulted . . . instead, she found herself warm with awareness. She swallowed. It had been forever since she had wanted a man. Why, now, was she responding to Mark?

"Look, Lindsey." His voice was different now. She could tell he had decided to explain. "His priorities became skewed. At first I thought he was just distracted and would get back on track, but that wasn't the case. Your father lost his business sense. I take my work very seriously. There are things I can deal with and things that I won't tolerate. There are distractions, and there are obstacles. Distractions can offer a needed break, while obstacles impede progress." He paused, looking a bit torn about his next words, before adding, "Your father became an obstacle."

She could understand his point, but it didn't change her position. "He's no longer capable of being an obstacle."

Mark shook his head. "He's still an obstacle I can't overcome, and you know it. He would cause me unwanted grief I'm simply not willing to take. Good thing you're an attorney, Lindsey. He always wanted you to follow in his footsteps and take over for him. Now you can."

"I'm not an attorney any longer," she stated firmly.

"I know you're still licensed to practice law."

She frowned, wondering how he knew that. "Only for convenience," she clarified.

"Are you afraid you've lost your touch?" The words were spoken softly, and were packed with far too much truth.

Lindsey felt the heat of her emotions like a pinch, sharp and quick. She ignored his question. "I don't want the firm. Don't you understand that?"

He gave her a level stare. "Seems you have no options."

Lindsey breathed in and out deeply. "Mr. Reeves . . ." she started to say, but he interrupted her.

"Mark," he corrected.

Her teeth ground together. "Mark, I want you to take over the firm."

He stared at her a long, tense moment, his expression indiscernible. Lindsey wished she could read him. It was damn irritating the way he managed to hide his thoughts, and lord knew she was trying. No wonder he did so well in the courtroom.

He shook his head. "That simply isn't an option."

Lindsey didn't try to hide her irritation. "Why?"

He didn't miss a beat, answering immediately. "I don't need a reason. Let's just say Edward and I disagree on a great many things."

She tried to keep the urgency from her voice. "Such as?"

Mark raised his glass and finished off the contents, setting the glass down on the table. "Clients, staff, you name it. We simply don't agree on anything."

She stiffened, feeling desperation, and hating it. "What if I told you he's given me full control of the firm, and I'm willing to hand it to you?" Lindsey searched his face for a reaction, but he wasn't allowing her to get even an inkling of what lurked beneath his surface.

His reply was short, giving her no hint of what he was thinking. "Why?"

"I don't want it," she insisted. "I have a job I love in another city."

His eyes probed, and silence lingered so long it made her uncomfortable. Then, "Still messed up over the Hudson case, aren't you, Lindsey?" His voice held no taunt, no accusation, just fact.

Just hearing the name Hudson made her skin chill. Her win of a not-guilty verdict had gotten another woman killed. It was the last time she stepped into a courtroom as an attorney. If there was anything this man could do to rattle her, it was this. To bring up her career-ending case was like a walk down nightmare lane.

And he did it in a voice both soft and familiar. Too familiar . . . and his words were far too knowing. Anger swept through her. She didn't like his quick dismissal of her offer nor did she like the way he sized her up and identified her weakness.

Lindsey stood up and walked to the window, looking out across the city, trying to shackle her temper, and regain some semblance of control. She wasn't even sure how to respond to such a remark. She stood there, deep in thought, unable to manage a reply.

"Lindsey?"

Without turning, she answered. "Yes?" She felt, rather than heard him move behind her, but she didn't turn

19

around. He was so close she could feel the warmth of his breath when he spoke. And somehow, as strange as it was, his presence comforted. It defied reason since he brought up the very subject that upset her. Besides, she hardly knew him.

"It wasn't your fault," he said in a voice laced with sincerity.

Her father had said those exact words too many times. "I got him off, and then someone died. He killed again, and it *was* my fault."

She felt his hands on her shoulders. The touch was a surprise, but somehow it felt right. He turned her to face him, and she didn't resist. She stood perfectly still, afraid of what she was feeling. An overpowering urge to lean into him consumed her.

"You did your job."

His words felt almost protective. "A job I no longer want," she said through tight, trembling lips.

He ran his hand through his hair before turning and walking back toward the couch, stopping with his back to her. The odd need to reach for him, to pull him back to her, was overwhelming. He was a virtual stranger, so wanting him near was crazy.

He turned to face her. "Look, Lindsey, I have obligations I've made since leaving the Paxton Group."

"I'll beat any price that's been offered," she said with hope in her voice. "My father has money."

He shook his head. "I don't want your money. The water between me and Edward is far too muddy."

She made a desperate effort at reasoning. "He's not capable of working now. You and I have no history. I don't resemble my father at all."

His eyes narrowed. "No, I don't believe you do, but I still can't come back."

Hugging herself with her arms, Lindsey turned to face the window. The pinching in the back of her eyes told her, that were he to look, there was a glassy desperation reflected there, the depth of which she preferred not to share with Mark. She half expected him to walk up behind her again, but he didn't. And if the disappointed and irrational desire she was feeling was any proof, she might just be losing her mind.

After a few moments of silence, Lindsey felt she had regained her composure enough to turn and face Mark. He hadn't moved from where he stood. Her words were soft and forced. "He has this case. Williams is the name. He believes the guy is innocent. It resembles the Hudson case. A lot." She paused and squeezed her eyes together as she inhaled a steadying breath. Then, forcing herself to look at him, she continued, "I can't handle it," she said shaking her head. "Daddy says he won't trust anyone but me to handle the case, but I just can't do it."

"You could still make the decision to hand it off to one of the staff attorneys," he offered.

Her eyes were hopeful. "Who do you recommend?"

He looked at her a long moment and then shook his head from side to side. "That was one of my issues with Edward, his choice of partners. None of them; I wouldn't recommend a one of them."

She said what was going through her mind, speaking half to herself. "This will be high profile. It could damage the firm if handled wrong."

"Yes." He sighed. "Look, Lindsey, you were good enough then, and you are good enough now." Then he added, "Paxton does have a few decent attorneys, but not for this type of case."

"Don't you understand, I don't want to do it?" Then

through clenched teeth, "Not—this—case."

Somehow, she felt he would understand. He walked towards her, closing the distance between them. Similarities in their histories alone made him know her in ways some never could. He stopped in front of her. Close. Attraction, warm and unnerving, danced between them like a flare gun ready to launch. Lindsey tried to crush this crazy rush she felt from his nearness. Yet . . . she knew he wanted to kiss her, and she wasn't sure if he tried, she would stop him.

Where was the woman who said no so easily and never showed her emotions?

Something about this woman got under his skin. Such a tough exterior, yet so much pain underneath. It made him want to touch her, to hold her. She looked into his eyes: emotions glistening in the form of unshed tears.

And somehow he knew he had been given a unique glimpse beneath her exterior. One very few ever saw.

He reached out and tipped her chin up, knowing he shouldn't touch her, but unable to stop himself. "I bet those green eyes can slice air in the courtroom." His gaze dropped and lingered on her lush lips. So soft, so full, so in need of being kissed. He couldn't remember ever getting his business senses blurred by a woman. Yet here he was, thinking about kissing Lindsey Paxton, daughter of his ex-partner.

A woman who was way too connected to a world he had no intention of ever revisiting.

"That was a long time ago," she said, yet her eyes held a distant look, as if she was remembering.

Mark reached out and playfully tugged at a long blond curl, wrapping it around his finger. Lindsey sucked in a breath, as if shocked. He suspected she wasn't. They both felt this strange tension between them. It begged to be acted on.

He offered her a soft smile, trying to convince himself to leave her alone. "You are very hard-headed. Maybe you do resemble your father in some ways."

Her eyes narrowed, and her response came quickly. "If that's the case, then you resemble him as well."

Mark couldn't hold back his laughter. "You are more interesting than your father ever was."

She took him off guard by offering a desperate plea. "Will you help me, Mark?"

He hesitated. For some crazy reason, he wanted to help her. He didn't have the time nor did he have the inclination to be involved with Paxton, but to be involved with Lindsey had appeal. He shoved aside the irrational thought. "I have commitments."

She reached out and touched his arm. He felt the desperation in her action. "Mark, I can't take this case. I can't. I know you don't know me and have no obligation to help me, but I really, desperately need you."

He couldn't help it. He liked the way that sounded. How many men had she ever said she needed? He would bet none. It fired up the wholly male part of him, and made him want to rise to the challenge. He tried to keep the heat raging inside in check. But his finger moved lightly down her cheek, as if on its own accord. She shut her eyes, and he knew she absorbed his touch, rather than fought it.

He leaned forward, near her ear. "You need me, do you?" he teased.

Lindsey opened her eyes. They stared at each other for long, intense moments packed with a potent undertone. Moments that had nothing to do with business and everything to do with attraction. "Yes, I do," she whispered. "I need you."

A seductive half-smile filled his face. Her lashes fluttered to her cheeks as if she was trying to hide whatever she felt. "I must admit, you're tempting me," he murmured, and his words had nothing to do with Paxton. He wanted to kiss her so damn bad it was killing him. But he couldn't, and he knew it. She was Edward's daughter. And she wanted something from him he couldn't give. With regret, he added, "But I can't go back to the firm."

Lindsey flushed red, taking a step backwards in a swift, jerky motion. "Damn it, my father is in a hospital bed. Do you not have a heart?" she demanded.

Well, hell, things sure went downhill fast. One minute he was near kissing her, the next he was being cursed. And try as he might, he couldn't fight the irritation her words evoked. "According to my reputation, apparently not."

Her cheeks flushed with anger. "You don't feel any responsibility to the firm after so many years?" she demanded.

If only she would be reasonable. He felt the flare of impatience. "My responsibility ended when I left the firm."

Her expression was murderous. "Damn you, Mark Reeves!"

"Yelling isn't going to get you anywhere," he told her, angry that she expected so much, and pissed that he was so damn attracted to her. He should have stopped this in the hallway. "Good thing you didn't use this tactic in the courtroom."

"I'm surprised you have won so many cases, Mark." Her tongue was taking on the sharp quality he had heard so much about at Paxton. She hated to lose a battle. Or so he had heard. "Seems you quit when things get tough."

Mark didn't immediately respond. This was getting

them nowhere fast. He saw no point in being dragged into the heat of the moment. Two people who loved to win engaging in hotheaded verbal sparring would only prove fruitless. No doubt, she would regret her explosion later. It was time to put an end to this.

"I don't believe I am the one who quit." Spoken in a low voice, his words held no anger, just truth. The impact was ten times more forceful.

Lindsey all but physically flinched at the remark. He watched the play of emotions on her face, and knew his comment had hit close to home. Her fists were balled so tightly in her hands that her nails were digging into her skin. "I never wanted to be an attorney in the first place. I only did it for my father." She was being defensive.

He shook his head from side to side, rejecting her words. Denial was killing her. If ever a person needed to face her past, it was Lindsey. Why he wanted to make her see the light, he didn't know. She wasn't his responsibility. Hell, he'd only just met her.

"Wrong," he said firmly. "You were too good to have only done it for your father."

She closed her arms in front of her body, assuming a defensive stance to match her attitude. "You wouldn't know. You weren't even around then, and you don't know me."

He let out a loud sigh. "Wrong again. I've seen your case files. I do know how good you are. And, like it or not, I see the love for battle in your eyes. You like winning, and that's what spooked you. You were afraid your desire to win killed that girl. You got scared, and you simply quit." He wasn't taunting her. He couldn't, even if he wanted to. Somebody needed to make her see the light.

Emotions flashed across her face. As her expression mimicked her pain, he wished he could pull his words back.

Anger flooded her features—another defense mechanism. She shot him a scowling look and exhaled as she clearly reached for control. "You're an ass, Mark Reeves. Daddy was right." Her words were soft; no longer was she yelling, but there was no mistaking the disdain etching her voice.

She turned on her heels, and stomped towards the door. Halfway there, she stopped. He lifted a brow, a silent question. "My briefcase."

Mark went to the couch and grabbed it, holding it up in the air, telling her she had to come get it. He couldn't help teasing her. She had stormed off so indignantly and now she had to face him again. Shoulders back, head held high, she stomped back towards him, and reached for her bag. He moved it just out of her reach. She all but growled at him.

"You give up easily, Lindsey. I'm disappointed." He meant to challenge her with his words. He loved the fire in her eyes.

"I don't give up easily," she spat angrily. "I analyze and choose worthwhile battles. My analysis is that this is not one of them."

Mark's head fell back as his rumble turned into a roar of laughter. "That stung. Very good, Counselor."

"Don't call me that. Give me my bag," she demanded.

He was laughing so hard she managed to take him off guard and snatch the bag from his grip. The minute she had it in her hand, she turned back towards the stairs. As she reached the door, he said, "Maybe you can stay longer next time."

She didn't turn and look at Mark. Instead she opened the door and exited, slamming it shut behind her with a loud bang. He loved her softness, her anger, her spunk, and, yes, her intelligence. The combination was alluring and way too appealing.

He regretted that he would probably never see her again. If things were different, he wouldn't hesitate to explore what was between them.

But they weren't. She was Edward's daughter. Case closed. The problem was, he didn't want it to be. He cursed under his breath, running his index finger across the stubble on his chin. Lindsey had been compelling in her pleas for help, too compelling. Mark remembered reading through the Hudson case when he first joined Paxton. Lindsey had done an exceptional job of handling the case, yet today he'd seen the pain the outcome had caused her.

She felt like she was a killer.

He had several consulting jobs he was committed to. But he wasn't as busy as he had led Lindsey to believe. Consulting was a lot less demanding than hands-on case management. Unable to help himself—his curiosity was piqued—he started walking towards his office. He flipped on the light switch and made a beeline for the computer.

A little research on Hudson, and this new Williams case, couldn't hurt.

Refreshing his memory, he skimmed through some materials about Hudson. He'd maintained his innocence over the years, never faltering in his insistence that he was framed. Even now, serving a life sentence—barely escaping the death penalty—he held true to his story.

Lindsey had defended him on four rape counts, all of which he was acquitted. The crimes had all fit a certain profile. Eerily, the women had all looked like Lindsey: blond, petite, long hair. He couldn't help but think that had to have rattled her a bit. A high profile criminal case was stressful. Add this little tidbit, and it got downright intense.

Reading his notes, he started remembering the details. A mere two weeks after Hudson was released, another woman

27

fitting the same profile as the prior crimes was attacked. But this time she was killed.

Hudson was picked up for the crime and later convicted, but Lindsey had refused to defend him. Mark looked up from his computer screen, pressing his fingers against his strained eyes. He vaguely remembered Edward talking about the circumstances around Lindsey's rapid departure from the legal profession. She had blamed herself. From what he could see of their strained relationship, he figured she blamed her father as well.

Mark flipped through the few articles he could find on Williams. He read a few minutes and then shoved his chair back from his desk, feeling a sickening dread. Something was very wrong. This case was almost identical to the Hudson case. Even the victims looked the same.

Like Lindsey.

Chapter Two

He'd hungered for her return for so long.

And now she was back. Just when he thought he might have to go after her, she had come to him.

His plan had worked. Recreating history had brought her home. A chance to undo her wronged past. A chance to catch him. Because he knew she really wanted him as he wanted her.

No one else had proven smart enough to see through his little game of hide and seek. Only Lindsey. She'd known Hudson was innocent, and she'd figure out the same about Williams.

At times, he was angry for the pain she had caused him. He tried not to think about it. The way she had left him alone had ripped through his very heart. But he'd vowed to push aside the fierceness of his devastation. Because now she was home with him where she belonged.

Oh, how he had missed her attention. Because Lindsey was his soul mate. The woman who knew how to find him, and make him whole.

For now it was enough to watch her, to see her in action. But soon they would be together.

And the darkness he felt would become light.

Lindsey stepped out of the cab onto the cement pavement of the cancer center's parking lot. Seeing her father always made her tense. She had only seen him once since her return, making work-related excuses for her absence when she called him each evening. But after a morning of forced attention on case files, she'd seen a disturbing trend.

Her father had been taking on clients who couldn't pay their bills. For a man who had always been motivated by money, it made no sense.

As she walked through the medical complex, Lindsey wondered if she should tell her father about her meeting with Mark, and decided against it. Bringing up a replacement for Mark seemed an even worse idea. But sometime soon it would have to be discussed. Lindsey found her father sitting in the courtyard, a large elm tree offering him shade.

When he spotted her, a tired smile turned up the corners of his mouth. "Hi, Lindsey. What a surprise. I'm so happy you came."

Lindsey bent down and kissed his cheek. It baffled her, the way he pretended three years of silence between them had never occurred. She forced a half smile to her lips. This place reminded her of her mother's car accident, and her death. Of the bedside prayers for her recovery.

"How do you feel, Daddy?"

As she waited for his answer, she examined him more closely. The cancer treatments were taking a toll. His hair was sparse, and he was too thin. The remaining hair that had seemed only peppered with gray on her last visit now seemed to be a cap of silver. She didn't want to think about him dying. She swallowed hard against the pain and fear. They might not have a good relationship, but facing his death wouldn't be easy. In fact, their strained relationship might make it harder.

She needed to make peace with him. And she would. Soon.

He reached for her hand. "I'm better now that you are here." Not a man who showed affection, his action took her off-guard. Her chest tightened with emotion. What was with the sudden change of temperament? God, was he going to die soon and he just wasn't telling her? Trying to act calm and controlled, she forced light conversation, afraid to hear an answer to the question buzzing through her head. "Aren't you hot out here? Do you want me to roll your chair inside?"

He patted her hand. "No, I asked the nurse to bring me out for some sun." He pointed at a woman who stood several feet away, and a scowl filled his face. "She watches me like I'm a child or something."

Lindsey almost laughed. Here was the Edward Paxton she knew. His bad temperament made her tension ease a bit. "She is just doing her job, Daddy."

He flicked a sneer at the woman and then lifted his gaze to Lindsey. "I know, honey. I just wish she wasn't so damn irritating as she did it." He paused a minute. "Anyway, it's so good to have you back home again."

Lindsey opened her mouth to speak and then clamped it shut again. This wasn't the time to tell him this wasn't her home anymore. "How are the treatments going?"

His response was cranky. "My stomach feels like I swallowed rocks, my head is almost bald, and I am stuck in this damn place. How do you think they are going?" Then he started coughing to the point that he hunched over and seemed to gag.

Lindsey looked towards the nurse in nervous desperation. She hurried towards them. Her father got a glimpse of her movement and pointed at her. "No, I am fine." He coughed again, and scowled at her. The nurse looked at him with a keen eye, and then stepped back to her original spot. Lindsey suspected she had backed off only because his coughing had subsided.

He settled back in his chair. "How are things at the firm, Lindsey?"

"Oh fine, I guess," she said, not up to the conflict of saying otherwise. Not after his little attack. "Ms. Moore hasn't changed a bit. I love her as much as ever."

He smiled softly at the mention of his long-term assistant, surprising Lindsey once again with the play of emotions in his usually cold eyes. "Yes, she loves you too. She's always asking about you. How's everyone else at the office?"

Lindsey leaned her bottom against the tree trunk. "Fine," she said with a shrug. "As far as I can tell. You know I really haven't had time to figure out much of anything."

He nodded and coughed again. "Yes, I suppose that's true."

She cleared her throat. "Daddy, I do have a few questions."

His eyes narrowed. "Ask away." His tone was cautious, contradicting the lightness of his words.

"Tell me why you think Williams is innocent."

He seemed to relax, his shoulders dropping a bit as if he had been holding himself stiff, waiting on her first question. "For one thing, the evidence is circumstantial. In my opinion, our wonderful police force had a lot of public pressure and needed someone to call guilty. He is as much a victim as the murdered girls." He looked at Lindsey's darkened expression and added, "Well, not as much of a victim, of course, considering he's alive and they aren't."

Lindsey nodded and pushed away from the tree, dropping to the grass Indian style, glad she had on slacks. Her expression was thoughtful as she pushed her fingers into the grass beneath her. "But there hasn't been another victim since he was arrested, correct?"

He grimaced. "Oh, come now, Lindsey, surely you don't think that means anything? Any smart person would take the arrest as a sure-fire way to get the heat off. I suspect the real killer moved along to another state or is simply sitting back laughing."

"He? Are you sure it's a he?"

"The police profile says yes." Ticking off items with his fingers, he went on, "White male, mid-twenties, likely to have a middle class background, white collar. Autopsy reports support the profile."

Lindsey took in the information, feeling an odd familiarity to the Hudson case. She sucked in a deep breath and then exhaled before continuing. If her father noticed, he didn't show it. "That said, have you gotten any certain evidence of his innocence?"

"Very little so far, I'm sorry to say. I fell ill just after taking the case." He started to cough again.

Lindsey hated the gruff-sounding cough. Leaning forward on her knees, she patted his back. "Daddy, are you okay?"

"Yes, yes fine. Stop acting like a worrywart. Now, back to Williams. I wouldn't have taken it if I didn't feel he was innocent. Have you reviewed the file?"

Lindsey moved to a squat position, feeling a nervous need to reposition herself, and then leaned back on the heels of her feet. "Not in detail," she said, and quickly thought up an excuse so he wouldn't guess she had been avoiding the case. "I haven't had time. Just wondered what your thoughts were, is all."

He frowned and succinctly reprimanded her. "Don't you

think you need to get the man's defense going?"

Lindsey clamped her jaws together. He had a lot of nerve acting as if she was slouching on a job she didn't even want. Irritated, she blurted out her next question. Speaking without thought wasn't her style. But then she wasn't quite herself, and she knew it. "Why did you part ways with Mark Reeves?"

His eyes darkened. "I don't want to talk about that man. Not now. Not ever."

So much for tact, thought Lindsey. Now he was defensive. "Wouldn't he be far more qualified than me to fill in for you? I haven't practiced law in years."

He shot her a look that would have most people squirming. For Lindsey it was just another one of his ways of intimidation that no longer affected her. "I refuse to have this conversation. Mark Reeves is out of the picture. Next question."

Her response was quick. She wasn't his little yes-girl any longer. "I want to finish with this subject first. Why not ask Mark Reeves to return?"

"Is this why you came here, to stir up a subject better left closed?" he demanded.

"You have a lot of time invested in Mark Reeves," she said, ignoring his question.

He snorted. "Wasted time."

Lindsey eyed him intently. "He's a good man. I need to understand what happened."

He waved a dismissive hand. "How would you know? You don't even know the man."

She sighed. This wasn't going to be pretty, but she might as well get all the ugly out in the open and done with at once. "I've met him, Daddy, and I know people. He is a good guy. Besides, just his reputation alone says he is an honest, hardworking man."

His eyes widened. "What do you mean you have met him?"

She shut her eyes a minute, grasping for patience before continuing, "It really isn't relevant how I met him." She gave him a hard stare. "Make me understand why I am here doing what he should be doing."

His face was pale, and his breathing rapid. "Lindsey, enough. We concluded our relationship on a sour note—the end. If you're such a damn good judge of character, stop blaming yourself for Hudson, and do what you're supposed to do. Run the damn firm."

Lindsey flinched. That was a low blow even for him. Anything to get his way. "I'm not taking over the firm, so I suggest you reconsider your position on Mark."

He crossed his arms in front of his body. "You belong here. Your home is in Manhattan."

She shook her head and pushed to her feet. "My home is in Washington."

He pointed at her, anger making his ears redden. His pale face seemed more chalk-like against their brightness. "You have responsibilities here, and you need to live up to them."

The nurse appeared at his side. Lindsey hadn't even noticed her approach. "Mr. Paxton, it's not good for you to get so upset. I'm afraid we need to break this up. You need your rest."

Not wanting to listen to her father chastise the nurse, she spoke before he could. "Fine, I'll leave." Lindsey touched his shoulder, guilt over upsetting him twisting in her stomach. "Get some rest. I'll check on you tomorrow."

By phone, she thought, and turned and walked away before he could say another word. She couldn't count on her control any longer. Distance. She needed distance from the suffocating pressure she was feeling.

Chapter Three

Her elbow hit the coffee mug, and it plunged into her lap.

Lindsey jumped as the hot liquid splashed her skin and seeped into her dress. "Great! Just great." She reached for a tissue in the top desk drawer. "Figures," she mumbled grumpily. "Bad day, bad luck, bad everything."

She blotted at the moisture on the silky material for a moment and then dropped her elbows to her desk, letting her face fall into her hands. She needed a minute. It had been a long night of no sleep, her thoughts and emotions raw from her argument with her father. Sighing heavily, she yanked more napkins from the drawer and stood up. Tugging at her dress, she lifted the damp cloth away from her skin.

"Need some help?" A deep, masculine voice came from nowhere, it seemed. Lindsey jumped yet again, one hand flying to her chest.

She looked up to find Mark Reeves standing in the doorway. Her eyes went wide at the sight he made. Sexy, powerful, and far too attractive for Lindsey's comfort, he seemed to fill the room with his presence. A warm awareness danced along her nerve endings. This man got to her without even trying.

She had forgotten what it was like to have sex—until now. Mark sent vivid, not-so-pure thoughts, racing through her mind. Just being near him seemed to remind every inch of her body what she had been missing the past few years.

She wasn't immune to her carnal needs. They just hadn't been stimulated.

Until now.

He wore a well-tailored blue suit with a powder blue tie. In some cases, a suit made the man. In this case, the man definitely made the suit. Looking like something out of *GQ* magazine seemed to come natural for him. Only he was flesh and blood and standing in her office. He was like a piece of Godiva chocolate, perfectly wrapped, and she was quite certain, even sweeter unwrapped.

"I take it I pass inspection?" he said, leaning a shoulder against the doorframe. The amusement in his voice made her eyes dart to his face.

A tinge of red filled her cheeks. Busted. Damn. Chewing her bottom lip, she tried to muster up a good response. What was it about this man that made her lose good sense? Trying to sound as normal as possible, she grasped for words but faltered. "Sorry, you look so, so . . ." she paused, wondering why she had forgotten how to use the vocabulary she had spent years of schooling to develop. Where was the cool attorney who could ice an ice princess in the courtroom?

Mark raised an inquiring brow, a challenge twinkling in his eyes.

She cleared her throat. "Different," she finished. "I didn't mean to . . ." She paused again. To, what? Dream about seeing you naked? Admire your hot body? What, Lindsey?

He laughed softly. "I didn't mind."

Any apprehension Mark had felt about coming back through the doors of Paxton was gone the minute he saw Lindsey again.

She needed him.

For some insane reason, that really mattered. There was simply something about her that called out to him. He'd seen the torment in her eyes when he'd watched her from the door. Before she had ever known he was there.

His eyes traveled her body in a slow inspection. Soft white skin peeked out of her black dress in perfect contrast. Even the dark smudges under her eyes couldn't hide the perfection of her complexion. Her dress was simple, but a woman like Lindsey didn't need a lot of frills. The soft material fell over her slim waist, accenting her luscious curves.

She was gorgeous, plain and simple. But her appeal came from inside out. His eyes moved back to her face. She was blushing. How many women, who had seen the things Lindsey had seen, could still blush? A woman with many facets, he thought, and he would love to unfold each and every one of them.

"What are you doing here?" She asked the question and then averted her gaze, feigning all-consuming interest in her already mopped-up dress.

He was making her nervous. "I was invited, remember?" He sauntered towards the middle of the room, watching her, trying to decide how to approach her. She was on edge, ready to attack.

"You declined," she said in a clipped tone. Swiping the tissues at her dress one last time, she tossed them into the trash.

"I've changed my mind," he said as he propped himself on the arm of a chair directly in front of the desk, remaining at eye level with her.

Lindsey's eyes jerked up to his face, her eyes narrowing. "Why?"

He chuckled softly. "You get right to the point, don't you?"

38

She just stared at him with those amazing green eyes. Damn, this woman got to him. He let one brow inch upward. "I thought this is what you wanted?"

Suspicion clouded her gaze. "It was," she agreed reluctantly. "But you made your position abundantly clear. You said you wouldn't come back, period. You don't strike me as a man who changes his mind without good reason."

"I guess that means I have a good reason."

She rested one hand on the desk, palm down, peering at him with intent. "Which is?"

She killed him. In a good way. She practically begged for his help, and now she demanded to know why he offered it. "Does it matter?"

There was a brief silence as she thought about his question. "Yes, I think it might."

He was here for *her*, plain and simple. She wasn't ready to hear that anymore than he was willing to say it. "My reasons are my reasons. You have what you wanted. I'm here, aren't I?"

He was attracted to Lindsey, but his reasons for being here were so much more immense. The shadows and fear he'd seen, still saw, in her eyes, had haunted him for days. She wouldn't like that, he was certain.

Lindsey's eyes narrowed. "Yes, you are, aren't you?" Uneasiness laced her tone. "You were adamant you wouldn't come back to Paxton. Make me understand your change of heart."

Mark was careful to keep his expression blank. Lindsey didn't want to need anyone. But she needed him. He didn't know why he knew this. He just did. He also knew she wouldn't take his help if he made it seem as if he thought she was weak.

Giving her another reason seemed critical. A strategy

formed in his mind. "Okay, if you must know, I care about my reputation. After some thought, I've decided the link between me and this place could hurt my consulting business, if I don't step in and get it under control."

He gave himself a silent pat on the back for giving her such a damn good excuse.

She gave him a measuring stare. "So you're here to protect your reputation?"

"Right."

"So you'll take the firm back?" She seemed skeptical.

He gave her another single, cool nod. "Under certain conditions."

She sat down behind the massive desk, as if she wanted the barrier between them. "Ah." She gave him a knowing look. "I figured there was a catch." Her arms crossed in front of her body as she leaned back in her chair.

Waiting.

He arched a brow. "Did you now?"

He saw a flash of frustration in her eyes. "Mark, please don't play games with me. I can't take games right now."

His eyes softened. He loved hearing her say his name. Everything male in him wanted to grab her and pull her into his arms and tell her everything would work out. But that wasn't what she needed. She needed help getting Paxton back in shape, and she needed help bringing her life back in order. "Here is what I'm willing to offer. I'll come back." He let his words linger in the air for several moments before adding, "But for no longer than six months."

Lindsey started to object, but he held up a staying hand. When he knew she was listening again, he continued, "I will mentor you to take back over the firm. A lot has changed since you were last here. We'll rebuild it together, and most importantly, I'll help you with the Williams case."

She sat up, hands on the edge of her chair, anger in her tone. "I don't want to be mentored for a job I don't even want," she blurted quickly, her face filled with exasperation.

He looked at her, completely unscathed by her declaration. He had expected as much. "Look, Lindsey, if you choose to leave after the six months, that's your choice. This way you'll know what you need to know to pass along the gauntlet. And don't forget, you'll have Williams behind you by then."

"No," she said. No compromise in her tone.

He hated having to put it on the line to her, but she left him no choice. Deep down, he knew he was helping her far more than she would understand until much later. "I'm not coming back to stay, and I'm not coming back without you being here. You really don't have a lot of options."

"I can't do it," she stated with a hint of desperation in her voice. "My job is waiting for me in Washington."

His voice was firm and unmoving. "You have to, Lindsey."

She balled her hands up at her sides as she pushed to her feet, and glared at him, desperation in her voice. "Why are you doing this?"

It was hard pushing her, knowing she hated him at this very moment. But he knew it was for the best. "You asked for my help. I'm offering it."

"Help?" she demanded. "You call this help?" She glared. "I have a job to get back to. I asked you to take back your old responsibilities, minus me. This," she waved around the room, "is yours, not mine. Take it back."

He kept his expression blank. She spoke like the firm was a material item to simply give or take. It was so much more complex. "I can't do that," he said softly.

41

Her hands flattened on the desk, her voice a low, angry promise. "I'm not staying. You can have this damn place. There is no use mentoring me because I'm not staying. Mentor someone else." Her voice softened. "Please."

Their eyes locked. There was a long, tense silence. "You and I both know Edward wouldn't allow me to take the firm without you."

"I'll convince him."

"I've got a news flash for you, Lindsey. I'm walking away from consulting work to do this. My being here is no small request. I am not the enemy." He paused, and then added, "I'm a friend."

Her lips pursed. "Yeah, right. Friend?" She crossed her arms in front of her body, and turned her face away from him. "I don't think so."

Mark pushed to his feet and covered the distance between them as she backed up against the credenza. He stopped directly in front of her, intentionally not giving her room to escape. She looked up at him, surprise in her eyes. She didn't move. He didn't move. They were so close that their legs almost touched.

He could smell the soft scent of her perfume. He could taste the torment eating at her. And he could feel the connection between them . . . and damn, it was hard to push her, when he just wanted to comfort. But he had no choice. "Do we have a deal, Lindsey?" he asked in a quiet, steady voice.

She closed her eyes. "What choice do I have?"

He grabbed her chin gently in his fingers, making her eyes dart open. "You have a choice. I can walk out of the door and never see you again." He paused to give her a minute to digest his words. Part of him wanted her to tell him to do just that. He was in uncharted territory. The very fact that he was here, unable to fight the urge to help her, was enough to make him want to cut and run. Another part of him knew he couldn't leave without seeing this through. "It's your choice, Lindsey. Do I stay, or do I go?"

She swallowed. "Can I have some time to consider?"

He couldn't help but smile. "What do you think?"

She sighed. "I figured as much." She diverted her eyes for a second and then looked back up. "Stay."

He smiled and released her chin. "So be it, then." He looked at his watch. "Unfortunately, I have to go see a client." He sighed and returned his gaze to her face. His hand went to her cheek, his fingers caressing her perfect skin. He heard her intake of breath with satisfaction. She was not unaffected by his touch.

Fighting the urge to see just how far he could push, he forced himself to take a step backwards. He turned and started walking towards the door. He turned to face her before leaving. "Line up a partners meeting for Wednesday at five-thirty." He wanted a plan to get close to her, to force her to start dealing with the past and the future. "I'd like to meet with you at five today to review how we will split things up."

Taking orders from him was eating her up. He bit back a smile as she nodded and gave him a terse acceptance. "One last thing," he added. "I want you to first chair the Williams case." She started to protest, but he held up a staying hand. "It's non-negotiable, Lindsey."

And then he turned and left her there, staring after him, and no doubt cursing his very existence.

In silence, they sat side by side at the conference table in Mark's office. He seemed to have slipped back into his old environment with comfort.

Lindsey watched as he tugged at the top button of his shirt and loosened his tie as if he couldn't stand it a second longer. Inwardly, she moaned, pulling her bottom lip into her teeth. The man was simply gorgeous. And smart. It was a damnable combination that seemed to wreak havoc on her desire to hate him.

Studying him, she noted the tightness of his jaw, now covered with light stubble. His hair looked as if he had been running his hands through it, perhaps from frustration. Somehow that only served to enhance his appeal. It also made her wonder what he'd found on his first day back to Paxton.

"So," she said stretching out the word. "Have you had time to make any assessments today?"

He leaned back in his chair, letting out a heavy sigh. The look on his face said he didn't want to tell her what was on his mind. He hesitated, and then, "The books are a wreck, and I still don't know what Edward thought he was proving by choosing some of these cases."

She shook her head and swallowed. "What exactly is the problem?" She was almost afraid to hear the answer.

A muscle in his jaw jumped. "Over the last few years, Edward started taking on cases for people who had zero financial means. It has gotten worse, not better, since I have been gone."

Her eyes went to the space above his shoulder as she thought out loud. "I noticed the oddity of the cases." Then, refocusing on Mark, "I was hoping you could offer some insight. Daddy was always about money."

"He took on a new philosophy this past year. Work for free is what it basically boils down to." The pure frustration in his voice was enough to set her on edge. He started rolling up his sleeves. Like he needed to get ready for some

44

serious work. "Let's set the subject of the books aside for now. Tonight we need to focus on the Williams case. He happens to be one of the few clients who actually can pay his bills."

A puzzled expression filled her face. "Yes, he does, which is odd considering the rest of the caseload."

He agreed. "Right. A professor at NYU who comes from a wealthy family."

"I can't figure out how he fits in with the other cases." She frowned. "If I understood the logic of the case choices, I might feel a little better."

Mark seemed to want to say something—she could see it in his eyes—but then he withdrew, as if he had talked himself out of whatever it was. She frowned, wondering what he was thinking and not saying.

"I reviewed the file today and nothing has been done," he said. "We don't have a choice but to file for a continuance."

Even a quick glimpse at the file had told her as much.

"I already have the papers being drafted."

He didn't acknowledge her words. Instead, he gave her a level stare and cleared his throat. "I've changed my mind. I want you to second chair."

"Wow," she said putting on the brakes. "Why the sudden change of heart?" She felt the pinch of indignation. "You think I can't handle it now?"

Surprise filled his face. "I thought you would be happy."

She waved off his words. "That's not the point." She jabbed her pen against the pad of paper in front of her as her agitation grew. "There's something you're not saying, and I don't like it. Not one bit. Are you afraid I'll collapse during trial or something ridiculous like that?" She didn't give him time to respond. "I won't, you know."

He shook his head in disbelief. "I do not think you will collapse in trial. Damn, woman, what does it take to please you?"

Lindsey grimaced, not liking the idea of being considered incompetent one bit. No, she didn't want to go back to court, but she wanted to fail even less. "Look, after you dropped your little bomb on me, and then ran out the door unwilling to face me, I might add, I spent all afternoon getting myself prepared to face this damn case. So don't go turning back the clock now."

He laughed in disbelief. "First of all, I did not run off. I had a meeting."

She smirked and crossed her arms in front of her body. "Uh-huh."

"To be clear," he said, his voice now more intense, his eyes direct as they held hers, "I trust your abilities in and out of the courtroom." He let the words linger a moment. "Probably more than you trust yourself."

"You have a terrible way of showing it."

Mark opened the file that sat in front of him. He spread five pictures out on the table, and leaned back in his chair. Watching her. "What do these girls have in common?"

The dark reality of the images made her swallow hard. She'd seen plenty of crime scene photos, but these brought back memories she preferred to avoid. "They're dead," she said flatly, her eyes lifting to his. She'd seen enough.

"What else?" Mark shot back.

She swallowed, and forced herself to look down. "They all fit a profile, of course."

"What profile, Lindsey?" he pressed.

"I've seen the file," she said in a clipped tone, giving him a hard stare. "I know these are the women Williams is accused of killing."

"They fit another profile too, though, don't they?" He was challenging her. Waiting for her reaction.

She glanced up at him and then back down at the photos, her stomach churning with realization. Her response was a harsh whisper. "They fit the Hudson profile." She dropped her pencil and ran her now-damp palms down her thighs.

His eyes narrowed. "We both know the other obvious factor." It was a question, but not really. They both knew the answer.

He wanted her to admit it out loud, and she knew it. Why, she wasn't sure. She stiffened, feeling the tension of the moment. And frustration, even a hint of anger. She didn't want to deal with this, but he was making her. "You think I don't know they all look like me?"

He leaned forward. "Then you understand why I am going to first chair."

She snapped, heat filling her gaze. "Stop trying to protect me. I am perfectly capable of handling this damn case."

Lindsey was, if nothing else, unpredictable.

Just this morning, she had all but refused to first chair the Williams case. She'd been ready to choke him when he had made his announcement. He'd seen it in her eyes. Who would have figured she would now be accusing him of being protective?

"You can scream, throw things, do what you will, but I am not—I repeat, I am not—letting you first chair." His eyes dared her to argue. She wanted to, too. After a long, tension-filled moment, he asked, "How well have you read the file?"

The question took the wind out of her sails. The truth was, and they both knew it, she hadn't even been able to bring herself to read it cover to cover. "I started to . . ." her voice trailed off.

"But you didn't." He let the words linger in the air. "I'll first chair. You can ease back into the courtroom, and deal with the implications of the past with less pressure. It's for the best."

"Just this morning—"

He cut her off. "I hadn't seen the pictures of those women." He reached for the photos, ready to get them out of sight. The way they resembled Lindsey was downright scary. "Now, I have. Now you second chair."

A knock sounded. Ms. Moore, her father's assistant, peaked around the door. "Sandwiches are here," she said in her normal, cheerful voice.

"Come on in, Maggie," Mark said, waving her forward as a boyish grin filled his face.

Mark had a soft spot for Maggie. She was like everyone's grandmother—a sweet, older woman with a nurturing tendency. Near sixty, she needed to retire, but refused. She liked being busy. Even seemed undaunted by Edward's constant harsh ways.

Maggie was smiling at Mark as she rushed into the room. "I have your favorite, Mark," she said smiling. "And I remembered: no mayo, extra mustard." Then she held up a bag of cookies. "And I got oatmeal raisin cookies. I know how you love them."

"Thanks, Maggie," he said. "You are always so good to me." She'd been one of the few bright spots at Paxton.

Maggie turned her attention on Lindsey. "I remembered what you liked, too. Egg salad on wheat."

Lindsey blinked. "I'm impressed. It's been years."

Maggie patted Lindsey on the back and winked. "I had to have a good memory to handle all the things your father

48

threw at me, honey. Besides, how could I forget my little Lindsey? Seems like yesterday you were a little one running around here with your Barbies."

Lindsey laughed. "Yes, well that was a long time ago. I was always at your desk bugging you though, wasn't I?"

Maggie buzzed around the table like a busybody, giving them each napkins. "Yes," she sighed. "I miss those days. You both," she waved a finger between Mark and Lindsey, "work far too hard, but I will shut up because neither of you will listen anyway." She sighed with regret as Mark and Lindsey exchanged an amused glance. "You both have tea to drink. I'll be leaving now, unless there is anything else either of you need?"

Mark chuckled. "I think we are fine now. Thanks again, Maggie. Have a nice evening."

"Okay, don't stay too late. See you both in the morning." Maggie started towards the door, but turned back. "It's nice to have you both back."

Lindsey smiled. "Thanks, Maggie," she said, with a hint of emotion in her voice. "Goodnight."

Maggie waved and left the room, humming as she pulled the door shut. Lindsey stared at Mark as he opened his mouth to bite into his sandwich. He stopped midway to his mouth and set his sandwich down on the wrapper. "What?" he asked as a puzzled look settled on his face.

She motioned with her head towards the door. "What was that?"

"What was what?" he asked holding up his hands in question.

"Maggie?" she questioned in astonishment. "Daddy never called her Maggie."

He grunted. "I'm not Edward. Never was, never will be."

"You were quite nice to her," she commented as she started opening the paper around her sandwich.

"And that surprises you?"

Guilt registered in her expression. "I'm sorry. That was bad of me. Your reputation says you like to win, not that you like to be mean while you do it."

"I guess you have a lot left to learn about me," he said, only half-kidding. Part of him was bothered that she would have thought him capable of being anything but nice to Maggie.

A few minutes passed as they busied themselves eating. Lindsey scribbled some notes as Mark thumbed through the file. "It really is amazing how she remembered what I always ordered so far back," Lindsey commented.

He gave her a half-smile "That's Maggie for you."

"Yeah, I guess so. She is one of the few things about this place I missed."

He rested his elbows on the table and watched her a long moment. "I bet there is more than you realize."

She glanced at him. "I doubt it." Changing the subject, she said, "We were talking about the Williams case. There has been no research whatsoever completed to date that I could see. Is that your take?"

Mark shook his head in agreement as he took the last bite of his sandwich and crumpled up his wrapper. He swiveled in his chair and shot the balled-up paper into the trashcan. Swoosh, it went into the can. "Yes," he said, about his success.

Lindsey rolled her eyes, and laughed. "King of trashcan basketball. Just where do your skills stop?"

He smiled, seeing an opportunity and taking it. "I'm good at lots of things." He leaned in a little closer to her, a sudden awareness between them. "Spend some time with me and you might be surprised what you discover."

She didn't seem to know how to respond. They sat here, attraction lacing the air, eyes locked, until she averted her gaze. "I was thinking I would do some field investigating tomorrow. We don't have time for someone else to do it. I'll hit the streets bright and early."

"*We'll* hit the streets," he said, drawing her gaze. "You aren't going without me. This is a murder investigation, remember?"

"I don't need a bodyguard," she said with irritation lacing her words. "I make my living protecting others."

He held up a finger. "Did you ever go out into the field alone while you were investigating a violent crime?"

She fidgeted in her chair. "Well . . ."

"Exactly. I'll pick you up in the morning. Write down your address for me. It's that or I'm hiring a buddy of mine to do the field work."

"We don't have time for someone else to get up and running."

Mark's tone was confident. "Royce Walker doesn't need time to get up and running."

"Royce Walker, as in the state security liaison?"

Mark grinned. "Yep, the one and only."

"I still think I can do a better job in less time."

He shrugged. "Then you will have to put up with me tagging along."

Lindsey grimaced but wrote down her address and phone number. "If you get lost, call me."

He gave her a you're-kidding look. "I won't get lost."

"Of course not. Not Mark Reeves," she mocked.

Mark ignored her. "Nine o'clock."

She nodded her agreement. "Lose the suit," she said pointing to his jacket.

Mark stood up and started to take off his jacket.

"Stop!" Lindsey shouted. "What are you doing?"

"You said lose the suit," he said, playfully dumbfounded.

"You knew what I meant," she insisted. "Don't wear a suit for the field work."

He frowned. "You sure? I'll be happy to lose it now." Amusement danced in his eyes.

She harrumphed. He rubbed his hand on his jaw. "What does that mean?"

Her brows went up. "Nothing." She paused a second. "Not really. I just didn't see you having a sense of humor, that's all."

He wasn't sure he liked that. In fact, he knew he didn't. He sat back down. "Let's back up here. Your early assessment didn't seem very flattering. Do you mind telling me exactly what you thought of me?"

She studied his sexy brown eyes, wondering what parts of her first impression she should share. "You know they call you a cobra in the courtroom. I thought they were right."

"I see." His words were long and drawn out. "A cobra."

He picked up the Williams file and started flipping through it, not one bit pleased. He'd put his life on hold to help a woman who thought he was a damn snake.

Lindsey frowned. "Mark?"

"Yes?" he said, without looking up from the file.

She reached out and touched his arm. Heat shot up his arm. His eyes lifted to hers. He was losing his freaking mind. No woman impacted him like this. He looked at her lips. Kissing her was on his mind.

"I was only teasing you about the cobra stuff, just because of the reputation you have. I admire you for your achievements. I told my father he was wrong about you."

He wasn't sure what to do with this new information. She'd talked to Edward about him. "I turned down your offer. Why would you defend me?"

She gave him a rueful smile. "Believe it or not, aside from the Hudson mess, I have always been a good judge of character. Just because you ticked me off doesn't mean you're a bad person. That's just one of the many differences between my father and me. He can't separate the two. Besides," she added, "if there's a cobra around, I want him on my side." She playfully poked his arm.

He smiled. Then, before he could respond, she added, suddenly serious, "I do appreciate you coming back, even if it isn't exactly on the terms I had hoped for."

"So," Mark said in a slow, playful voice. "How much do you appreciate it?"

She eyed him. "What?"

"How much do you appreciate me being here?" He grinned.

She rolled her eyes. "Why do I know you are being bad, Mark Reeves?"

He laughed. "I'm good when I'm bad, baby."

She gaped at him. "You're out of control."

A glimmer of heat sparked in his eye. "Hmm, I am. I think you should do something about it."

She shook her head. "That," she said sharply, "would be dangerous."

"I thought you liked danger, being FBI and all."

She glowered at him. "Will you be serious?" she said, abruptly changing the subject. "Please. Now, I want to know how bad the books really are."

He longed to pull her back into her playful mood. But it was too late. With a brief moment of regret, he answered.

"I do my job well. It will be fine."

"That bad?" she asked apprehensively.

He sighed. "It could be worse."

"Oh," she said flatly. "*That* bad."

"Don't worry, it will be fine." And it would be. He was going to make sure of it.

Irritation flickered in her eyes. "Mark, don't protect me. I hate being coddled. Tell me how bad it is."

"I'm not protecting you. I'm simply not done with my analysis," he countered.

Her eyes narrowed. "You are too. You've said as much."

He laughed. There was no fooling Lindsey. "I'm sure. Look, let's make a deal."

"Another one?" she asked incredulously.

He slanted her a plaintive look. "I never make a promise I can't keep, so let's compromise."

She jumped in. "I don't like the sound of that."

"Let's try this again," he said with forced patience. "Where I come from, a compromise is better than a lack of one. Should I continue?" He crossed his arms in front of his body and waited for her answer.

She made a face. "Fine."

"When it comes to business matters, I'll tell you the cold, hard facts. However, I can't and won't promise not to be protective in matters involving rapists and murderers. It's just not in my chemical makeup."

"Fine. I'm too tired to argue." He tone was tense. "Do you have the Hudson file?"

"Yes. Why?"

"I just want to look through it tonight," she said quietly.

He studied her expression. "The similarities are bothering you?"

"The marks on the girls' arms." Lindsey grabbed the file

and pulled the pictures out again. She held up several pictures, one at a time, and pointed to each girl's arms. "The markings on their skin, the similarities in the girls' appearance . . ." she paused deeply in thought, "I don't know. It just bothers me."

It bothered him too. The way Lindsey resembled the victims bugged the hell out of him. "Yeah, I have to admit something doesn't feel right. I did some research after you left my apartment the other day. There are too many parallels in the two cases for comfort."

Her face was filled with concern. "Yeah, I know. I think we should go interview Williams before we do anything else tomorrow."

"A good plan," Mark said.

She glanced up at him. "I scheduled the partners' meeting. Everyone had a lot of questions, but I put them off for the most part. I figured you might have your own approach to things."

Mark leaned back in his chair, his hands resting on the arms. "Yes, actually I do."

Exhausted both mentally and physically, Lindsey stepped in the front door of her one-bedroom apartment and wearily discarded her belongings on the foyer table. She started walking towards the living room when a sudden wave of unease stopped her dead in her tracks. She turned and walked to the door and flipped the locks into place. She pushed to her tiptoes and looked through the peephole.

Nothing.

An inescapable shiver slid down her body. This damn case was messing with her head. She turned away from the door, determined to shake whatever was rattling her. She caught a glimpse of herself in the hall mirror, and paused.

Leaning forward, she examined her image. She exhaled heavily. Okay, so it was a little creepy to look so like the victims. With Hudson, she was so certain of his innocence she had never given it much thought. She should have, of course, because his innocence meant the responsible person was still free. But that was rape, and this was murder. That changed things.

What have you gotten yourself into, Lindsey?

She shook her head and turned away from the mirror, refusing to spend one more moment acting like a frightened kitten. A few minutes later, with sweats and a T-shirt replacing her business attire, she sat down on her bed with her briefcase in hand.

Scouring the Hudson and Williams files for some semblance of answers took hours. She'd been so certain Hudson was innocent, and looking through his file those old gut feelings about him came roaring back to life. Tunneling her fingers into her hair, she made a frustrated sound.

He couldn't be innocent. It was crazy to even think such a thing.

Determined to handle the Williams case without flaw, she began scanning his file. Thus far, there were four dead women, all of whom were students at the college where Williams taught. The evidence was all circumstantial. She frowned. Williams could be a fall guy, as her father had suggested.

Or he could be a cold-blooded killer.

And he was a common denominator. He'd tutored each and every one of them at some point. In two cases, the girls were killed on nights he had met with them. Sounded like guilt. Yet there was no physical evidence.

Reaching for the Hudson file, she laid it on top of the

Williams file and flipped it open. Hudson's situation had been similar in many ways. He managed a restaurant near the NYU campus, a hotspot for late nights. The victims had all been visitors the night of their attacks. Yet not one could identify Hudson. Their attacker had worn a mask. But, the police needed a conviction, and he had been a common denominator with no alibi.

Lindsey had all but chewed her pencil in half. "Damn, I am far too tense," she murmured, dropping the pencil on the bed as she wrapped her arms around her knees.

Shoving her files back into her briefcase, she decided to attempt to sleep. It was, after all, two in the morning. Her mind was racing with many uncontrollable and unsettling thoughts. She wondered if Mark was awake. The urge to call him was strong. Which was crazy. Why would she call Mark?

Chapter Four

Lindsey sat straight up in the bed, hand going to her chest.

A loud noise filled the air, penetrating her sleep-fogged mind. Her heart was beating a million times too fast, and her T-shirt was damp. She eyed the nightstand, and let out a breath.

The alarm.

She reached over and turned it off, as images began to form in her mind. As she shoved her hand through her bed-ruffled hair, she felt frustration build. Even in her sleep, she was battling the past. She'd been having a nightmare. A man was chasing her. She tried to make out his features but couldn't. Running . . . she'd been running from him.

Desperate to get to Mark.

Mark? Why was Mark in the equation? It was strange. She struggled to bring back the images, but her memory failed. Her mind was a blur where she wanted it to be vivid. But the feeling of fear, of being in danger, was as clear as the new day now here. She shoved the blankets aside and eyed the clock, determined to shake the darkness of her feelings.

Coffee. She needed coffee. It was her first-line cure for most things. If it didn't work, she went for the sure fix. Chocolate. Once the pot was brewing, she took a speedy shower and dressed. She wanted to call her ex-partner from the bureau before Mark arrived.

Dressed in faded jeans, a tan, fitted knit shirt, and boots

almost the same color, she walked to the living room, coffee cup in hand. A few moments later, she leaned against a small walnut-stained desk and dialed the phone.

A moment before she heard his voice, she felt a sick feeling of dread. She'd been a crappy friend and knew it. "Steve here." Hearing his answering voice only made that feeling worse.

"Steve," she said a bit too softly, "it's Lindsey."

She could hear his smile through the phone. "Hey partner, or maybe I should say, stranger?"

There was a reprimand in his tone, but it didn't lessen his welcome. It only served to make her feel guiltier. "I should have called before now."

"Yes, you should have. Don't expect me to say anything different. I'm just glad you are calling now."

"I'm in town."

"You're kidding? For a visit or to stay?"

Talking about this was hard. In the past, Steve had been one of the few people she told about her life. It should have made it easier. It didn't. "My father has cancer. I'm running his firm until he is through the worst of it." She stopped there. What if he didn't get through it? A moment of silence passed and she knew Steve was thinking the same thing. "Or until someone else takes over."

"I had no idea," he said with sincere emotion in his voice. "I'm sorry. I wish you would have let me know. I know this is hard for many reasons."

His understanding nature made her guilt flare again. "I'm sorry, Steve." And she was. He was a good friend, and she had turned her back on him along with the city. It wasn't necessary to explain what she apologized for. They both knew.

He was silent for several moments. "If anyone knows

why you needed out of here, it's me."

"But it didn't mean I had to turn my back on you. I . . ."

"Don't have to explain," he finished for her. "I'm happy to hear from you now."

She sighed. "I won't repeat the past. Hearing your voice is like a breath of fresh air. A needed one."

"Good," he said. "I'm going to hold you to that. How about lunch today? Let's start catching up."

"I wish I could, but I have a case. It's a problem."

"I'm listening."

She smiled into the phone. He expected her to want his help. It was the partners thing. There was a bond that never went away. "Williams is the guy's name."

"Doesn't sound familiar."

"Accused of killing a group of women. The profile, well, the profile fits . . ."

"Fits what?"

Her doorbell rang, and she was thankful for the reprieve. Talking about the similarities of these two cases was harder than she would like.

"I need to answer my door. Hang on for me."

With his quick approval, she set the phone down and rushed to the door. She pulled the door open and waved Mark forward, but not before she felt a rush of awareness. A quick look told her he looked as he had the first day they met, James Dean casual, and way too sexy to be safe.

For her.

She turned away from him, not wanting to keep Steve waiting. "I'm on the phone," she told him, looking over her shoulder. "There is coffee in the kitchen, if you want some."

Lindsey grabbed the phone again. "I'm back." She turned to find Mark standing in the archway overlooking the living room. Propping one shoulder against the wall, he studied her with a watchful eye. She studied him back. Didn't mean to. It just happened. When they looked at each other, she seemed to forget everything else.

Steve had said something. Damn. "I'm sorry. What was the question?"

"What about this case?"

"You're going to think I'm crazy." Mark's eyes narrowed at her words. She turned and gave him her back. "It's a lot like the Hudson case."

A moment of quiet. "How like it?"

"Very."

"Can't someone else take the case?" he asked, concern in his voice.

"I'll be fine, Steve. The problem is—Lewis, the male chauvinist pig himself, has been assigned to help the local authorities."

"Lewis?" He laughed. "You won't get much information from him, that's for sure. I told you to be nice to him."

"I tried."

"Calling him a red-faced, perverted pig was nice?"

She sighed. "He deserved it, Steve, and you know it. He treated all the females in the bureau like they were ornaments, not professionals. And may I remind you he had played a nasty little joke on Rebecca—who happens to be a damn good agent—and almost got her fired in the process."

"I know, but you do tend to speak your mind a little too bluntly at times."

"But I tell the truth," she argued.

"Yes," he said with a smile in his voice. "That you do. I'll see what I can find out and call you later today."

"Thanks, Steve." She gave him her number and said a quick goodbye.

Lindsey turned to lock gazes with Mark. The impact was nothing less than magnetic. So much so that there was simply no use fighting it. The attraction was too magnetic, too powerful. She'd spent a good hour in bed the night before thinking about this thing between them.

To act on it or not had been the question she battled to answer. Finally, she had decided to act . . . only on her terms.

"Don't you want some coffee?" she asked with a nod towards the kitchen.

He didn't care about the damn coffee. He wanted to know who she had been on the phone with. He followed her, his eyes admiring the soft little sway of her curvy hips. She looked like pure temptation in her snug jeans. He'd thought she looked amazing in business attire. In casual wear, she was even more alluring. Perhaps more approachable.

The woman lit him up like a match. Never, ever had he wanted someone the way he did her.

Mark never mixed business with pleasure. In Lindsey's case, he wouldn't be at Paxton if it weren't for her. In his mind, that justified pursuing Lindsey. And he had every intention of seeing where their attraction would lead.

He stepped into the doorway of the kitchen, feeling the unwelcome, but undeniable, white-hot flare of jealousy. "Friend?" he asked, unable to keep the question from flowing from his lips.

A puzzled expression filled her face. "What?"

"On the phone."

"Oh," she said. "My old partner." She set her cup on the counter and reached into the cabinet and pulled out another as she added, "Before I moved to Washington." She poured coffee into both cups, and turned her attention to Mark. "Cream or sugar?"

"Black is fine. Thanks." He stepped forward and took the cup from her. "Partner or boyfriend?"

"What?" she asked, acting confused. It seemed sincere. He wanted to believe it was. "Boyfriend? You mean Steve?" She laughed. "My old partner, my boyfriend?" She reached for her cup, seeming more amused than angry at the questions. "He's married. In fact, his wife's a dear friend. Steve's digging up some insider info on the case for us."

"That's good." Mark relaxed a bit. "Anything would be helpful at this point."

He leaned an elbow on the counter, and set his cup down, surprised when she did the same. They faced one another, the look they shared like a live charge of electricity. Her soft smell floated across the steaming coffee, carrying with it a sensual wave of heat.

A silent understanding passed between them, a mutual need that surpassed words. The question was—did either dare cross the line of business and pleasure? For Mark, he had already decided, yes. He could only hope she too would allow them to explore what was so evidently, so potently, a mutual attraction.

He knew the moment she reached for escape. Something—a hint of fear—flashed in those way too alluring eyes. And then she spoke, and he knew her intent was to change the mood. "I'm going to call him back and ask him to run a national search for crimes that match our profile since Hudson went to jail."

"Hudson?" he arched a brow.

She shrugged. "The two profiles fit—Williams and Hudson. Who knows at this point? I even considered they could both be innocent and the real criminal is still at large."

He had been afraid she would revisit the past rather than focus on the present. It appeared she was. "You think Hudson is innocent?"

Lindsey looked down at the floor, and he could tell she fought with her emotions. "Just covering my bases."

"Lindsey?"

She raised her eyes and looked at him. The rich color of green took his breath away. Or maybe it was the simple awareness he felt each and every time their eyes locked. He watched with admiration as she reached for control and overcame her emotional state.

This time he changed the subject. "You look good today."

Surprise lit her eyes, but, to his satisfaction, not displeasure. Then, to his utter amazement, she let her eyes roam down his body and back up. A bold move no doubt meant to send him a message. She was considering . . .

"I suppose you pass inspection," she teased.

He raised an eyebrow, laughter in his eyes. "You suppose?"

"You'll do," she said, and started to walk past him.

He sidestepped, blocking her way into the small kitchen. "Perhaps I should show you how well I will do?" His voice was low.

"Do you always feel the need to prove yourself?" she challenged.

He gave her a hot look. No way could he hide what he was feeling. Not that he intended to. He wanted Lindsey, and he wanted her to know it. And yes, he had an agenda. One he wasn't hiding anymore than he was his desire. "With you, it seems I do."

Her lashes fluttered to her cheeks, dark crescents against the ivory of her skin. As if she was thinking, perhaps struggling with her response. She looked up at him, her eyes now darker. Hotter. "Why, Mark? Why do you want to prove anything to me?"

He never blinked, nor did he hesitate in his response. He'd given this very question a lot of thought. "I admit, I can't explain it. I'm not one to dance around a subject. You do things to me, Lindsey. I came back to Paxton for you, and only for you."

Her eyes widened. "And your reputation, of course."

No more games. He didn't like them, and he wanted the air clear. Honest. "I could have dealt with the reputation thing without coming back, and we both know it."

There was a long, drawn-out silence as they stood there, so close they were practically touching, staring into each other's eyes. He wanted to kiss her so damn bad it was like a need as critical as his next breath. He swayed towards her, his head tilting downward, closer to her. Lindsey's lips trembled ever so slightly, and he could almost taste his anticipation.

But then she stiffened, and he knew she had talked herself into getting spooked. The dismissal came next. She delicately cleared her throat. "We need to get going, Mark."

He ran a hand through his hair, trying to offset the rage of his body with the movement. "You and I both know what's between us, but if you need time, I'll give you time." With that said, he stepped aside to let her pass.

She appeared stunned by his statement, standing there, staring, unmoving. When she started walking, he let her come parallel with him, and then he grabbed her arm. His face moved very near hers, his eyes fixed on her face. "I don't know what's going on in that head of yours, but I'm not what caused those shadows in your eyes. I'm here now, not a part of the past, and no matter how hard you push me, I won't run."

His eyes bore into hers, his intent to let her know he meant business. He'd decided he wanted Lindsey, and he was going to do what it took to earn her trust. After several potent seconds, he released her.

And she took off like a scared cat.

Chapter Five

The décor-free, musty room surrounded them like an empty shell.

A single metal table and four chairs sat in the middle of the lifeless walls. Lindsey impatiently tapped her pencil on the table, which in turn made a loud thud every time it hit the metal.

Mark reached out and grabbed the pencil. "Why don't you sit down? It might calm your nerves a bit."

Lindsey shot him a glowering look. "My nerves are fine. I just hate wasted time. I wish they would hurry the heck up. It's not like we have all day."

Mark eyed her, opening his mouth to comment, but lost the words when the wide, steel door opened. A burly, toothless guard held Roger Williams by the arm. The guard grunted and pointed at a chair, watching with stone-cold eyes as Roger sat down. Then the guard stepped to the hallway, never saying a word, leaving Lindsey and Mark alone with their client. Roger Williams was a slight man, not taller than five feet seven inches, with sunken cheekbones and weary green eyes. Lindsey studied him, seeking an answer.

Guilty or innocent?

She had seen the eyes of many criminals, in fact, looked into some of the deadliest eyes known to man. Roger Williams had gentleness in his. And fear. Not guilt. Of course, she had said the same thing about Hudson. Frustrated at her own thought, she shoved away her self-doubt. If she was going to defend this man, she had to stay focused on this case and this case alone.

"Who are you two?" Roger asked, his fingers entwined on the table. His nervousness was like a live charge in the room. It laced his words and made him fidget.

"I'm Mark Reeves, and this is Lindsey Paxton," Mark offered. "We will be representing you."

"Yes," Lindsey added. "We're your new attorneys."

Roger's face clouded with confusion. "Where is Mr. Paxton?"

"Mr. Paxton, my father, has taken ill," Lindsey explained. "Mr. Reeves and I will be taking over."

"Excuse me for being blunt, but I trust Mr. Paxton. How do I know I can do the same with the two of you?"

Lindsey was a bit surprised by the question, considering the meekness of his exterior. "I understand your concerns."

Mark reached inside his portfolio and slid a piece of paper onto the table. "I brought a copy of a resume for you, Mr. Williams. It includes credentials for both Ms. Paxton and me."

Roger picked up the paper and started reading. Mark continued, "There are a lot of questions we need answered. If you accept our representation, then we hope to get started today."

Lindsey was irritated that she didn't know what it included, and made a mental note to have a little talk with Mark. "You both appear more than qualified," Roger said, looking up from the paper. "I don't mean to be difficult. This has been a horrible experience, being accused of such horrible acts."

"Murder," Mark said. "You've been accused of murder.

I think it's important we speak frankly about what we are up against."

Lindsey gave Mark a warning look. She was quite sure Roger knew what he was accused of, and didn't need to have it crammed down his throat. "Mind if we sit down?" she asked, indicating the table with a wave of her hand. Roger nodded, and Lindsey and Mark sat down, side by side, directly in front of Roger, each pulling out a legal pad and pen.

"The first thing we need to do is get the facts straight and get your side of the story. Forgive me, but I really have to ask this question. Did you kill those girls?"

His eyes widened. "No," he said vehemently, hands slamming the table. "I did not kill anyone, Ms. Paxton."

"Then why do they think you did?" Mark asked, leaning forward, a challenge in his voice.

Roger sank back into his chair, his fight seeming to evaporate. "I guess they need someone to blame." He exhaled loudly and then rested his forearms on the table as he leaned closer to them. "Look, I would like to think my own attorneys have confidence in my innocence. Mr. Paxton believed me. What do I need to do to prove to you that I'm innocent?" There was no mistaking the desperation in his voice.

Mark set the pencil he held on the table. "I assure you, we are aware of Mr. Paxton's feeling on the matter." Mark paused and ran a hand over his jaw. "Look, I'm going to be honest with you because you are facing some tough times and you need to be ready. A jury will want to believe you're guilty." When Roger started to speak, Mark held up a staying hand. "Just hear me out." Roger sat back in his chair and reluctantly nodded. "The jury will want vindication for those girls. Crying parents and friends in the courtroom will only make matters worse. We," he waved a finger between him and Lindsey, "are human, just like the jury. The only difference is that we have a job to do. And that job is to provide you with the best defense available. In the end, guilty or innocent, we are protecting the system that protects the people of our nation by offering you our best. We are good at our jobs and neither of us likes to lose."

Roger started shaking his head, distress in the depths of his eyes. "You think I'm guilty."

Lindsey leaned forward, giving Roger a direct look. "We don't have any opinions at this point. None. But in reality, our opinions don't matter. It's what the jury thinks that counts. Our job is to make sure they vote not guilty."

"But if you believe in me, it will affect how you represent me. Do you deny that as fact?" he challenged.

Lindsey swallowed. He was right, but an attorney never admitted that out loud. Mark saved her the discomfort of answering by jumping in with a quick reply. "Actually, I do. You will get the best defense possible, regardless of our opinions."

"That's right," Lindsey said in quiet agreement. It was really true. Lindsey and Mark were both good at their jobs, a lot better than a lot of attorneys ever hoped to be. Years off the job made her no less confident in her ability to deliver results.

When Roger didn't reply, Mark flipped open his notebook and pulled out a piece of paper, then slid it in front of him. "This is a list of questions. I need you to take the time and answer them in detail. Today if possible."

Roger picked up the paper and scanned it. Lindsey discreetly eyed it herself. She didn't know Mark had prepared the questionnaire, but she couldn't help but be impressed. Still, she would have liked to have known in advance.

"There's a lot of questions here," Roger commented.

Mark nodded. "Yes, there are. Everything I could think of, up to this point, that opposing counsel will target or ask in any way, shape, or form. There are some key questions we need to go ahead and discuss. Once we review the completed questionnaire, we will be likely to have a lot more to discuss as well."

Lindsey cleared her throat. "That said, let's get those key questions answered." She looked at her notes. "Did you know any or all of the victims?" She knew the answer already but it was good to hear it from him, the way he would tell the prosecutor.

"They were students in my classes," Roger responded. A flash of pain dashed through his eyes.

"Two of them died on nights that you tutored them," Mark commented.

"I know, but I didn't kill them. Someone must have been watching. I tutored all of them at least two times, but not during the same semester." He looked from Lindsey to Mark. "I swear, I feel like someone is framing me."

His response did little to help his defense, and Mark dismissed it with his next question. "Is there anyone you suspect? A student who knew them all, another teacher?"

"My classes are huge," he said in a defeated tone. "We are talking a major university here. I don't even know all of the students' names. The ones who take advantage of tutoring are really the only ones I know well."

Mark's expression remained indiscernible. "Where can we get a list of everyone you tutored?"

"I'm required to key tutoring information into a database at the university, but I keep records at my house as well. My sister is watching over my place, so if you need the list, she can help you."

Lindsey was desperate for some sort of bone, a tidbit to help her defend him. "We need another common denominator other than you. A place the girls hung out, a person they all hung out with, something, anything?"

He shook his head as he spoke. "There are popular hangouts for the campus crowds, but as I said, NYU is a big school with a massive student body," he said in a defeated tone and then added, "and a multitude of hangouts to match."

Mark leaned back in his chair. "What about the last victim, Elizabeth Moore? You were seen going into her home the night of her murder."

Roger ran a hand through his hair. "She was getting over losing her mother to cancer. I was like a father figure to her, I think. She was having trouble with her grades and really life in general." He frowned, his eyes seeming to replay the past. "She started crying during the tutoring session that night, so I offered to walk her home. To be honest, I was worried that she was on the brink of a real disaster."

Lindsey interjected, "What do you mean disaster?"

"She was partying a lot, drinking too much. I knew because she was late to class several times, and she had fallen asleep during lectures, that kind of thing. I confronted her during a tutoring session and told her she was making it hard as hell for me to pass her." He shook his head. "The girl was headed for trouble."

"Do you know where she usually partied?" Lindsey asked.

He grimaced. "I'm afraid not. It was out of character for me to even speak of personal matters with a student." He glanced from Mark to Lindsey as if he was trying to read their thoughts. "It doesn't look good for me, does it?"

Lindsey responded in a calm, matter-of-fact tone, carefully avoiding promises of any sort. "The evidence is fairly circumstantial from what we can tell." She held up a finger. "However," she said with emphasis, "it would help if we had another angle on the murders, another suspect perhaps. That's what we're going to look for over the next few days."

"Mr. Williams," Mark said and then paused. "Roger," he corrected before continuing. "We do need you to know, people have been convicted on far less evidence. Though Lindsey is absolutely correct, the evidence is fairly circumstantial, the reality still stands as mentioned before; the jury will want justice for those girls. You are the common denominator, and without anything else for us to latch onto, it will be hard to create doubt in their minds." Mark spoke the cold, hard truth. Though she had gotten Hudson off in similar circumstances, he hadn't had some as incriminating as the visit to Elizabeth Moore's house.

"Do you have any enemies?" Mark asked.

"No, none," he said adamantly. "I keep to myself."

Mark's expression held skepticism, as did his tone. "None? Come now, everyone has some enemies."

"Really," Roger insisted. "I keep to myself."

Lindsey thought he seemed a bit of a hermit. "Have you ever lived out of state?"

"No, why?" he asked in a puzzled voice.

"Just being thorough," she commented. "Can you think of anything else we should know?"

"No," he said in a defeated tone. "I wish I could say I did."

Mark stood, and Lindsey followed his lead. Roger's head flew up to watch their movement, but he didn't stand. "We'll be in contact," Lindsey told him. "We're filing a continuance to get more investigation time. We feel optimistic we'll get it under the circumstances, but we'll keep you posted."

Mark added, "Finish that questionnaire."

Walking around the table, Mark knocked on the door as he hit a buzzer. Lindsey frowned. The double-kill action indicated impatience, but upon examination of his features, Mark was nothing but calm.

Something had him uptight. She wondered . . .

Mark hated interrogation rooms.

Walking, Lindsey by his side, he was damn glad to be done with Roger Williams.

Opening the passenger's door to his black BMW, he let his hand drift to the small of Lindsey's back as he guided her into the car and tried not to stare at her very long, very addictive legs. A much-needed distraction from the edginess that had built during their little chat with Roger. He shut the door and walked to his side of the car, Lindsey on his mind.

Damn, how he wanted to pull down her walls and see the real woman. There was no doubt in his mind they would sizzle together.

Working by her side only seemed to ignite the heat he felt for her. Something about the way she handled herself . . . her confidence was sexy as hell. And he'd taken every opportunity possible to touch her, to remind her of the attraction between them. As soon as he was in the driver's seat, she twisted around to face him.

"What do you think?" she asked, her eyes wide with anticipation.

He rubbed his temple and sighed, intentionally turning away from Lindsey. He needed to focus on Roger Williams rather than getting Lindsey undressed. "I think," he said, "I have a headache."

"Is that why you were so impatient to get the door open?"

Mark's head jerked around in surprise. "How did you know that?"

Lindsey smiled. "Never underestimate me, Mark Reeves. Have you always been claustrophobic?"

His eyes narrowed. No one had ever guessed his phobia. He was very good at hiding it. That Lindsey had, only served to make her more alluring. "Since I was five and got locked in a cellar for four hours. Those interrogation rooms always seem to bring it back. I know damn well I wasn't obvious. How did you guess?"

She shrugged. "I had a friend in high school who was claustrophobic. When you knocked and hit the buzzer at the same time, it set off a light bulb."

A slow smile filled Mark's face. He had to respect her sharpness. No wonder she had been so successful in the courtroom. Mark flipped the air conditioner on high and then turned his attention back to Lindsey. "You know what I think, Counselor?"

She gave him a questioning look.

"You haven't lost your touch," he said, and then reached out and ran his fingers down a strand of her long blond hair.

"How would you know?" she questioned. "You've never even seen me in action before."

Mark's eyes danced with a dangerous challenge. "I'd like to," he said in a low voice, not taking his eyes from hers.

He saw her swallow, and knew she was nervous. But he also had seen the flare of heat in her eyes. Abruptly, she looked away. "Is he innocent, Mark?"

He chuckled lightly at her change of subjects, letting her know he was onto her. "What do you think?"

She turned her gaze to him and frowned. "I don't know. I'm not comfortable going with my gut anymore."

"You think he is innocent," he stated flatly. He already knew the answer.

She shrugged. "My instincts—for what that's worth—tell me he is innocent." She refocused on him. "What's your gut reaction?"

His lips firmed. "I never go with gut feelings. As for facts, we don't have enough for me to make an educated guess." He turned towards the steering wheel and then glanced back at her. "We need that list of students."

Lindsey pulled her briefcase from the backseat and removed a small file. When she'd finally gone to bed the night before, she hadn't been able to sleep. After an hour of staring at the ceiling, she'd gotten up and done something productive. "I printed maps and directions off the Internet last night for anyplace I thought we might need to go." Lindsey shuffled the papers in the file. "Here," she said pulling out a map. "Home address and a map." She handed the paper to Mark.

His brow arched up. "You're quite thorough, aren't you?" His lips turned up.

Lindsey cocked her head to one side and peered at Mark, a smile slipping onto her lips. "Did you expect less?" A hint of flirtation laced her words.

He smiled, feeling a wave of satisfaction. "Oh, no, definitely not."

Her smile widened. "Well then, let's start at our client's home."

They arrived at the townhouse, finding it to be only a few blocks from the NYU campus, in a quiet neighborhood. Roger Williams' home was located on street level with a small patio entrance. Lindsey scanned the streets as Mark pushed some ivy aside to punch the buzzer on the door.

When there was no response immediately, Lindsey reached across Mark and punched it again.

He gave her a look. "Now who's impatient?"

She shrugged. "I admit it," she said, and reached out and jiggled the doorknob, only to find it locked. "Damn," she muttered.

Mark shot her a scowl. "That's breaking and entering," he reprimanded.

She shrugged again. Years in the FBI had taught her to push the envelope at times. A lot of agents did, they just didn't admit it, and they damn sure made sure they didn't get caught. "Arrest me, but . . ." she paused and wrinkled her nose, "get the charge right. It was attempted breaking and entering. And . . ." she held up a finger, "if it had been unlocked, there would be no breaking-in to be done." Lindsey scanned the street and then turned back to Mark. "Watch the sidewalk for me for a minute, and tell me if anyone is coming."

She headed for a window with a cluster of bushes offering coverage. Mark reached out and grabbed her arm. "What in the hell are you doing?" he demanded.

She shot him a glowering look and yanked her arm free. "Getting that list." She pointed towards the street. "Watch for people."

"Lindsey, no," he said in an abrupt voice. She rolled her eyes, and darted away before he could grab her again. Men. Steve had hated some of her tactics, but he'd eventually learned to accept who she was. No way was she letting a criminal get away because she was afraid to push the envelope. She'd let Hudson escape, and that was her one and only mistake.

If she got in trouble for going above and beyond, so be it. Better that than the guilt of seeing a killer go free. She had every intention of getting this case right. No way was she letting it turn out like Hudson's. Stopping in front of the window, her hands planted on her hips, she looked at Mark, her instincts telling her he was going to be a problem. "Mark, trust me. I know what I'm doing."

When she turned back to the window, she heard him grumble something inaudible. No doubt a complaint. This had to be done. She pulled the screen off the window and then jiggled the bottom of the seal. A smile slipped onto her lips the instant she found it unlocked. In a quick jerk, she raised the window and climbed through it.

Once inside the house, she leaned out of the window. She peered out at Mark who was scanning the street, his body stiff with tension. "Psst," she whispered. "Mark."

He looked up, his eyes sharp with anger as he moved towards her. She pointed to the screen beneath the window. "Put it back in, and I'll let you in the front." She shut the window before he could refuse and headed towards the door.

Lindsey found herself in a small, quaint, living area with a rock fireplace, and filled with high-back, woodsy furnishings and lots of bookshelves. She grimaced. Didn't look like a psychotic killer's home to her. Of course, what do the homes of psychotic killers look like?

Moving through the room with a swift, catlike motion, she was at the front door in seconds, unlocking the deadbolt. Pulling the heavy wooden door open, she frowned when she didn't see Mark. Peeking outside, she found Mark messing with the window screen. She rolled her eyes at his back. "What are you doing?" she asked in an irritated whisper. "Just leave it!" He dropped the screen to the ground and started moving towards her. "Are you trying to look suspicious or what?"

"If you wouldn't have bent the damn thing, it wouldn't be a problem," he said in a whispered reprimand as he shot her a glowering look. In a few crisp steps, he followed her through the door, pulling it shut behind him. "You're killing me, woman," he said through clenched teeth.

Lindsey gave Mark her back, moving through the hall to look for an office area. She could feel Mark's eyes on her back as she disappeared into a room, and almost feel his frustration across the distance. She was already sitting at a small computer desk booting up a computer when he entered the room. A plump, white Persian cat came up and started rubbing on her leg.

"Oh, damn," she muttered with irritation. She looked at Mark. "I'm allergic to cats," she explained as she shoved the animal away with her leg just as the first sneeze hit her, followed immediately by two more. She sniffed, feeling the itching in her eyes already starting. "Damn, I'll be sneezing all night."

Mark didn't comment. He was just standing there, staring at her. His expression said she was a major pain-in-the-ass. She didn't care. "I don't think this is a good idea," Mark said, watching her tab through computer files.

She glanced up at him and then back to the computer screen. "We're trying to help our client," she reasoned. "He told us to get this information from his computer." Then to herself, "Let's see, what would this be called . . ." Her voice trailed off as she quickly thumbed through files.

"Here," she said, punching Enter. "I think I found it." She shot Mark a look that said I told you so, which only served to deepen the scowl on his face.

A few more keypunches and Lindsey sent the document to print. Mark sighed behind her and started rummaging through the desk. Lindsey smiled to herself. She turned to look at him. "Find anything?" And despite her effort, a hint of laughter slipped into her voice.

He straightened and eyed her. "No, nothing." He rubbed his jaw. "In fact, the guy seems pretty darn uneventful."

Lindsey pushed to her feet and pulled the papers off the printer. "Ten names," she flicked the paper with her thumb and forefinger. "Only two of them are men. We have names, addresses, and phone numbers. Mission accomplished."

Mark nodded and reached for her hand. "Perfect, let's get out of here."

Lindsey dodged his hand and made a face. "Let's dig around a bit more."

Before Mark could comment, Lindsey buzzed past him and disappeared into the hall. Lindsey found what she thought was the master bedroom, and slipped inside, flipping on the light switch as she entered.

Surveying the room, it appeared normal enough to her, with all the basics, and nothing exceptional. Bed, dresser, lamp, Ansel Adams pictures. On the surface, nothing stood out. She headed towards the dresser, intent on checking out the contents.

Mark's voice drew her eyes to the doorway. "What are you looking for?"

She gave him a look of disbelief. "Even if you weren't a criminal attorney, there would be no excuse for that question." She plopped her hands on her hips. "The bedroom or the closet is where the weird stuff always is." She dropped her hands. "If there is any." She pointed to the closet. "Looks like a manly place to start your search, if I ever saw one."

He made a frustrated sound, but didn't argue, moving

towards the closet. Lindsey figured he just wanted to get it over with. Lindsey searched drawer after drawer. When Mark finished the closet, he turned to face her. "Nothing."

Lindsey sighed. "Same here."

"Good, then it's time to go," he said firmly.

She tried to glare, but it was lost in the midst of another sneeze. "The damn cat must sleep in this room."

Mark's expression was dark. "Let's go."

Lindsey knew she had pressed her luck with Mark. It was time to do what he wanted. Besides, her nose was killing her. "Fine, let's go."

They made it to the hallway when the lock on the front door started to rattle. "The sister," Lindsey whispered.

They scanned the room for their best escape route. Mark grabbed her hand. "Quick, the kitchen," he whispered tugging her behind him. "Maybe there's a back door."

They stopped in the center of the kitchen. "Nope," Lindsey said. "No exit."

Mark yanked open a small door to reveal a tiny, well-kept pantry, barely big enough for one person. He reached for Lindsey, pulling her with him as he stepped into the closet and pulled the door shut. They were standing face to face, their thighs pressed together. Mark leaned against the wall, shifting Lindsey with him, and Lord help her, she felt it in every inch of her body.

He looked down at her, and despite the dimness of the light, she could see the desire he felt, just as she had seen it in her kitchen. She'd talked herself out of acting then, a flare of second thoughts making her bolt. Afraid he would be as controlling as the men in her past. Afraid she was lost to him if she gave in to her attraction.

But there was no way to hide from this moment.

Flattening his hands on her back, pulling even closer, he

molded them together. And she didn't fight him, silently giving her approval of his actions. Her heart was racing, pounding so loudly in her chest, she wondered if he could hear, or at this proximity, feel it.

Her hand settled on his chest, fingers spread. They stared at one another, a mutual understanding, a need, shared in those moments. Both knew what the other wanted.

"Hey there kitty, how are you?" A woman's voice made Lindsey stiffen as she listened, never taking her eyes from Mark's. The voice was loud. Close. "I brought you your favorite food. You miss Roger, I bet, huh?"

Mark slowly moved his hands up her back, sliding them around her waist, and then up her sides, barely skimming her breasts. Lindsey almost gasped from the sudden, intimate touch. Mark smiled down at her with a challenge in his eyes. Surely, he knew he'd already won. She was ready to surrender.

It was pure madness, but standing in a closet, about to be caught for breaking and entering, his every little move impacted her with such intensity, it took Lindsey's breath away.

His eyes were full of suggestion, and Lindsey felt her body responding with a resounding YES. The only thing keeping Lindsey from completely losing control and attacking Mark was the voice on the other side of the door.

"Little kitty, eat up! I can't stay tonight. I have to go see your Daddy." The woman was talking in a baby voice to the cat. Lindsey started to roll her eyes, but then she heard the sobs. The woman was crying. Lindsey's heart sank. She felt the pain of Roger's sister as if it were her own.

Suddenly Lindsey felt the tickling of a sneeze. Panic formed and overwhelmed her as she struggled to stifle her urge. Just as suddenly as the sneeze had snuck up on her, so did Mark's lips. Hungrily they met hers and she accepted them, her sneeze disappearing without a trace, passion replacing it in equally uncontrollable dimensions.

It was a long, sweet kiss that tasted of desire and temptation. His flavor was perfection, even better than she remembered, and she wanted him to keep kissing her. God, she wanted to do a whole lot more than kiss.

For a few moments she forgot they were in a stranger's house, forgot the investigation, and even forgot Paxton. His kiss was like a drug, making her out of control, consuming in its potency. Whatever walls her mind built to protect her from Mark, her body dismissed. The chemistry between them was like a live charge. Leaning into him she could feel every inch of his long, hard body. The sound of a door slamming jerked their lips apart. For several seconds they stared at each other, both breathing heavier than normal.

"She's gone," Lindsey whispered but didn't move out of his arms.

His answer came slow. "Yes, I believe she is."

"Uh, we should get out of here." She all but stammered the words. Still she didn't move.

"I suppose we should," he said, in a husky voice as he pulled her tighter against his body and lightly brushed his lips against hers. Then, nuzzling her ear, he whispered, "Mission accomplished."

And she knew he was talking about winning her surrender.

Standing at the door of Elizabeth Moore's apartment, now maintained by her former roommate, Lindsey felt a tightening in her chest. One of the things she hated the most about her involvement in criminal law was the pain of the family and friends of the victims. At the same time, it was that very thing that had driven her to get out of bed each day. Fighting for justice was the only thing that could be done to help. And if that meant getting an innocent person set free, then so be it. At least, then, attention would be turned to finding the real criminal.

The door opened, revealing a young woman with dark hair and eyes, and a less than welcoming expression on her pale face. "Can I help you?" Her tone mimicked the look on her face. Dressed in sweatpants and a T-shirt she appeared to be in typical college hangout attire.

"Ms. Vicky Kencade?" Mark asked.

"Who wants to know?" she shot back, propping one foot on top of the other, arms hugging her thin body.

"Au-choo." Lindsey sneezed, covering her mouth in an abrupt action. "Excuse me," Lindsey said with a sniffle. "Cat allergy," she explained trying to fight off another sniffle. "We are investigating the murder of Elizabeth Moore. I'm Lindsey Paxton," she said and waved a hand towards Mark, "and he's Mark Reeves."

"I've already told the police everything I know."

Lindsey really wanted to hear what this woman had to say. Telling her they were defense counsel wasn't likely to help. "Can we just ask a few more questions? We're attorneys and it's our job to go to court and help the jury make a good decision." Lindsey hoped Vicky would assume they were prosecutors.

When the door was suddenly opened to them, she was relieved. Success. She and Mark exchanged a look before Lindsey stepped into the apartment with him at her heels. Quickly scrutinizing her surroundings, Lindsey found it typical college living: small, with homemade wall hangings and posters, as well as second-hand furniture.

Feet planted in the middle of the living room, Vicky faced them. "I'm so glad that freak is in custody. I want him to hang for what he did to Elizabeth. Tell me what I can do to help."

She motioned towards a plaid, worn couch, and Mark and Lindsey sat down. Vicky dropped to the floor as if to gain a comfortable distance from them. She pressed her knees to her chest and wrapped her arms around them.

"Ms. Kencade, did you ever meet Mr. Williams?" Mark asked in a quiet voice.

"Yeah, the night Elizabeth was killed. He came in for coffee after a tutoring session."

"You were here when Mr. Williams came by?" Lindsey asked, as she pulled a pad of paper and pen from her briefcase.

"Yes," she said with a deep sigh. "He seemed nice enough. I would never have guessed what a real bastard he was." Her voice reeked with bitterness.

"Why did you think he was nice?" Lindsey asked.

"He seemed to really care about Elizabeth. She was hurting over her mother's death and had these crying spells. Something set her off in the tutoring session. She was upset. He seemed really concerned that she get home safely."

"Were you here when he left?" Mark questioned.

"Yes, actually I was."

Lindsey's expression held surprise. "So you saw him leave, and Elizabeth was unharmed?" Mark put a hand on her shoulder as if in warning. She understood. Vicky might decide they were the enemy, if she wasn't careful, and then they wouldn't get anything more from her.

Vicky was frowning. "Well, yeah, but Elizabeth decided to go out after he left that night. I guess he followed her."

Mark raised a questioning brow. "Out?"

"Yes, to a club called the Pink Panther," the girl stated.

"Did you two go there often?" Mark asked.

Vicky nodded. "Yeah, it's the spot we hang at, if you know what I mean."

"Did you know any of the other victims?" Lindsey asked.

"I knew of one of the other girls. I saw her around a lot. Mandy Gibson. We didn't hang or anything."

"Was Ms. Moore seeing anyone?" Mark asked.

"Her and her boyfriend broke up a few months before . . . um," she paused and looked down at her hands which started to shake, "you know, she died."

Lindsey's voice softened. "I'm sorry. I know how difficult reliving all of this can be. We'll try and hurry." When Vicky nodded, seeming to pull herself together, she continued, "This guy she was seeing, was the breakup easy, hard . . . ?"

"As good as breakups can go, you know," she said with a shrug. "He was a nice guy. Elizabeth just wasn't the same after her mother's death."

"What's his name?" Mark asked.

"Tom, Tom Maloney. He goes to school with us."

"This Mandy Gibson, you said you saw her around," Lindsey said. "As in where?"

"School, out," the girl stated.

Mark frowned. "Out?"

Vicky opened her mouth to answer but Lindsey interrupted, "Ah-choo." Lindsey covered her mouth and sniffled. "Sorry, again. Go on, you were explaining what 'out' means."

"Parties and stuff."

"The Pink Panther?" Lindsey asked.

"Yes, actually, I think so. A few times."

"Do you have an address for this ex-boyfriend?" Mark asked.

Pushing to her feet, Vicky walked over to the kitchen and pulled out a pad. "Yeah, he lives on campus." She wrote something down, ripped the page off, and walked back towards them. She handed the small piece of paper to Mark. "This is his address."

Lindsey and Mark exchanged a look, silently agreeing they were through. They both pushed to their feet. "Well, thank you for all of your help," Mark said offering her his hand. "We may be in touch again."

Vicky shook Mark's hand and then Lindsey's. "I really want him to pay," she said, wrapping her arms around herself again.

"We know you do," Lindsey said as they reached the door, and then had another thought. She turned and faced Vicky. "How long had Elizabeth and Tom been dating?"

Vicky gave Lindsey a puzzled look. "Almost a year."

Lindsey calculated in her head. The dates of the murders, the time frames. Often serial killers had normal lives, including wives or girlfriends. It was an excellent cover.

She wanted to know more about this boyfriend.

Chapter Six

Lindsey sat down on the floor of Mark's apartment and rested her back against his couch.

She felt comfortable here, and she couldn't figure out why. It reminded her of the first time she had met Mark, the way she had felt so drawn to him. Something about him just called to her.

Trying to focus on work, she pulled files out of her briefcase, and plopped them on the coffee table. Glancing at the pile of paperwork, she let out a weary sigh. It had been a long day and exhaustion was making a fast sweep through her body.

She wasn't sure she was up to doing anymore work tonight.

Besides they had accomplished a lot in a relatively short window of time. Her only regret was they hadn't managed to track down the ex-boyfriend. They had dropped by his house and even called him several times, to no avail. They had made it through a big portion of the students on the tutoring list. Not that it had offered them much to go on.

So far they were just as much in the dark about what had happened to those girls as they were before.

Lindsey had agreed without hesitation to have dinner at Mark's place while they reviewed the day's notes, knowing full well what being alone with him meant. Her morning second thoughts were gone. A day with Mark had made her desire abundantly clear. No way was she going to walk around this thing between them for six months.

She would simply make sure she kept things firmly in her control.

Standing behind the bar, Mark pulled out two wine glasses and then froze, his eyes locked on Lindsey. He was still reeling from her easy acceptance of his dinner invitation. Surely she knew his intentions. The closet kiss was a sure tell-all, and man, what a kiss it was. It took Herculean strength not to take her right there in the closet. He had felt her submission like a sweet reward. She wanted him as badly as he wanted her.

Perched against his couch, she looked completely at ease in his home, a fact that filled him with an odd surge of pleasure. It also made him want to show her how good they could be together. With that thought in mind, he popped the corkscrew from the wine bottle.

Mark stood above her, with glasses in hand, finding himself spellbound by the sight she made. Her long, blond hair streamed over her shoulders, soft and silky. Her eyes, green as grass, seemed lit with a seductive message. He handed her one of the glasses and enjoyed the openness of the smile she offered in return. His voice came with effort, his mind and body so weighted by the things this woman made him feel.

"Italian take-out okay by you?" he asked.

She nodded. "Yes, I love Italian."

"What do you like?" he asked, anxious to get any distraction out of the way.

"Something with chicken. You order for me, will you?"

Mark didn't say another word. Funny, but the little bit of control she had just given him made him smile. It was only her dinner choice, but somehow he thought it was symbolic of more. She held onto control, especially around men. It was significant that she had given even a little to him. And he wondered if she recognized what she had offered.

He made quick work of ordering the food before joining her on the floor. Lindsey was staring out the window, sipping her wine, ignoring the files on the table.

"Thanks," she said and tipped her glass at him. "I needed this." She took another sip before leaning backwards across the couch in a catlike stretch.

The action draped her soft, blond locks across the black leather and Mark couldn't help but wish it were his chest. Tearing his eyes away from her profile was an impossible task he didn't even attempt. "Your sneezing seems to have stopped," he commented softly, barely keeping his hands from reaching for her.

She darted him a quick smile. "Yes, but my eyes are still burning." She tipped her chin towards the window. "The view here is amazing at night. I had forgotten the appeal of this city."

Mark turned his head to the view, sharing her love of the Manhattan skyline. It was his solace on many an evening, giving him peace after a tough look into the world of crime. He had taken great pride in moving into his home, and building a successful life. But lately something had been missing, a void in his life. He glanced back at Lindsey, and realized she somehow filled the hole that had been demanding recognition. Why or what that meant, he didn't know. Or maybe he just wasn't ready to face it.

There had been plenty of women in his life, but Lindsey somehow seemed different. She needed him, even if she didn't admit it. But then again, she didn't depend on him. He found her independence and strength admirable.

"Yes," he agreed. "I love this view."

He turned his gaze on her, rubbing his fingers across his jaw, feeling the bristle of one-day-old whiskers. God, she was something. From the first moment he'd seen her, he'd known he was in trouble. She did something to him. He wished he knew what. Then maybe he could control it. But he didn't, and he couldn't, and right now it simply didn't seem to matter. Unable to resist any longer, he moved closer to her, his hand running down the back of her hair and lingering.

He heard her swift intake of breath as she turned to him. Her words surprised him. He'd expected her to shy away, to resist. But she did just the opposite. "Thank you for today," she whispered, and ever so softly touched his face before dropping her hand.

His eyes narrowed, and his senses reeled. Her response, her touch, shocked him and set him on fire. "For what?"

"I thought meeting Williams, talking about the crimes so like those involving Hudson, would be harder than it was. It's strange, but just being with you somehow made things easier." She looked down at her lap as if she wasn't sure how he was going to respond.

Using his index finger, he tilted her chin up so he could see the expression in her eyes. And so she could see his. He knew what she would see in them. But it was what he saw in hers that took his breath away. Emotions, raw and hot, danced in her gaze, there for his viewing. Now, while she was in this mood, he wanted all he could get from her. "That was a major confession for you, wasn't it? To admit needing me?"

She nodded, her lips trembling. For a fleeting moment, he thought he saw fear in her eyes. He smiled at her, intent on making it go away. "Well," he said, "guess what?" He didn't wait for her to answer. "I'm damned honored."

Her face was blank for a moment before her lush, tempting, sexy-as-hell lips curled into a smile. Her hand moved to his cheek, cupping it. There was something so tender about the action, it pressed him over the edge. With a low growl, he wrapped his arms around her waist and pulled her close to him, their mouths so near their breath intermingled. "I want you more than I remember ever wanting a woman."

"You do?" she whispered.

"Yes," he said. "I do."

Her reply was so soft he barely heard it. "I want you, too."

He absorbed the words as he would a needed breath of air, taking them in, and allowing them to fuel his desire. His lips brushed hers, once, twice, a third time—soft, tender, and passion-driven. She tasted like wine and a special something that was simply, perfectly her. With sensual strokes, their tongues met, languidly caressing each other.

His hands cupped her face as he pulled back to look into her eyes, dipping his head for one more taste. He slid his hands down her neck and started making soft circles with his thumbs. This woman was connected to him in some way beyond Williams, beyond Paxton, and beyond understanding.

For now, he just wanted to experience all that they could be together, here, now, tonight.

Lindsey rested her hands on his chest and allowed her head to slowly roll backwards. Her breasts tingled with his nearness, making her wish he would move his hands. Thinking she could deny herself this amazing man had been crazy. His lips pressed against the sensitive flesh of her neck, making a shiver of desire dance along her skin.

She wanted this, wanted him . . .

He nuzzled her ear, his tongue and teeth both touching the lobe. "I can't begin to explain what you do to me."

Lindsey pulled back a bit, wanting to see into those fascinating brown eyes of his. She liked knowing he wanted her. This gorgeous, sexy man wanted *her*. Of course she had seen desire in a man's eyes before . . . but not the live, heated burn she saw in Mark's. "Tell me why you want me, Mark?" She looked at him, waiting for his answer. For some reason, she needed to know.

Maybe she wanted him to say something wrong, to push her so she could run. Deep down she knew she was scared of Mark, of his powerful nature, and the way it resembled other men in her life. Yet . . . he was tender, and sensitive, and made her feel respected but still sexy. Was it real or just a good act, this way he treated her?

"I wish I could answer that question," he told her, and there was so much honesty in his voice and eyes, it made her stomach flip-flop.

She so wished she knew the answer as well. Right now, she wanted Mark, and she wanted him in a way that went beyond words. No more holding back. He'd passed her test. "Mark," she said, and the one word said so much. It was packed with her desire.

She moved then, rotating so that she straddled him. His hands went to her hips, helping her settle on top of him, feeling the evidence of his arousal. Their eyes locked, and the knowledge of what was to come passed between them and gave her a rush of pure heat. And it empowered her. This take-charge man was now here, under her control, and she liked it.

She bent her head, and let her lips linger above his,

feeling the warmth of his breath as it touched her mouth. But she didn't kiss him. Instead, she trailed her lips along his jaw, and then further to his neck, her nose flaring with his very male, very provocative smell.

Moving her lips near his ear, she whispered, "Why, Mark?" She flicked his earlobe with her tongue before leaning back to see his face. "Why do you want me? I want to know."

His hands settled on her cheeks, his eyes holding hers. "You want to know why, Lindsey?"

"Yes, tell me." Her voice had a breathless quality.

His voice was a deep, sensual play on her nerve endings. "It's way beyond your looks, but I think you know that."

She didn't say anything. Couldn't. He simply took her by storm. Her intention had been to take control of this night. Instead, it felt more as if she had given it away. But it wasn't a bad feeling like it had been in the past. With Mark, it felt . . . different.

"But you know you're beautiful," he said as his thumb moved across her bottom lip. "I know you do."

Her lashes fluttered to her cheeks. She hated being told she was attractive. The corporate world had taught about politics and manipulation, and often looks played a key role. She hated it. "No," she whispered.

"Look at me," he said gently. She forced her eyes to meet his. "How can you say no?"

She wasn't going to explain. "Kiss me," she said instead.

He seemed as if he might refuse, but then his hands were in her hair, his lips pressed to hers, warm and wonderful, making her forget the past, and the future. Now was all that mattered. Their lips connected first, pressed together as if they were absorbing the very essence of the other. She felt the moment in every inch of her body. Her nipples tightened, and her body seemed to melt.

Then his tongue slid into her mouth, sliding against hers in a slow move meant to savor, not tease. One stroke after the next, they tasted one another, slow and hot. His hands slid beneath her shirt, and along her back. Her hands moved from his shoulders, to his neck, to his chest, pressing against him as their kisses seemed to deepen, their bodies molding together just as their mouths were.

Her need for him intensified, and her hands moved along the fine lines of his muscular body, and settled at his tie. "Take it off," she whispered against his lips, and then leaned back to make eye contact. "And the shirt."

He reached for the knot, his stare bold, and fierce with passion. "You too," he said.

"You first," she responded, grabbing hold of the moments of control she could. Something told her with Mark, she would have to take them where she could get them. She reached for his buttons, starting with the bottom ones. He pulled his tie from his collar as she said, "I'll help."

His hands fell to his sides as he willingly let her take over the task. There was a huge part of her that wanted to grab the shirt and rip the buttons loose. Another wanted to savor each inch of skin as it was exposed. Dark hair ran from his belt to his navel and she ran her finger over it, eager to explore. The action seemed to make him grow impatient, and he finished off the buttons. She shoved the material aside, fingers flattening on his chest, feeling the soft hair that invited her touch.

"Now you," he said, his hands going to hers. "Now you." This time there was a challenge, even a dare, in his voice. As if he thought she was afraid to act.

She reached for the bottom of her shirt, and, in one easy

move, pulled it over her head, tossing it to the floor. His eyes dropped to her breasts, and without looking she could feel her nipples pucker against the thin ivory lace, responding to his stare as they might his touch. Or perhaps begging for it.

He took both his index fingers and ran them in a barely-there touch along the lace framing her breasts. "Beautiful," he murmured, his gaze on his fingers, or rather what they touched.

Before she knew his intentions, he pulled the silk down and exposed her nipples. Sucking in a breath of air, she whimpered as his fingers pinched and teased. Her lashes fell shut, her head tilting backwards.

And then his mouth was on one, warm as it suckled, sending waves of pleasure to her breasts and along her skin. Her hands moved into his hair, cupping his face. Without warning, Mark rolled her to her back, using his legs to part hers, and settling between them. His mouth was on her, his tongue hungrily sliding against hers, his body pressed into hers.

Her leg slid over his, trying to pull him closer. For long minutes, she was lost in his kisses, his flavor, his touch. . . . but in some far recess of her mind she registered a knocking on the door. "Mark?" Lindsey murmured against his lips, only to find herself thoroughly kissed again.

"Mark," she whispered, his teeth nipping her bottom lip. "The door."

"They'll leave," he said, pushing his weight to his elbows, and staring down at her, and then making a low sound before kissing her again. She tried to keep a hold of reality, but his hand cupped her breast, and kneaded, pulling her back into the haze of their heat.

But the doorbell rang, and then someone knocked. "Mark, you better get it."

Mark buried his head in her shoulder. "Damn it."

She ran her hand through his hair, urging him to look at her. When his eyes lifted to hers, she said, "I'm not going anywhere."

His eyes flashed with debate, and then he sighed and pushed to his feet, reaching for the buttons on his shirt as he walked towards the door.

Lindsey sat up, trying to gather her thoughts. He tugged her bra back into place and put her shirt back on. As she moved to sit on the couch, she could hear Mark exchanging words with a man at the door. A few seconds, later he returned, eyes taking in her replaced clothing, as he set the bags on the table.

Mark reached for her hand, and pulled her to her feet. "Let's finish what we started in the bedroom." She let him pull her into his arms and kiss her, a slow exploration that promised so much more to come.

Then he led her towards his room, and she followed. Anticipation burned inside, making her both eager for what was to come, and also nervous. It had been a long time since she had been with a man, and never before had it felt quite so exposing but yet liberating. Mark seemed as if he could make love to not only her body, but her mind.

The bedroom was lit by the moon and stars shining through a full wall of ceiling-to-floor windows. The shadows in the room seemed to add to the intimacy as she looked towards the massive bed framed with four huge posts, and covered in mounds of blankets.

Stopping beside it, Mark turned to her, his hands going to her waist. "I would love to have you lying naked right in the center of my bed."

Her brow lifted. "Would you, now?"

He nodded. "Very much," he said and lifted her so that she sat on the side of the bed, then nudged her legs apart, urging her back to the mattress. He leaned over her, palms pressed into the mattress. "What do you want, Lindsey?"

Her voice was slight. His words had her warm with possibilities . . . "You naked with me," she said, as her arms went around his neck. "Can I have my wish?"

He kissed her then, his mouth closing over hers, hot and demanding. All she could think was more. She wanted more. It would never be enough. She tasted him with frenzied, burning need, her tongue sliding against his, savoring the flavor. His flavor. So male. So unique. So addictive.

They shuffled, minds working within a shared desire, shifting farther onto the bed. His hands were all over her, moving up her blouse, flat on her bare skin. "Take this off," he said hoarsely.

"Okay," she whispered, "but you too. Take yours off." On second thought, "Take it all off."

He stared down at her, their eyes locking and holding. She felt a connection then, something that made her aroused from head to toe, but it was so much deeper than just physical. Or was it? Could they have an attraction so potent that a mere stare could make her sizzle from head to toe?

She could hardly catch her breath. What she felt, so raw and alive, scared her, made her feel out of control. Desperate to gain control, trying to break the spell that was taking it, she said, "Get undressed."

His gaze narrowed a moment, as if he knew what she was doing, but he didn't argue. He pushed to his knees and started unbuttoning his shirt. She sat up and pulled her shirt over her head as he tossed his aside . . . She stared at the perfection of his broad chest, the sprinkling of light brown hair, and perfect biceps, with admiration.

She wet her lips, feeling the urgency to explore, to touch, to feel. But he moved. She wanted to reach for him, but he pushed off the bed. Before she could complain, he halted her words, as he bent and took off his shoes. She liked the direction this was going. Her boots were gone in mere seconds, tossed to the floor, and drawing laughter from Mark.

He smiled. "Don't stop there."

"You either," she said, smiling through the heat of desire, wanting to say, *Be fast about it.* Instead, she quickly slid her pants down her legs, leaving her panties in place.

She looked up to find him gloriously naked, and . . . hard. Swallowing took effort. He was gorgeous. Leaning back on her palms she watched as his knees hit the mattress. He stayed that way, gently urging her legs apart. His eyes dropped to her legs, and slowly moved to the center and settled on the tiny piece of lace. Then, on the move again, they traveled up her stomach, and to her breasts.

When his eyes finally settled on hers, she was wet with desire, feeling as if she had been completely, seductively touched. "You are so beautiful," he said, with obvious arousal etching his low voice.

His palms, which still rested on her knees, began to move, sliding up her thighs in a seductive caress. When his hands reached the top of her legs, he slid his thumbs on her inner thighs, moving them so that they brushed the silk covering. The effect was like a jolt of pleasure dancing along each and every nerve ending of her body.

"Mark," she whispered. He looked at her. "Please come here."

"Not yet," he said, his thumbs stroking her panties, and

then dipping beneath to touch her sensitive core. Then he bent, taking her off guard as his lips pressed on her stomach. She fell back on the mattress, letting the soft cushion absorb the impact of her body, hands going to his hair just as his tongue dipped into her navel. At the same moment, his hands went to her panties, pulling them over her hips and down her legs. She kicked them off as his mouth traveled upward, mouth closing over her bra, teeth scraping her nipple through the lace even as his fingers popped the front clasp.

Moments later his hands were covering her breasts, his lips pressing to hers. All her promises to control how they came together were gone. She was lost in him, begging for more, unable to stop herself. Her body arched into his, his arousal nuzzling her thighs, his fingers pinching her nipples until she whimpered into his mouth.

His lips trailed along her jaw, to her ear. "You make me crazy, Lindsey," he whispered.

She made a sound of pleasure as he nipped her lobe. "You're making *me* crazy."

He moved so that his lips lingered just above hers. "Good," he said, and his eyes locked with hers. "Then we're even."

Something about the way he said the words made her hand go to his cheek. "What?" She blinked, trying to clear her passion-fogged mind.

"You and me," he said. "We're even. I want you. You want me."

It was as if he sensed her need to have some semblance of control. "Yes," she said. "I want you."

"And I want you, Lindsey." His words were packed with emotion. "Very much. From the first moment I met you."

"You did?"

"I did," he said, the air around them heavy with their breathing, their desire, their shared emotions.

In that moment, she wanted to share her feelings. Wanted him to know what he did to her. In that moment, thoughts of later, of control, of beyond that moment simply didn't exist. "I wanted you, too."

His lips brushed hers in a soft, delicate caress. "And now?" he asked. "Do you want me?"

Her lashes fluttered to her cheeks, and then lifted. "You know I do."

One of his hands moved to her hair, and his other slid to his erection. He slid it along her wet, sensitive flesh, drawing a whimper, then a sigh. Her eyes fluttered shut, as he teased them both, sliding his hard length back and forth like a sensual game of pleasure. One that built need and urgency, and when she thought she could take no more, he dipped the tip of his penis inside her.

His mouth covered hers, swallowing her gasp of pleasure as he slowly slid deep, until he was completely inside her, and they rested together as one. He kissed her long and deep, but slow. She clung to him, one leg moving over his, her hand going to his back.

His hips lifted and he began a slow rhythm . . . in and out, kissing her, his tongue mimicking the movement of his body. For long minutes, they clung, touched, explored with their hands, their bodies, their mouths. But then it changed. Their kisses grew hotter, deeper, and the intensity fierce. They were pressing themselves against one another as if they wanted to get beneath each other's skin, passion gone wild, bodies moving as one, together, harder and harder, and faster and faster.

And suddenly, Lindsey was in the bittersweet climb to the top of the waterfall . . . ready to fall over the edge into satisfaction, but not wanting to let go of the moment. She called his name, arching her hips into him, as she silently begged for the moment to last.

And then it happened. The first spasm literally made her body shake, and words, even sounds, were impossible. It felt as if her body absorbed him as her own. She heard him moan, and call her name, and then he shuddered and shook. She was easing into the aftermath as he entered his moment of utter pleasure.

His head tilted back, his eyes shut.

One last lunge into her body, and he buried himself deep, his face moving to slide against hers . . . and her name whispered on his lips.

They stayed like that for long moments, pressed together, arms and legs entwined. Lindsey began to feel reality, but shoved it away. She didn't want to think about why he felt so right or why he made her heart flutter in such a funny little way. He moved, rolling off her, but pulled her with him so that she rested on his shoulder. His arm was around her, holding her close to his side, and her hand settled in the soft hair of his chest.

And for just tonight, she wanted to pretend they were really special.

How long they rested, wrapped together, Mark didn't know.

Lindsey was amazing and he wanted to hold her forever. His eyes went wide. Forever. Where the hell had that come from? He was getting way out of control, way too fast. Lindsey had him tied in knots like no other woman ever had.

She nuzzled his chest, and he found himself running his hand down her hair. "Hungry?" he asked, thinking food and a bit of distance, as much as he didn't want it, would help him snap out of whatever spell she had him under.

"Starved," she said, pushing herself up on her elbow so she could look at him. The movement put her bare, sexy breast directly in his line of view.

He swallowed. "If you want food, you better cover up, because it won't take much to detour me." Because he simply couldn't help himself, he entwined his hand in her hair and pulled her lips to his, kissing her with slow, caressing strokes.

When he tore his lips from hers, he stared at her. "Damn woman, we better go eat. I think we both might need the energy."

She smiled at him, soft and alluringly sweet. Very unguarded, and he praised the moment. Something told him they were few and far between. "I think you might be right."

Lindsey sat on the kitchen counter, wearing Mark's shirt, and loving the way it smelled like him. And how intimate and perfect it made her feel, wearing his clothes.

Mark moved around the kitchen, pulling out plates and glasses and pushing buttons on the microwave. Deeply absorbed in the task of heating up their take-out, he looked almost boyish. Not easy for a dominating presence like Mark.

The man was a powerhouse who walked into a room and drew attention, and even more so, respect.

"Can I do something?" Lindsey asked, smiling at his efforts. Thus far he had made her promise to let him do the work. It was as if he wanted to wait on her. Not something that seemed to fit his personality. She wanted to condemn him as just like her father, but he kept doing things that didn't quite compute in the formula.

He gave her power where she thought he would take it.

Mark looked up from the plate he was filling, and returned her smile. "If you really want to help, you can grab the wine from the bar and fill our glasses."

Lindsey pushed off the cabinet, happy to perform her assigned duty. A few minutes later, wine-filled glasses in hand, heading back to the kitchen, she found Mark exiting the kitchen, two plates in his hands. He motioned towards the living room with his chin. "I thought it would be nice to enjoy the view while we eat."

She bit her bottom lip and nodded her approval. It would be very nice indeed. Fear inched into her stomach. Mark was really getting to her. Where was independent Lindsey who didn't need or want any man? Because this Lindsey, the one following a man wearing only boxers on a sexy body into the living room, was really wanting this one.

Like beyond the night.

Lindsey set the wine glasses on the table, and she sank to her knees. Mark put the plates on the table side by side. "Mmmm, it smells so good. I'm so hungry. Chicken Marsala?"

"My favorite," he said sitting down beside her. "I hope it works for you."

"I love chicken Marsala. You did well." Lindsey picked up a fork, and took a bite. "It's terrific."

"Or you're just hungry," Mark offered with a laugh.

Lindsey shrugged. "Maybe, but it tastes good, whatever the reason."

They ate in compatible silence for several minutes until Lindsey turned to study him. "Can I ask you something kind of personal, Mark?"

He laughed. "Well, I'd say we're about as personal as two people can get, so go for it."

Lindsey frowned. Sex wasn't an indicator of how well

two people knew each other by her book. Granted, what had passed between her and Mark had been unique, and far more moving than pure, physical lust . . . but it didn't make them progress beyond simple possibilities.

The chance for more between them was farfetched. And getting to know him could make her like him more. A risk she would have to take, because finding out more could also help her put things into perspective and keep her heart detached.

So, she took the plunge, and started asking questions. "Did you always know you wanted to be an attorney?"

Mark digested Lindsey's question with interest. He set his fork on the table, and looked at her, long and hard. Her question said a lot. She was close to letting down a small barrier. The very fact that she was trying to get to know him said a lot. "My father is an attorney just like yours, so I suppose some might say it was in my blood. Then again, I have a brother who's a computer programmer, and a sister who's a nurse."

After several thoughtful moments, and a sip of her wine, Lindsey asked, "Did you consider other career options?"

"No, I didn't." And he hadn't. Being like his father had been his dream. "Did you?"

She stared into her glass, gnawing on her bottom lip a long moment before looking at Mark again. "I guess I didn't."

Mark crooked his index finger under her chin. "Why do I sense that answer bothers you so much?"

Her eyes widened, and then her chin jerked slightly, her eyes averting from his. "I didn't mean to turn this into a probe about me."

Mark moved a little closer to her, sensing her inner turmoil, and wanting to help her calm it. He wasn't sure what it was about Lindsey, but he felt her pain like his own. His hand moved down the back of her hair. "I'm not probing, just talking." Perhaps exposing more of his inner workings would help her open up. "I couldn't work with my father anymore than you could. I wanted to be an attorney, but I learned early on that working with him was impossible."

Her eyes focused on his, suddenly alert with interest. "You tried working with him?"

He nodded. "I did and that lasted all of thirty days. It was a disaster. I moved to Houston and worked for a firm there until your father recruited me."

Lindsey tilted her head to the side. "Where is home?"

"Austin."

"Has it been hard being away from your family?"

"Not really. My brother and sister are married and busy with their lives. My father, well I talk with him often enough, and see him on holidays. We have more in common than you realize—you and me. My mother is gone. She died when I was four."

Pain flashed in her eyes. He wasn't sure if it was for him or for her loss. Maybe both. And suddenly he wished he hadn't brought up the subject. "How?" she whispered.

He paused, hating what came next. "Cancer," he said softly. "Sorry. Bad subject."

Lindsey smiled but it didn't reach her eyes. She reached up and touched Mark's jaw. "No worries. I've, of course, thought of his death. The other day, when I went to see him, he didn't look good." She seemed to fret a moment. "Do you think it is harder to lose someone you are close to or someone you, well, someone you never seem to get it right with?"

He took a sip of his wine and thought about the best way to answer her. "I don't know, Lindsey, but if you can manage to put your relationship back together with him, this would be a good time to do it."

A wave of emotion danced in her eyes. "The only way to make things better with him is if I live my life his way."

Mark set down his wine glass. "I'm not suggesting you make choices that aren't your own. Just be careful you don't make choices just to defy his control. You've had some time away, and deep down you, and you alone, know what you really want. Make him understand and accept your choices."

Lindsey turned abruptly and tucked her knees to her body, chin on her knees. "That's just it . . . I don't know what I want anymore." She eyed him. "I can't believe I'm even telling you this."

His fingers gently touched her cheek. He wasn't going to comment on what she did or didn't tell him. He was just glad she was opening up to him. "You don't have to make decisions right this minute. Give yourself time, but give him time too. Start talking to him about why you feel like you do. The worst that can happen is he doesn't listen."

Lindsey looked at him, her eyes probing as they held his. "What do you want from me, Mark?"

It was a vast question that he could have answered so many ways. Simple seemed best. "Nothing you don't offer freely."

Her lashes dropped to her cheeks, dark circles against her perfect, ivory skin. When she opened her eyes again, fixing him in a stare, she smiled. "I'm glad I'm here tonight."

"Me too," he whispered, and he lowered his mouth towards hers. "I really want to make love to you again, Lindsey." His lips lingered just above hers. "Can I?"

"Yes," she whispered. "I'd like that very much."

And his mouth covered hers, their kiss one of tenderness, passion, and possibilities.

Chapter Seven

Lindsey woke to the warm feeling of Mark's strong arms wrapped around her. Nuzzled against his shoulder and chest, his scent wrapped around her like a cozy blanket. Running her hand through his chest hair and down his flat stomach she couldn't help the satisfied smile that settled on her lips. There was never a time she could remember feeling so perfectly wonderful nor could she remember ever wanting a man the way she did Mark.

Needing her own identity, not wanting to be defined within the confines of a relationship, it had been years since she had even been with a man. Somehow, Mark seemed different from the men in her past. Would things change when he became more comfortable with her?

Was he simply like the rest but with a better disguise?

The dull ringing of her cell phone broke into her thoughts. It was in her purse, which was still in the living room. "Damn," she murmured as she moved to get out of the bed only to feel Mark's arms tighten around her.

"Where are you going?" he whispered, half-asleep.

Lindsey smiled and kissed his cheek. "My phone's ringing. I'll be right back."

He nodded. "Hurry back," he murmured.

Lindsey grabbed Mark's shirt off the floor, and pulled it over her head. The ringing had stopped, so she didn't rush. Once in the living room, she sat down on the couch, removed her phone from her purse, and checked the caller ID.

Just as she thought, it had been Steve. Lindsey hit the callback button and he picked up in only one ring. "Listen," he said without saying hello. "I've got some interesting information. There was a string of rapes in Vegas last year that fit the Hudson profile."

"Really?" Lindsey paused, her mind racing with possibilities. "They fit the Williams profile then, too."

A moment of silence and then, "Except they were raped, not raped and then murdered."

At this point, Lindsey was convinced there was reason to check out the possibility of a connection. She dismissed his comment and asked, "What information can you get me?"

"I can give you names, addresses, and general information on the victims, but not much more. I know they have no suspects."

"When was the last attack?"

"Almost a year ago—here's the odd part—not long before the first victim in your case was found."

Lindsey's mind raced with options. The possibility of the Hudson and Williams cases being related had just moved to the possible scale. The implications the new knowledge represented made her stomach churn. "I have a bad feeling about this."

Steve's voice held a warning. "Lindsey, I think you need to turn this information over to the right people. The Williams murders were violent. I don't want you taking crazy risks."

She squeezed her eyes shut. "I need some time, Steve, please. Once the prosecutors know about this, I'll have a much harder time uncovering what is truth and what is colored over."

"You have a history of pushing beyond what you should. Lindsey, these girls all look like you. I don't like it." He made a frustrated sound. "Not one bit."

Lindsey knew she pushed the envelope. "I'll be careful. Just give me a couple days."

He was silent a moment, then in a softer voice, "How long are you going to pay back the world for Hudson? When are you going to forgive yourself?"

She swallowed back the threatening emotion. When she felt she had herself in check, she said, "Give me a few days."

His hesitation was silent but it reached through the phone line. "Three days and no more, and I want to be kept in the loop. The minute you shut me out, I shut you down."

Lindsey didn't like being held captive by Steve or anyone else, but her options were limited. "Fine," she conceded.

"How about we meet at that coffee shop you love, and I'll give you what I have. Say," he paused as if looking at his watch, "in an hour?"

A quick goodbye later, Lindsey hit the end button on her phone, and curled her legs underneath her body. Her thoughts were running wild. Could Hudson and Williams be innocent? She hated to even think such a thing. What if she was wrong?

But what if she wasn't and she didn't pursue the real criminal? How many women might die?

"What are you doing?"

Lindsey looked up to see Mark standing a few feet away; dressed in only his boxers, he was a picture of rippling, perfect male. It took her a minute to find her voice. Mark so took her breath away. "Just sitting here thinking."

He walked to the couch, and her eyes followed his every step. He sat down beside her, and pulled her legs across his lap. It was an intimate, comfortable act that made her smile inside. His hand ran up her bare leg. "You look good in my shirt."

She smiled and spread one hand on his chest, loving how it felt to touch him so freely. "You look good without it."

Mark laughed and brushed his lips across hers. "Who was on the phone?"

She drew back slightly, eager to tell him her news, and watch his reaction. "Steve," she said. "Get this. There was a string of rapes that fit the Hudson and Williams profiles in Vegas last year. They never connected anything to Hudson, of course, because he was in jail."

"What do you mean they fit both profiles?" he asked. "Be specific."

"Same exact profile, they all looked . . ." She let her words trail off, wishing she could take back what she had started to say. But it was too late. Mark was no fool. He would guess, or he would insist she explain.

"Like you?" he asked tensely.

"Yes, I suppose they do." She swallowed back a feeling of sickness. "I wish you wouldn't put it that way. I was going to say like the local victims." A pregnant silence followed. Unable to take the wordlessness between them, she said, "Steve is meeting me in less than an hour to give me everything he has on the cases."

"I'll go with you."

"You have to get dressed and go to the office. I'll go by my place and change after I meet Steve."

Mark's lips firmed. "I'm going. Besides, we have to be in court at ten o'clock, so it will be just as well to already be together."

"Five-thirty is the partners' meeting. You remember?" she asked trying to distract him.

Mark shot her a look that said he knew what she was

doing. "I'm coming with you."

Lindsey felt her temper start to flare. "Mark, don't start trying to keep me under thumb."

She tried to move her legs and he held them with his hands. "I saw the way you hopped through that window, Lindsey. I'm worried about you."

Men who tried to control her got nowhere. Mark included. "You're starting to really tick me off. Let go of my legs."

Mark wrapped his arms around her and pulled her close, his mouth moving just above hers. "If you're going to get mad because I care, then go ahead. It's not going to make me back off."

How he managed to deflate her anger, she wasn't sure. In its place, a sizzling awareness settled, and when his lips pressed against hers, she was lost. Desire spread inch by inch, like a warm spray of water, rich with depth.

And when he pressed her back into the couch, and she felt his weight settle over hers, she forgot everything but him.

Still flush from the pleasure of their lovemaking, Lindsey scrambled for her clothes. Mark was in the shower, so she had a mere few minutes to make her escape. No way was she taking Mark with her to meet Steve. The last thing she needed was Steve getting all tight-lipped about what he knew.

And just because she and Mark made love, that didn't mean he was now her sidekick.

If anything, his insistence on joining her only made her more determined to go without him. She liked Mark. Maybe too much. But Mark, or any other man, for that matter, was not going to start controlling her. Been there, done that, already had the T-shirt.

Besides, she would be going home to Washington. That, in and of itself, was a good reason to keep things light. Once dressed, Lindsey quickly scribbled a note to Mark and grabbed her purse before she headed for the door. She paused as she reached for the knob and sighed, a bit of regret filling her mind and making her stomach flutter.

She hated to end their night with this kind of departure. But what option did he leave her?

Mark stepped out of the shower, towel wrapped around his waist. He had just finished lathering his face with warm shaving cream when he realized how quiet Lindsey had become. A bad feeling made him step into the bedroom. "Lindsey?"

Something moved on the bed, caught in the draft of the ceiling fan. The instant he brought it into focus he cursed, and moved towards the bed. It was a damn note. She'd taken off without him. He grabbed the paper.

I had to go alone. Steve won't tell me everything he knows with a stranger present.

Sorry, Lindsey

He crumbled the note in his hand. She was killing him. As amazing as their time together had been, it was abundantly clear he had no control over her. Why did everything have to be so damn complicated with her? And why in the hell couldn't he just walk away?

Lindsey walked into the coffee shop, and immediately spotted Steve.

He was, after all, pretty hard to miss, considering he was

the only guy in the place linebacker big, black, and dressed in a suit. He pushed to his feet the minute he saw her, and held out his arms, offering her one of his teddy bear-sweet hugs that so didn't match his intimidating physical presence.

After a few moments of heartfelt happy greetings, they sat down at the table Steve had been holding for them. A cup of steaming hot coffee sat in front of Lindsey. Steve grinned. "I got your favorite. A venti Carmel latte."

She felt the ache of her past actions both in her stomach and the ache in her heart. He was a good friend, a close one, and she had turned away from him. "Thanks, Steve," she said, trying not to choke on emotion. "How are Louise and the kids?"

"The kids are kids. Tommy got suspended for pulling the fire alarm and Sally put gum in her hair. Louise, on the other hand, is mad as hell at you for forgetting about us."

"I know," she whispered. "I don't even know what to say. Everything sounds like an excuse. The bottom line is I was afraid of anything that tied me to the past. I needed a new life. But I regret making you a part of what I shut out."

His expression softened at her honesty. "I know it's hard for you to be back here, faced with running the firm."

She reached for her cup. "And this case." The warm liquid seemed to soothe her nerves. Some people claimed caffeine put them on edge. Lindsey felt it gave her life. "Mmmm," she said, "I missed this. No one makes a Carmel latte like this place." She set her cup down, "And, believe me, I have tried to find a match."

"I guess you haven't broken that caffeine habit of yours." Steve chuckled as he reached for his orange juice.

She crinkled her nose at him. Years of working long hours had pretty much made coffee a food group by her standards. "I see you haven't broken your healthy eating habit."

Steve leaned back in his chair. "Yes, still got that bad habit." He laughed. "You are a piece of work, Lindsey."

She laughed. "So you have always said."

"What are you going to do about the firm?"

She took another drink of coffee, and another. Just thinking about her situation made her agitated. Mark really did have her captive. "Trying to get Mark Reeves to take it back."

"And?"

She sighed and set her cup down. "He's agreed to help me for six months, but swears he won't stay beyond."

Surprise registered in his eyes. "You're staying for six months, or he's letting you go back to Washington?"

"He won't help unless I stay." Her tone was one of frustration. "Not at all how I want this to play out. But for now, I am stuck with this case, and will at least see it through."

Steve leaned forward. "I don't know Mark, but I know his reputation, and it's a strong one."

"Oh, he's good at what he does. Too good for my dad to have lost him. I can only hope time will work in my favor and Mark will decide to stay."

"And if he doesn't?" he asked.

"I don't know if my father will practice again. He certainly can't run the firm. I will have to find someone to take over."

"But not you."

"No," she said firmly. "Not me."

Ready to change the subject and concerned about time, she said, "I have to shower and be to court by ten. What do you have for me?"

Steve pulled a large folder out of a notebook sitting on

the table. "Three girls in Vegas raped and killed. All three look . . ."

She shot him a reprimanding look. "I know," she paused for a beat, "like me. We all know this. What else?"

He gave her a measuring gaze. "You need to just chill, Lindsey. I don't like that these girls look like you. It would be too damn easy for you to become a target." He paused as he looked her over closely. "Make sure you're not being followed. Those girls were all grabbed from behind. Be aware of your surroundings."

She grunted. "First Mark and now you. Stop. I know how to take care of myself."

"I'm damn glad to hear Mark has some sense. This is serious stuff."

She snapped, "Stop acting like I am some novice, and show me the file."

Steve sat back in his chair and crossed his arms in front of his wide chest. "What gives, Lindsey?"

Lindsey looked at her coffee cup, and then back at him. "Sorry, Steve. I guess I'm more on edge than I realized."

He stared at her for several seconds, and then nodded. "I know you have a lot on you right now."

"It's no excuse for me snapping. I'm sorry."

He waved a dismissive hand. "Let's talk Vegas," he offered, giving her an escape from the moment, which she appreciated because she knew it was his intent.

"You said there were no suspects, right?" Lindsey asked.

"No one. They came up dry. The girls went to the same school and hung out at the same bar."

A chill raced up her spine. "Bar? So far I have confirmed at least two of the girls in the Williams case hung out at the same bar."

"Could be a lead," he said. "I included a lot of general

information like drivers' license pictures of victims, and contact info for the detectives on the case."

Lindsey took the folder. "Did the detectives here locally follow up on the Vegas lead? If they searched the national database, they would have found this."

"The grapevine is pretty tight-lipped, but the word is that yes, it was examined but ruled out."

Lindsey frowned. Steve asked, "What?"

Lindsey sighed. "You know what I am thinking. The obvious."

"There was no way to tie Williams to the cases, so someone pushed Vegas under the rug." His tone was grim with the potential truth. He and Lindsey both knew those types of things happened if someone had a political agenda and needed a conviction.

Lindsey nodded and then asked, "What time do you have?"

He glanced at his watch. "Eight forty-five. You better hit it if you're going to shower."

Lindsey took a big swig of her coffee and dotted her mouth with her napkin. "Yeah, my first day back in court. I better dress the part."

"I won't ask why you are wearing wrinkled clothes."

They both knew she was meticulous about her appearance. Not only that, the very fact she was rushing home to change confirmed any assumptions he might make.

"And I won't explain." Lindsey stood up and grabbed the folder and her briefcase. After giving Steve a quick kiss and promising to check in that night, she started for the door.

Steve reached out and grabbed her arm. He grabbed her hand. "Be careful," he said looking at her with concern etched in his face.

She nodded and turned to walk away but suddenly had a thought that made her turn back. "Hudson, the last trial I didn't handle, can you find out how conclusive the DNA evidence was?"

He eyed her. "I can. You think it was a plant?"

"Maybe," she said. "It's a long shot, but worth looking at."

Lindsey started stripping the minute she walked into her apartment, leaving a trail of clothes leading to the shower. Late to court wasn't an option. Twenty minutes later, dressed in a stylish black suit, her hair twisted into a neat bun, she walked out her front door, dialing her phone as she pulled it shut behind her.

The receptionist at Paxton answered in two rings. "I need Mark. This is Lindsey."

"Oh, dear," she said in a panicked voice. "Mark has been grumbling about you."

"I imagine." Lucky for her, court would make it impossible for him to yell at her.

Music came on the line, and then, "Damn it, Lindsey, where are you?"

"Temper, temper," she said. "I'm on my way to the courthouse now. I'll meet you in front."

"If you ever pull a stunt like this again I swear I . . ."

Lindsey interrupted. "You'll what?"

"Just get your ass to the courthouse." The line went dead.

She stared at the phone. "That went well." She sighed and hit end.

Lindsey stepped out of the cab to find Mark pacing the steps of the courthouse. The minute he saw her, he stalked in her direction looking like a hard-nosed, perfectly-dressed attorney who happened to be breathtaking sexy, and so angry he looked like he could kill.

The instant he was within hearing range, he started his verbal lashing. "You could have made us late." He tapped the face of his watch.

Her chin lifted defiantly. "But I didn't."

Mark grabbed her arm, not hard, but no less forceful, as he leaned down, his mouth near her ear. "Don't pull a stunt like this again."

Lindsey's eyes lifted to his, a challenge in the direct stare she gave him. "Or what, Mark?"

He looked her squarely in the eye. "Or I won't stay around to deal with it."

Her eyes widened with disbelief. She didn't think he would hold his presence over her head. "You know what?" she asked, her tone low, but packed with fury. "I want your help, but I won't have it held over my head. If this is how it's going to be, then forget it. I don't want your help. Give me the file, and I will take over."

His eyes were so dark brown they were almost black, and she could see a muscle in his jaw jump. She could almost hear him count to ten in his head. Then, as if the anger she had just seen in his eyes had never existed, an aloof coolness filled his face. His hand dropped from her arm. "This isn't the time or place for this discussion. We're due in court."

For a moment, she actually had the crazed desire to tell him to go to hell, demand the case file, and march up the courtroom stairs by herself. A moment was it. After that, sanity took over. She didn't want the case or the firm. "Fine," she spat, because no other words came to mind. Not ones that wouldn't greatly hurt her chances of keeping Mark at Paxton.

They eyed one another, a stand-off of sorts, and without another word, turned and walked, side by side, up the courthouse steps. A few minutes later, not a word spoken between them, they stepped into the courtroom. As they approached the defense table, Lindsey momentarily stopped walking. She could hardly believe who was representing the state.

Mark's head jerked in her direction. "What?"

She swallowed, and started walking again. "Prosecutor change. Not a good one."

Mark followed her lead. "Meaning what?"

She eyed him as they sat down. "Meaning Greg Harrison is not one of my favorite people." In fact, he was one of her least favorites.

Mark leaned close. "I'm not in the mood for anymore surprises."

She gave him a hard stare. "He's my ex-fiancé, Mark."

He shut his eyes a minute, and then refocused. "Let me guess? He isn't going to play nice?"

"We'll see, I guess."

Mark pulled the case file out of his briefcase. "Wonderful. This day gets better and better." He looked beyond her shoulder. "Don't look now."

Lindsey turned as Greg was almost upon them. Dark hair, blue eyes, with a tall, athletic build, most found him attractive. She'd seen the man beneath the outer shell. He was far more beast than beauty. "Hi, Greg," she said, before he could speak, eager to take control of the conversation. She knew Greg. He was big on commanding the room. She indicated Mark with her hand, pushing her chair back so they could see each other. "Do you two know each other?"

"We know each other," Mark said with cool politeness.

"Why didn't you tell me you were back in town?" Greg said, focused on Lindsey, ignoring Mark.

She didn't even try to smile. It would have taken too much effort. "Now you know."

"All rise for the Honorable Nelson Dearman."

Lindsey turned towards the judge, dismissing Greg with her action. "Catch you after court," he whispered, leaning down far too close to her ear. And then he was gone.

Lindsey felt Mark rise next to her. It was strange letting him take control. She was used to controlling the courtroom, not watching another take charge. Forcing herself to ease back into her chair, she watched Mark in action. He presented well, compelling but not overbearing. It wasn't long before a thirty-day continuance was in the pocket, and they exited the courtroom.

Her name rang out through the hallway, but Lindsey didn't turn; she already knew it was Greg. She tried to ignore him, but he was persistent, simply increasing his volume. Just before she hit the elevator button, she exchanged a glance with Mark. His expression held both irritation and a demand: Shut the man up.

She turned, teeth clenched, as she willed herself to stay cool. "Lindsey?" Greg said, a bit out of breath as he stopped beside her. As if he had been half-running. "I thought we were going to talk after court?"

The elevator door opened. "When did we say that?"

He ignored her question. "Are you here to stay?"

"No," she stated, her tone flat.

"How long?" he asked.

The elevator doors closed. "Too long."

He stared at her. "Lindsey, please ease up."

He glanced at Mark as if he was trying to decide what he should say in front of him. Then he took a step closer and leaned his head closer to Lindsey. "Have dinner with me."

Even in a low tone, Greg came off demanding. Lindsey bit back her words, wanting to tell him what he could do with his dinner. "Not going to happen," she said, stepping backwards so close to Mark she was almost touching him.

His eyes flashed with irritation. Maybe even a hint of anger. "I'll call you," he stated.

"I would rather you not." Lindsey glanced up at Mark and then back to Greg. "We're in a rush." She punched the elevator button a little too hard, as if it would open the doors faster. Luck was on her side because it worked. The doors opened. "Goodbye, Greg," she said, and gave him her back as she stepped into her escape car.

As she turned to face forward, Mark by her side, Greg's eyes locked with hers. "You can't get rid of me that easily."

And then the doors slid shut.

Mark stared straight ahead. "This is going well."

Lindsey shot him a glowering look. She was up to her chin with men for the day. Silence filled the elevator except for the ding at the floors, then, "I can't see you with him."

She laughed. Bitter. "That makes two of us."

He didn't ask anything more and she didn't offer. By the time they were in the back of a cab, Lindsey was about to scream for the strain of their silence. She turned to him. "Yell at me or something. This tension is driving me nuts."

Mark was leaning against the seat, his body relaxed. "It's done." As if that was it.

"Okay," she said, turning away from him. "If that's how you want it, so be it."

She felt his eyes shift to her, but she didn't look at him. "I don't like these little games you're playing."

Her head turned. "Games?" she demanded. "What games?"

"That stunt this morning."

"You can't just demand to go with me, and expect me to do your bidding."

"When it comes to Paxton or this case, I damn sure can." His lips thinned, eyes narrowing. "Tell me I'm wrong, Lindsey." A dare laced his words.

She turned away, staring out the window, fighting the roll of anger burning inside. Oh, how she wanted to tell him to go to hell. "You are so like them."

"Like who?"

Damn. Had she said that out loud? Her arms crossed in front of her body. "No one." She refused to look at him.

His hand went to her arm. "Who?"

"My father," she said, her temper getting the best of her. "Greg." There, it was said. Her voice was lower now, but no less intense, her eyes hard as they met his. "Men who have to be all and control all."

Surprise registered in his face. "What does Greg have to do with this?"

"He and my father had it all planned out." Her voice held bitterness. "Greg was just the kind of man my father wanted attached to me and Paxton."

"But you didn't see it that way?" he asked, speculation in his tone.

She felt the regret of her past mistakes. "I got smart. When Greg proposed, I declined."

He raised a brow in question. "Just like that?"

"You make it sound simple. It wasn't. It took a dead girl for me to see the light. Until then, I would have done anything to please my father."

"Including marrying Greg?"

She looked away, unable to face the truth, let alone admit it out loud. "I didn't. That's what counts."

He was silent for so long it was hard not to turn and look at him. Finally, he said, "I'm not like them."

She wanted to believe that, but today he had tried to keep her under thumb. She didn't respond. What good would it do?

Mark didn't accept her silence. "Can you say something, Lindsey?"

She turned to him. "What am I supposed to say?"

His eyes flared. "Why is it wrong for me to worry about you when some crazy person has been killing women who look just like you?" His face hardened. "Does that make me controlling? Does that make me a jerk? If it does, I'll live with it rather than see something happen to you."

Lindsey swallowed, almost choking on her own guilt. "Mark." He didn't look at her. She didn't know what to say. Turning to the window, she tried to make sense of the roar of confusing messages running through her head.

She didn't know what to do about Mark. Maybe he was just worried about her. But, then, maybe his concerned words were simply a manipulation tactic.

The minute they stepped into the lobby of the Paxton Group, Judy greeted them with messages in hand. "The phone is ringing off the hook," she said, her voice frazzled as she stuck a pencil behind her ear. "Everyone has heard the two of you are back." Her attention went to Lindsey. "Your father called, sounding rather grumpy."

Lindsey made a face. "So, he sounded normal."

She laughed. "A little more on edge than usual," she said, and thumbed through several messages, and a memory flashed in her face. "Oh, yeah, some guy called several times. Said his name was Todd but wouldn't give me a last name or leave a message."

Mark and Lindsey looked at one another. "The boy-friend?" Lindsey frowned.

"Maybe," Mark said. "We did leave him several messages."

"Yeah, but why not leave his last name and a number? It's strange." She shrugged. "I'll just try and call him again."

He nodded. "I'm going to have Maggie order some food. Want something?"

"Yeah, sure. She'll know what to get," Lindsey said, her thoughts still lingering on the oddness of Todd's call.

Entering her father's office, Lindsey let her body hit the chair with a loud thud, wishing it was her office, her space. Somehow it seemed as if that would be accepting a future at Paxton. Still, sitting in her father's office was like being suffocated by his wishes.

The ones that included running her life.

But what was really upsetting her was fighting with Mark. Her teeth sunk into her bottom lip. Her night with him had been amazing. For the first time in a long time— no, maybe ever—a man had made her feel feminine and special, but also, she grasped for the word . . . equal. Yes. She had felt as if what they had shared was just that. Shared. Give and take.

So what happened in the light of a new day?

Being honest with herself wasn't always an easy task. No one wanted to face hard truths about their own choices and decisions. Or their fears. And Mark scared the hell out of her. He made her feel things she didn't want to feel. Things she didn't want to put names to. Fighting with him messed with her head far more than it should. Deep down, she knew, way too fast, she was developing feelings for Mark.

As if that wasn't complicated enough, stepping back into the courtroom had been like a rush of memories. She'd expected as much. The big surprise was that they weren't all bad. In fact, they were—for the most part—good. For the first time in years, she was questioning what she thought she knew. Being in the courtroom again had felt invigorating. A part of her had felt more alive than it had in years. And she had just been sitting behind a table: watching Mark, imagining her own performance.

The truth was, she had loved the challenge of each and every case. The high of winning had been exhilarating. Dropping her elbows to the desk, she buried her face in her hands. If only that woman hadn't been killed. The hell of that murder had haunted her for years.

A stream of bright sunlight was suddenly at her window, as if a cloud had moved. Hot and heavy, it rested on her face, making her more uncomfortable than she already was. She pushed to her feet and moved to the window, pulling the cords to release the blinds, and turning the room into a darkened box. A perfect match for her mood.

She hadn't called her father back, and she knew she had to. Judging from the mood Judy had suggested he was in, he'd probably heard about Mark. The firm needed Mark, but her father wouldn't see it that way. What would he do if she refused to run the firm? Squeezing her eyes shut, willing herself to pick up the phone. Her fingers dialed. She tried Todd again. No answer. She left another message. And that was the end of her excuses. She dialed her father.

The minute he heard her voice, he went on the attack. "Lindsey, what in the hell is going on over there?"

She went for a matter-of-fact voice. "We had a good day in court."

He growled into the phone. "You know damn well what I mean. Why is Mark Reeves in my offices?"

This was going well. "Daddy, listen—"

"No, you listen," he huffed. "I want him the hell out of there now!"

Twisting the phone cord around her hand, she forced out her response. "I can't do that."

There was a pregnant silence, and she knew he was stunned at her open disregard for his wishes. "You can, and you will."

She was firm on the outside, but arguing with her father had always been difficult. "I can't."

"Don't cross me, Lindsey," he warned.

This time she crossed the invisible line never to be crossed. She put it on the line. "He stays or I go."

Silence, thick like a heavy blanket, fell between them. "What?"

Her voice was low. "I can't handle the Williams case without him."

He didn't care. "You can, and you will," he said in a biting tone. "I'm warning you, Lindsey Paxton, get rid of him by tomorrow or I will. I don't care if I have to have security carry him out."

She clenched her teeth. "I won't do it, Daddy. We're a package deal. He stays or I go."

"Get rid of him." And the line went dead.

Her stomach twisted in a knot. Holding the receiver, a bit stunned by the outcome, she couldn't seem to get herself to move. A knock on the door made her jump, and she dropped the phone. It crashed against the desk and hit the floor. "Come in," she yelled, as she reached for it.

"Look, what I have for you!" Lindsey knew Judy's voice without turning. She replaced the receiver and turned to find her rushing towards the desk with a vase of roses. "Someone sent you flowers."

Setting them on the corner of the desk, Judy stepped back and surveyed the arrangement with approval. "They're so pretty," she beamed.

It didn't take reading the card to tell Lindsey who sent them. They were Greg's signature pink roses. She swallowed, trying to fight that old feeling of claustrophobia the combination of Greg and her father combined had always evoked.

Reality hit hard. The courtroom hadn't driven her away. They had.

"Aren't you going to look at the card?" Judy asked, her eyes sparkling with excitement.

Lindsey's lips thinned. "No," she responded. "I know who they are from."

Maggie walked in at that moment, Lindsey's lunch in hand. She froze in the doorway. "Oh, dear," she said and then began walking again. "Greg knows you're back, I see."

Lindsey grunted. "Yes," she said in a strained tone. "Would you believe he's prosecuting Williams?"

Maggie's face filled with understanding as she set the bag of food down on her desk. "Sorry, dear," she said and patted Lindsey's hand. "I know this is not easy for you."

Lindsey gave her a look of appreciation.

Judy now stood with her hands on her hips. "Who's Greg?"

Maggie shot her a reproachful look. "No one interesting." Maggie directed a rare frown at her. "Who's covering the phone?"

Judy's hands flew to her chest. "Oh goodness. The flowers distracted me, and I completely forgot the phones." She turned to exit and peeked over her shoulder. "I'm sorry," she added and dashed away.

Maggie focused on Lindsey. "You okay?" Lindsey nodded. Maggie wasn't satisfied. "You don't look okay, you look pale." Maggie indicated the food with a nod. "Perhaps eating will do you good."

Lindsey eyed the bag. "I'm not very hungry. Why don't you see if anyone else wants it? I'll take the drink though." She offered a weak smile.

"Are you sure?" Maggie asked, with concern falling over her features.

An unconvincing smile filled her face. "Yes, I'm sure." A thought came to mind. If anyone knew what the past held . . . "Maggie, what happened between Daddy and Mark?"

"Well dear, I'm not completely sure. It comes down to one simple fact. No one crosses your father and gets away with it."

Lindsey sighed. "Right. How did Mark's leaving impact the firm?"

"I know our billing dropped more than fifty percent." She hesitated and then said, "I heard them argue just before Mark walked out. Something about the wrong type of clientele and people who don't pay their bills."

It made sense. Mark hadn't been the bad guy. He'd been trying to save the firm. "Is Mark in his office?"

Maggie nodded. "Yes, I just took him his food."

"Okay, thanks Maggie." She pushed to her feet. "I'm going to go see him."

"Mark?"

Mark's eyes lifted from the file in front of him. He'd know Lindsey's voice anywhere. He'd been thinking about her. If thoughts could will someone to appear, his had willed her to his office.

"Do you have a minute?"

He could see the tension lines in her face. Leaning back in his chair, he waved her forward. "What's wrong with you?"

"My father," she stated.

That said it all. "He found out I'm back and wants me removed immediately."

Lindsey's eyes widened as she settled into the chair in front of his desk. "Yes, exactly. How did you know?"

"I expected as much." Edward, was, if nothing else, predictable.

"He threatened to have security escort you out."

Mark pushed away from his desk and stood up. He walked around the desk and leaned on it, facing her. Close but not too close. Edward wasn't his concern. "What do you want?"

She didn't hesitate. "I want you to stay."

"You're sure?" he asked. Her accusation still ate at him. "You said I was just like him."

She looked down. "I was upset." Her eyes lifted again.

He needed to know where they stood. "That doesn't tell me anything."

"Mark, I . . ." Her words faltered.

His eyes probed her face. "What did you tell Edward?" Her answer would say a lot.

Her chin raised a notch higher as if she wanted him to see the truth in her gaze. "I told him if you go, I go."

He reached for her then, taking her hand and pulling her to her feet, and then into his arms. She came without hesitation, hand on his chest, looking up at him with those soft, too-green eyes. "And he said what in response?" Mark asked.

A wave of distress flashed across her face. Unaware of

her action, her hands tightened on his shirt. "He hung up on me."

Mark couldn't help feeling a hint of amusement. He would have loved to have been a fly on the wall when Lindsey had laid it on the line. But she was distressed, and he understood why. His hand ran down her back. "Everything will work out. I promise. Let me think things through, and we'll talk before the meeting. Is that fair enough?"

"How can he expect me to do this alone?" she said, as if a wall had come down and she had decided to unload on him. "I've never even touched the books, and dealing with the partners is new to me. I can't do this Williams case alone—"

Mark cut her off by kissing her, a soft, reassuring press of his lips to hers. When he lifted his head, he smiled at her. "It'll work out, I promise."

"Why does he hate you so much?"

Mark was silent. He hadn't told Lindsey what had happened between him and Edward, and now didn't seem like the time. "He and I simply don't agree on business matters."

She grabbed his tie. "Don't shut me out, damn it."

His hand went to her face. "Then don't shut me out. Give me a chance before you judge me."

Her eyes registered her guilt, but her words were defensive. "I had a good reason for not taking you to the meeting with Steve."

"You ran out on me while I was in the shower. That was a low blow."

She paled. "If you hadn't demanded—"

"I was worried."

"I can take care of myse—" He swallowed her words with his mouth, kissing her as if he was drinking her in, with long, sensual strokes. Lindsey was like a fine wine, perfect from the very first drop, and addictive from there.

Whatever she was doing to him, he wanted more. The instant his tongue touched hers, she relaxed into him, arms inching around his neck, body leaning into him. She felt what he did. This irresistible need to explore what was between them. Right or wrong, what they shared was too alive to ignore.

When they came up for air, he leaned close to her ear. "I wasn't trying to control you."

"I know," she whispered.

He leaned back to see her eyes. "You're sure?"

She smiled. "At this very moment, in your arms, having just been kissed very well," she said, "yes."

He laughed. "I guess I will settle for that answer."

"Do you have time to hear what Steve had to say?" She pointed at the untouched bag of food on his desk. "You can eat while I talk."

He smiled. "Sounds good."

"Then we can figure out how to handle my father."

"I'll take care of Edward."

She fixed him in a look. "Not without telling me how. We do this together or not at all."

Mark smiled to himself. Lindsey had no idea how much she had just given him.

Chapter Eight

If one more cab passed her by as if she wasn't standing at the curb with her hand out, she might just throw something at it.

As if in acknowledgement of her words, a car screeched to a halt in front of her. "Finally," she muttered to the air as she yanked open the door and slid inside.

"Where to, lady?" the driver barked, never looking at her. Lindsey reached for her briefcase. "I said, Where to, lady?"

"Just a minute." Her response was terse as she dug for Todd Rogers' address and found it.

A few seconds later, she sunk back into the seat as the car jerked forward. It didn't take much to tune out the horn-honking and cursing that went on in the front seat. It was just as much a part of New York as pizza.

Her thoughts went to Mark. How easy it had been to fall back into his arms, and forget their earlier fight. She'd even enjoyed exchanging thoughts about the possible Nevada connection. But when he'd finished his lunch, he'd seemed eager to get away from her. And secretive about why. The more she thought about it, the more she wondered if he hadn't manipulated her to see his way by way of his kisses. Which meant he had done the very thing she hadn't wanted . . . controlled her.

So, bothered by the idea that Mark was keeping her under thumb, she had to get out of the office. Since Todd couldn't be reached by phone, she'd decided to try another in-person visit.

The cab stopped at her destination way before her whirlwind of thoughts were in order.

Todd Rogers lived on Bleecker Street smack in the middle of Greenwich Village, the heart of the art district. Considered to be one of the more expensive areas of town, Lindsey assumed Tom had family money or a whole heck of a lot of roommates. Stepping from the cab, she took in historic buildings with fondness. The particular area of town was full of shopping, fine dining, and elegant architecture. Close to campus, it was busy with skateboarders, bikers, and a scurry of walkers. Busy during the day, it was even busier at night. Clubs and bars lined the corners, as did restaurants and stores.

Todd's apartment complex sat nestled between a pizza parlor and a hairdresser. It was a small complex, not more than ten stories, versus the many high-rise towers so common in the city. There was no doorman so Lindsey was able to push through the street door and enter the small hallway that housed the mailboxes and the downstairs apartments. Glancing at the narrow stairs that led to the other apartments, with no elevator in sight, Lindsey was thankful Tom lived on the bottom floor.

Almost the instant she knocked on the door, it flew open, taking her off guard. Tall, lean, and denim-clad, the man who greeted her was a full-fledged cowboy, complete with a Stetson on top of his head. The hat shadowed his eyes, but she felt his gaze, hot and heavy, as it made a slow slide down her body. Uneasiness pricked at her nerve endings. Despite the perspiration dampening her skin, she felt a cold chill sweep over her skin.

"Todd Rogers?"

Using his knuckle, he tapped the brim of his hat backwards, exposing the well-defined sharpness of his cheekbones, along with sharp, sea blue eyes. "Nope, but sure wish I was," he said, plopping a shoulder against the doorframe and crossing one booted foot over the other.

Lindsey fought irritation. Damn if the man wasn't going to make her ask the obvious. "When will he be back?"

"Well, now, that depends on who's asking," he drawled in a slow, Texas accent.

"Lindsey Paxton is the name and I am investigating the death of Elizabeth Moore. Now," she said succinctly, "when will he be back?"

He gave her a long, assessing stare. "Too bad about Elizabeth."

His voice seemed sincere enough, but something about it didn't sit right with Lindsey. Perhaps, the words rolled out a bit too flat. As if they didn't matter all that much. Lindsey's eyes narrowed. "You knew her?"

"Hard not to. She dated my roommate for a year. Party animal that one there, though. I told Todd he needed to get her under control. Appears I was right. Never safe for a girl like that to run around like she did."

Lindsey opened her mouth to speak when footsteps alerted her of someone's approach. She turned as a man stopped beside her. "Hey, Rogers. You got a visitor," Cowboy announced.

Used to quick assessments, Lindsey sized up her new visitor. Medium height and build, he was nothing like his roommate. Glasses sat on top of his nose, encasing light brown eyes. Dark hair, conservatively cut, matched his yuppie-style clothing. Opposites attract, as they say, and Todd Rogers and his roommate were indeed just that.

She extended her hand. "Mr. Rogers, I'm Lindsey

Paxton. I'd like to talk to you about Elizabeth."

She watched as his eyes went wide. Her thoughts went to Jack the Ripper, a conservative businessman who had a nasty side. Could that be the case with Todd Rogers? Was there a nasty side hiding behind Mr. Prim and Proper?

"Who do you represent, Ms. Paxton?" he asked tersely.

"I'm with the FBI." Which wasn't a lie. She was. She was just on leave. "Care to see my badge?"

He nodded and walked past her. "No, come on in."

Cowboy pulled his hat off his head and flattened himself in the doorway, allowing Todd to enter. Waiting for him to move, she was surprised when he didn't. Instead, he waved her forward, a dare in his eyes. Lindsey raised one eyebrow. "Forget it, Cowboy. Step aside."

He laughed and slowly complied.

Once inside, Todd motioned towards a small, wooden kitchen table. Sliding into a seat, she pulled out a pad and pen from her briefcase. "Sorry for Rick," he said, motioning towards the door. "He is a real ladies' man."

She assumed Rick was Cowboy. "And you're not?"

He laughed. "No, hardly. In fact, had Elizabeth not approached me, I might not have had the good fortune of knowing her."

Rick's comment about her wild side came rushing back. "How did you meet?"

"At a bar."

"The Pink Panther?"

His eyes widened. "Yes, did Rick tell you?"

Behind her Rick responded. "Nope, I didn't say a word."

Lindsey didn't turn. She'd already known Rick was there. She could feel his gaze riveted on her back. Ignoring him, she focused on Todd. "Why did you and Elizabeth break up?"

He took his glasses off and rubbed his eyes with his thumbs. It was a long moment before he replied. "I guess it just wasn't right between us."

Rick interjected, "He means she wasn't satisfied with one man. She liked to play."

Lindsey watched Todd's eyes as they seemed to cloud over. "Look, Ms. Paxton, I loved Elizabeth, but I don't see what any of this has to do with her death. Isn't Williams going to trial?"

Lindsey nodded. "Yes, but the evidence is circumstantial," she said truthfully. "Without more evidence, he could go free."

His expression registered understanding. "So tell me what you need from me."

He was making things easy on her. His willingness to help without asking too many questions kept her from explaining her role in the case. And she was damn thankful for that little prize. "I need you to tell me every little detail you can think of that might help."

They spent the next hour talking about Elizabeth and her habits, likes, and dislikes. Things her parents wouldn't know, because college-age kids didn't show that side to them. Rick's frequent interruptions, though irritating, did offer insight. Several times, things Todd left out of his stories, Rick brought to light, and then Todd would elaborate. When she felt she was out of questions, she stood and stretched. "Well, you have given me a lot to check out. I appreciate your time."

Next stop, the Pink Panther.

Lindsey arrived at the Pink Panther only minutes later. Located a few blocks from Todd's place, she had walked. She wasn't surprised to find the front painted pink, which made it stand out amongst the row-to-row buildings. She stuck her sunglasses in her purse as she pulled the doors open. Her eyes strained against dim fluorescent lighting. Blinking several times, she stood still and willed her eyes to adjust. Shadows danced along the walls, and she searched for a source. Odd, rainbow-colored spotlights were placed in each corner of the room.

Taking several tentative steps forward, she let her eyes drift around her surroundings. Barstools and tables lined a large dance floor. A doorway at the far side of the room gave her a glimpse of what appeared to be several pool tables with pink velvet coverings. "Classy," she muttered under her breath.

A bar ran the length of the far wall. Smoke climbed into the air from a lone ashtray sitting near the cash register. Bingo. Signs of life. She made her way towards it, ready to get answers and be on her way. This place gave her the creeps. Knowing it was somehow linked to four dead women—maybe more, if Hudson and Williams were innocent—made the feeling worse.

Lindsey leaned across the bar, trying to see inside an open door directly across from her. "Hello," she called. No response. She tried again but louder. "Hello."

This time a gruff-looking, overweight man came through the door with a cigarette hanging out of his mouth. He looked at Lindsey and then down at the ashtray. "Damn, if I didn't do it again."

He moved forward and stubbed out the cigar. His eyes went to Lindsey, irritation clear in his look. "What do you want, lady?"

Nice, she thought. "I want to ask a few questions about some girls who have frequented your place of business."

He snorted. "Hey, if their ID says they're legal, we did our job."

Guilty bastard. "I hadn't given your ID procedures any thought, but you're full of great ideas."

His reply was quick and vehement. "Don't play games with me, lady. What exactly do you want?"

Lindsey watched his face. "I want to know about four dead girls who just happened to party here the night they were murdered."

"I don't know nothing about any dead girls," he said roughly.

"I see we have a visitor."

A slight accent laced the voice that came from behind. Lindsey turned her back to the bar, facing the newcomer. He was tall, deeply tanned, with a menacing presence that crawled up her skin like a snake. Slowly he sauntered towards her, his movements graceful, his demeanor arrogant. His tan pants and matching blazer were expensive and well tailored. He reeked of money, power, and something more sinister. The word "evil" came to mind.

"She's talking some murdered girls," the bartender grumbled.

"Is that so?" the dark stranger asked, sauntering across the room and stopping way too close to Lindsey. He stared at her with eyes as black as coal, his deep, heavy brows framing them in a forbidding way. To some he might have been attractive. To Lindsey he felt dangerous. "Paxton isn't it?"

Lindsey almost gasped. For him to know who she was seemed impossible. She managed to keep a blank expression. Showing any sign of weakness seemed imprudent. "And you are?"

"Victor Ruzo, Ms. Paxton," he said coolly, almost too

139

coolly, "the owner of the Pink Panther." He motioned with his hand to indicate their surroundings.

"Just the man I need to speak with."

He leaned against the bar, his eyes watchful, intent. "About the murders," he said, as if he found the subject intriguing.

Lindsey's composure started to waver, and she was thankful for her practiced, courtroom poker face. "Yes," she said leaning on the bar herself, trying to seem as cool as he did. "Why don't you tell me about the murdered girls?" She paused for a beat. "Did you know them well?"

"Would you like a drink?" he asked, changing the subject, as he flagged the bartender.

"Need something to calm your nerves?" she asked.

He brushed aside her question. "Vodka, Larry, and bring the lady one as well." Then he turned back to Lindsey. "I didn't know any of those girls, Ms. Paxton."

She rejected his response. "They all knew this place."

Larry set down the drinks. Victor reached for his, taking a slow sip before his eyes met hers above the rim of the glass. "I make it a point to know about certain things." Victor gave her a challenging look. "Especially things that directly impact my business."

Lindsey's eyes narrowed. "And how exactly has your business been impacted?"

He set his glass down with a clank and propped his foot up on a metal rail. "My bar was mentioned in the news several times. There was a huge write-up about you as well. About how you got him off so he could kill again. Stunning picture of you, by the way. A beautiful young attorney who knows how to get killers off certainly got my attention."

Lindsey felt the words like the slap they were meant to deliver. She stared at him, struggling to pull herself together. For his painful remark, she lashed out. "Each and every one of the victims was at your bar the night of their attacks. That's a pretty damning scenario, if you ask me."

He smiled. "You seem very tense." He shoved her glass towards her. "I think you should drink this."

How could he act so nonchalant about a string of murders connected to his bar? "You haven't heard the last of this." Feeling the need to escape, Lindsey started towards the door.

"Come back again, Lindsey," he said from behind her. She cringed, hating how he said her name . . . so familiarly. He continued with arrogance, "Next time, we can get to know each other better."

Lindsey walked faster, forcing herself not to run, relieved when she reached the front door. She shoved it open and darted towards the street, only to run smack into something hard. Big hands closed on her shoulders, retracting the blow of her charging form.

"Wow, now, pretty lady."

Lindsey's eyes shot up as shock washed over her. Todd's roommate Rick stood before her, his hands lingering on her arms. She stepped back, feeling as if she had been attacked. She didn't like the man, and after her encounter with Victor she was feeling more than a little freaked out.

Forcing words from her lips took effort. "Ah, sorry," she muttered.

He gave her a grin. "Anytime you want to bump into me," he said with a smile, "feel free."

Any remnant of diplomacy Lindsey might have managed disappeared. "Why are you here?" she demanded.

He laughed. "Well now, little darling, my heart is broken." He held his hand over his chest. "Obviously you're not as pleased to see me as I am you."

Lindsey repeated the question, a demand in her voice. "Why are you here?"

He grinned. "I work here, of course."

Mark walked through the front door of the long-term care facility where Edward Paxton was being treated with a predatory-type stride. He carried himself with confidence through the hall, only remotely aware of the curious stares he received. Stopping at the front desk, he was greeted by a young brunette nurse who gave him Edward's room information.

It was well past time he and Edward had a long talk.

Mark found Edward's room empty. Frustrated, he started to turn away, intent on going back to the front desk and asking for more information. But his eyes caught on a figure outside the window. Edward sat in the courtyard beyond, his profile to the room. To say Mark was shocked at Edward's appearance would have been an understatement. The man had made a complete physical transformation. Thin and pale, he looked so unlike the robust man he had been only a short time before, that the change seemed almost impossible.

With a strained sigh, Mark turned away from the window and headed towards the courtyard. No matter how ill Edward was, there were matters that had to be discussed. A short walk later, preparing for a bitter welcome, Mark stepped to the front of the wheelchair.

Edward's eyes went wide. "What in the hell are you doing here?" He half-yelled the words.

A nurse eyed them and started forward. He shot her a glare that stopped her in her tracks, and refocused on Edward. "We have a few matters to discuss." Mark's tone was sharp, yet calm.

"We have nothing to discuss. Get the hell away from me and my company, and especially my daughter!"

"You handed your daughter a damn mess, Edward. Paxton is six months, at most, from bankruptcy."

"That's crap, Reeves. Besides, my daughter is very capable." He spat the words at Mark as his forehead fell into deep creases.

Mark stared at him with utter disbelief. Where was the man's sense? This was not the person he had gone to work for years before. He was putting his own desires above his daughter's happiness. Not only that, he was putting the employees and partners of the firm at risk.

"Lindsey doesn't even want to work at Paxton, let alone run it. For god's sake, she has never even looked at the books. She is hardly prepared to deal with bankruptcy, irate partners, or anything of such devastating magnitude."

"My daughter is a good attorney," he stated in an almost childlike fashion.

Mark's eyes grew wide and he sighed. His next words were spoken a bit more gently, but still with enough firmness to make an impact. "Lindsey's ability as an attorney is not in question by anyone but her. Think about this clearly, Edward." He hated what came next but it had to be said. "What if you don't pull out of this? Do you really want to leave Lindsey with a load of problems?"

His eyes looked wild for a moment, even panicked, before he inhaled and exhaled several times. Then, through clenched teeth, he said, "I *will* make it through this." No mention of Lindsey.

It was clear he wasn't dealing with someone who had a grip on reality. Despite his differences with Edward, seeing his old friend in such a poor state was hard to swallow. There had been a time when they had been close. Lindsey needed his help, and he intended to give it to her, however, he had to go about making that happen. "Look, Edward, I offered to buy your stock from you, but you refused. Now you are so deep in shit, you can't wade out. Your options are few and far between." Mark paused to see if he would get a reaction. When he didn't, he continued, "You will go bankrupt without me. Be logical about this."

"This is none of your damn business," Edward ground out through clenched teeth.

Mark's frustration was building. "Lindsey can't stay with Paxton if it shuts down. The only chance you have of keeping Lindsey on board is to save the business. Lindsey has handed over the reins to me, along with full control."

Edward's eyes went wide, anger flashing in his face. He held up his fist, and shouted, "And I am taking the control away from you."

Mark kept his voice steady. "If you interfere, you will lose any chance of getting your daughter to move back to Manhattan. She'll close the shop and go back to Washington."

Edward glowered at Mark, his eyes darkening. "I suppose you want the stock too? You bastard, you think you can just take over my company and my daughter?"

Mark stiffened, but he kept his expression blank. As much as he hated playing hard ball with a sick man, he had no option left. The man was too damn stubborn for his own good. "I know I can, and so do you. What options do you have? Lindsey and I have worked out an arrangement that guarantees her presence here for an extended period of time. If nothing else, that should make you happy."

Edward pointed a long, thin finger at him. "You'll run her off, is what you'll do. You'll make her hate the world of

law. She wants it to matter. It's just money to you. Leave
her alone."

Mark was silent a long moment. If the man only knew
how much he wanted Lindsey to stay, how truly on the
same page they were for once. "Your strategy of working for
free certainly hasn't worked, now, has it?"

Mark let his words linger in the air, watching Edward for
a reaction. For the first time since he had known Edward
Paxton, the man seemed unable to find words.

"Now," Mark said. "I need a commitment that you are
going to back off." When Edward started to speak, Mark held
up a staying hand. "Otherwise I am going to recommend
Lindsey file for company bankruptcy."

Edward's face reddened. "Damn you, Mark Reeves."

Mark's voice was low, no pleasure in his victory. "We
have a deal, I take it?"

"What choice do I have?" His voice was weak with resignation.

"You don't, but what you do have is a chance to keep
your daughter in Manhattan. Your way was a worthless effort. One day I hope you'll see the truth. Lindsey needs
your acceptance for who she is, not who you want her to be.
I can only hope you get smart before it's too late to make
amends with her."

When silence filled the air for a long moment, it was obvious to Mark that Edward wasn't going to respond. "I'll
leave you with your thoughts. Good day, Edward."

The phone on her desk started ringing the minute she
stepped into her father's office.

She had hoped for a few minutes' peace to get her
thoughts together. Apparently that was too much to ask for.
She began scurrying across the office when she heard

Maggie over the intercom. "Lindsey?"

She forced the irritation out of her voice. It wasn't Maggie's fault that she couldn't get any peace and quiet. "Yes, Maggie?"

Maggie cleared her throat nervously. Not good, Lindsey thought. "Greg on the line."

Caught between a choice of avoidance and head-on collision, she pondered her options with no easy answer. Damn it, she didn't feel like dealing with Greg, but she knew she wouldn't later either.

"Ah, Lindsey?" Maggie questioned, letting Lindsey know time was up.

Grimacing, Lindsey gave in. Better to get it over with. "Put him through," she said, sitting down, as she deposited her things on the desk.

"Good luck, honey."

"Yeah, I need it," she mumbled under her breath. Lindsey took several deep breaths and then picked up the phone line. "This is Lindsey."

His voice made her flinch. "Hey, beautiful. How are you?"

Lindsey rolled her eyes. Spare me the sweet talk, please. Her response was clipped but polite. "Thanks for the flowers."

"Just like old times, right?" he said in a soft voice full of intentions that didn't match Lindsey's.

No way was she letting him go down this path. "No, Greg, it is not like old times, and it can't ever be like old times again."

He ignored her in favor of his own agenda. That part was indeed just like old times. "Go to dinner with me, tonight."

It wasn't a question, which set her nerves even further on edge, if that was even possible. What part of "over" did the man not understand? "I can't, Greg. I have a lot of work to do."

"That's an excuse, and we both know it," he said. "Go to dinner with me and you can find out what I know about the Williams case."

Typical Greg tactic. Dangle something she needed as bait. Silently she cursed him. Lindsey bit her bottom lip, thinking hard. It was tempting to milk him for information. He owed her at least that for the hell of their past. Still, could she put up with Greg for an entire dinner? After only a moment of contemplation, she decided she couldn't. "Greg, I really can't."

He paused as if considering his next attack method. Greg was, if nothing else, a practiced overachiever. The word "no" was not in his vocabulary. "Okay then, coffee. We'll go to your favorite little spot." His voice dropped. "I haven't forgotten any of your little pleasures."

Every muscle in her body tensed. The very thought of him understanding anything about her, let alone her pleasures, was a joke. Yet logic told her she could get a lot more scoop about Williams if Greg was playing to win her back. She hated being a user, but turnabout was fair play; and she'd been a token in his game for years. "Well," she said slowly. "I guess we could do coffee."

She could picture his cocky grin as he responded. "Good. How about seven?"

"Fine, seven."

"I'll pick you up at your office." He didn't give her a choice, which was so Greg. "See you then, Lindsey." And he hung up.

No! Not the office. What would Mark think? Lindsey looked at the phone, realizing her grip was like a vise. He couldn't come to the office. Her fingers punched the telephone buttons, dialing his number, which was embedded in her brain like every other bad memory he represented. Seconds later, she was informed that he wasn't in his office. Slamming down the phone, she sat unmoving, mulling over her predicament.

Why in the world did she say yes to anything with Greg? He would just cause her trouble.

After a few minutes of beating herself up, she resolved to make the best of her situation. Lindsey swung around in her chair and grabbed the Williams file off her credenza. If the man was going to screw up her life, she might as well do a good job of milking him. It was time to roll up her sleeves and study and make a complete list of questions.

Reviewing files and calling witnesses took up the rest of her afternoon. A call to the NYU Dean's Office proved difficult at best. Convincing them to share any student information was like pulling teeth. It took threatening the school's reputation to get any semblance of information. A few other phone calls proved completely fruitless. If Williams was innocent, there was a link to those girls somewhere else. And she knew there had to be.

He was innocent, just like Hudson.

Her instincts said so, and as much as she feared trusting them, as always, they drove her actions. Regardless of the past, she had to go with what had always worked for her. And if Hudson was innocent, then her instincts had really never failed. She'd just thought they did. Getting back to her roots was the only way she would succeed.

She was looking through the police investigation reports on the Williams case, lost in deep concentration, when a noise made her jump. Her eyes darted upward, and she was shocked to see Mark standing in front of her desk. It scared the hell out of her that she had been so absorbed that she'd never even heard him enter. "Do you know how to knock, Mark?" she asked sharply.

Mark's eyes immediately flashed to the roses sitting on Lindsey's desk and then back to her face. "Funny, I thought we were past certain pretense." His voice was sweetly sarcastic.

Lindsey avoided looking at the roses. He was angry, but he had it tucked neatly behind his business mask. Still, it was there, in his eyes and in his tone of voice. And that made her angry. Between her father, Greg, and the men she had encountered in her field investigations, she was well past her quota of the overbearing opposite sex for the day. She didn't need Mark sending her into overload.

"One romp in the sack does not discard my right to privacy at work," she threw out sharply.

Mark's eyes narrowed and a flash of anger darted through them before he carefully offered her a blank stare. "So that's how it is, is it?" He thumbed a rose petal.

Lindsey pushed her chair back and stood up. "You know, at the moment I have had it to about here," Lindsey put her hand to the top of her head, "with men and their territorial claims on me and my time."

Mark's eyes darkened into deep pools of heat as he stood completely still, not moving a single muscle, just staring at her. There was a long, awkward silence before he turned and headed to the door. If he had said something, anything, it would have been easier to deal with than his cold silence. Lindsey felt regret like a sharp pain, and her chest tightened. "That's it?" she demanded to his back. "You're not going to say anything?"

Mark stopped walking but didn't turn around for several beats. When he did, she hated the cool detachment that filled his face. His voice was brittle and low. "I am not playing this game with you, Lindsey. Press me, and I'll leave you with this mess."

As much as she knew she shouldn't lash out again, she couldn't seem to contain her temper. Crossing her arms in front of her body, she stared back at him. "Ah, I see. Looking for an out."

The muscle in his jaw jumped, but he kept his expression emotionless. "If I was looking for an out, I wouldn't have dealt with your father today. I have every intention of keeping my word to help you, but I will only put up with so much."

Her eyes grew wide. "You fixed things with my father?"

He nodded and then turned back towards the door.

Lindsey stepped out from behind her desk and started crossing the room towards him, once again speaking to his back. "What happened? Mark?"

Mark's hand was on the doorknob, his words spoken without turning. "We're late for the partnership meeting, Lindsey." He opened the door and left before she could stop him.

All eight partners were already seated when Lindsey entered the conference room several moments later.

Mark sat at the head of the table, a sturdy business face securely in place, ensuring she had no hope of reading him. She regretted how she had treated him. Her feelings for Mark were confusing, and she'd allowed her own inner turmoil to escalate her temper. He didn't deserve to be smashed because of what other men in her life had done to her, yet it was so hard to separate him from them.

And terrifying. What if he turned out to be like them?

Mark was so stone-cold it was like watching a stranger. He was aloft and cold, with his cobra-like instincts alight in his dark eyes. He was prepared for battle, and she wondered if it was with her or the partners. Without speaking, she found her way to the empty seat next to Mark.

"Well now that we are all present, let's begin." Lindsey knew Mark's words were aimed at her tardiness, and she felt her cheeks turn red with an anger that she managed just barely to tuck beneath her surface. She was late. No question about it. It had taken her a few minutes to pull herself together after his abrupt exit from her office.

Speaking to the group, Mark continued, "For those of you who don't know, I've taken control of Paxton."

There was whispering around the table. Several people made remarks about being happy to see him back. Mark went on to explain the state of financial distress the firm was experiencing. Going into detail about caseload and expectations, he ignored the mumbling around the table.

Then he put everything on the line. "We are going to have to make big changes around here. If you don't like these changes, you are welcome to leave Paxton. Your shares will be purchased at a fair price."

Mark picked up a stack of papers and asked Lindsey to start passing them around the table. "The requirements for each partner's performance are detailed in this literature. If you can't meet your billing requirements, you simply won't be here. We're not a nonprofit and we do not do charity work," he paused for a beat, "contrary to what our current caseload indicates."

Heads dropped in concentration as each partner read the material. Mark let his eyes trail around the table and then stop on Lindsey. "Questions thus far?" he asked the room without looking away from her.

Lindsey met his gaze squarely, her eyes full of respect. It wasn't difficult to see why Paxton needed him. His tactics were hardcore, but she admired his ability to control the room and the firm. There was an inner strength, a power to Mark that drew her like a magnet. Sitting in the midst of a room of her peers, Lindsey understood why he rose to the top. Others found him as compelling as she did. His enemies found him dangerous, a true threat. His clients found him competent, a true defender. His lovers found him caring, as she did. The thought made her pulse quicken as vivid images of their bodies naked and wrapped together swirled through her mind.

Mark's eyes narrowed as he watched her, as if he sensed her mind was on their relationship and not the business of the meeting. For a moment, they sat absorbed with one another. It was Mark who broke the eye contact as he looked around the room.

"No questions?" he asked again.

Todd Walker, a gruff-looking man Lindsey guessed to be in his fifties, spoke up at that point. "What does Lindsey have to do with this?"

Mark answered. "Lindsey will take over in six months. I won't be staying. Next question."

The man sneered. "What? You are going to leave us with some young broad who appears more into style than law?"

Lindsey opened her mouth to offer a tongue-lashing, her eyes throwing daggers at the man, but Mark was already responding. "I assure you, Ms. Paxton's exterior assets only work as an added plus in the courtroom. She is not only a fine attorney, she's a member of the FBI. Cross her and you might find yourself learning more about her skills than you'd hoped."

The room filled with laughter. Lindsey sat dumbstruck by Mark's sharp response on her behalf. Clearly considering the subject closed, Mark began reviewing case files. It was several hours later when he adjourned the meeting. Lindsey was one of the first to leave as several partners stopped to speak to Mark. She walked through the lobby, ready to get some alone time, deep in thought.

"There you are, Lindsey." She looked up to find Greg. "I was afraid you might have backed out of our date."

Lindsey stood face to face with Greg, wondering how she'd forgotten something she so dreaded. "No," she said in a strained voice. "I just need to get my stuff. I'll be right back."

Lindsey walked with a quick, long stride, nervous as hell that Greg and Mark would cross paths. And her worst fears were confirmed as she found her way back to the lobby. Mark and Greg were talking. She tensed the minute she saw them, Mark's stiff demeanor telling her all she needed to know. He'd condemned her without knowing the whole story. Rigid coldness etched his features, and he refused to make eye contact with her. She wished she could explain, but somehow she doubted he would listen. The cobra had not stayed in the conference room. He was alive and well in the lobby.

Greg smiled as she joined them. "There you are, Lindsey," he said. "I was just asking Mark what your father did to convince him to come back."

Lindsey's eyes darted to Mark's face, but he still didn't look at her. "What did he say to that?" Lindsey asked tentatively.

"Actually, I don't believe he answered me," Greg said.

Mark stared at Greg a moment and then turned his gaze on Lindsey. She hated the coldness in those dark eyes of his. She longed to see them tender and aroused like the night before. And when he spoke, his voice was downright frigid. "If you'll excuse me, I have work to do. I'll let you two be on your way." He turned on his heels and disappeared without another word. Lindsey felt her stomach churn with downright nausea. It took Herculean strength to fight the urge to run after Mark and explain. Yet she also knew she shouldn't have to explain. Should she? She had no commitments to Mark Reeves, and he had no commitments to her. Yet she couldn't shake her need to explain things to him.

"Well, let's go, Lindsey." Greg smiled with a hint of satisfaction in his eyes. As if he knew what he had just done.

Only a few minutes later, Greg and Lindsey settled into the coffee shop chairs. Lindsey felt a ping of displeasure as Greg ordered her a drink, no request for her preference. Steve had done the same thing, and it felt like a friendly, courteous gesture. From Greg, it felt like he was assuming. Try as she might, when he set it in front of her, she couldn't bring herself to drink it.

"So Lindsey, how have you been?"

She couldn't manage to hold back a biting response. "Well, my father has cancer, I am handling a murder trial similar to the Hudson case, and I've given up my career at the FBI. How do I sound?"

He leaned back as if slapped, but his eyes looked more amused than anything. "Touché." She could feel his eyes on her even as she averted her eyes to the table.

"Perhaps," she said, but she wasn't about to apologize.

"You look beautiful," he said. She lifted her gaze, but she didn't speak. There was an uncomfortable silence between them. He leaned back in his chair, one arm dangling behind him. "I thought Mark left your father's firm for good. I even heard it was a nasty departure."

"I asked him to return."

Greg raised a brow. "Why?"

"I was, and still am, not prepared to take over the firm."

"Why didn't you come to me, Lindsey?" There was irritation, even a bit of heat, in his voice.

"Greg, please don't make things more difficult than they have to be." It took all of her willpower to make the words sound civil.

"I would have helped you."

Lindsey knew his form of help, and it was all about power and control. She wanted no part of it. She leaned forward, using every bit of mental fortitude she owned to hold back full-blown anger. "I didn't need help. I needed experience at Paxton, which Mark has. In case you didn't notice, I am quite capable of taking care of myself." Though he'd tried damn hard in the past to make her feel she couldn't.

"Lindsey . . ." he started to speak, but Lindsey held her hand up to stop his speech. "Greg, stop. Let's change the subject."

He was silent a long moment, shifting in his chair. "I tried to call you in Washington. You never returned my calls."

"I know."

He looked pointedly at her left hand, which cupped her coffee. "I take it you're not married."

"No, not married."

"Me either. I'm still waiting on you, Lindsey." His voice was a seductive purr.

Lindsey's narrowed on his, her discomfort heavy. "We are the past. Gone. We both know that."

"You never even told me why you ended our engagement. I deserved, correction . . ." he leaned forward, "deserve, to know what happened."

She shrugged, and leaned back in her seat wanting distance. "It wouldn't change anything, so it's pointless."

A wave of vulnerability flashed through his eyes, surprising her. "Two people in love can deal with whatever comes their way."

Lindsey shifted in her seat and cleared her throat, not liking the direction he was going with this. "Greg, please drop this. Tell me about the Williams case. Seems pretty circumstantial to me."

He stared at her in disbelief. "So does my guilt at this point." He lowered his voice and put his hand on hers. "Lindsey, I love you."

She stiffened and pulled her hands to her lap. "No you don't, Greg. You never even knew me."

He ground his jaw tightly. "What?" he asked, disbelief in his voice. His eyes narrowed. "If anything, I knew you better than you knew yourself."

She shook her head from side to side. "No," she said adamantly. "You knew the Lindsey my father created, the Lindsey you helped him feed and keep alive." She pointed at her chest with her finger. "I am not that person." She enunciated each word.

He glared at her. "Lindsey, this is crazy. We were in love."

She met his gaze with an unblinking stare. One of the things she always hated about her relationship with Greg was the way he told her what she felt. Didn't she deserve to decide her own feelings? "No," she said with ruthless intention. He didn't understand any other tactic. "We were not in love."

Greg just stared at her like he didn't comprehend her words. After a long moment, he fell back in his chair as if the wind had been knocked out of him, emotions darting across his face in wild array. His face settled into hard lines of anger. "I see," he said through clenched teeth. Squaring his shoulders, he continued, "Obviously you came here to talk business, so let's talk business. Williams is guilty. Life, with no parole. That will spare him the death penalty. Take it or leave it."

"Circumstantial evidence is all you have. That's not going to fly," Lindsey shot back.

"You have to make the offer to your client," he pressed.

"He will decline," she retorted.

"You can't win," he declared immediately.

"I will win, you can count on it," she stated firmly. Lindsey stood abruptly, pushing her chair back from the table. "See you in court, Greg." She turned and left the coffee shop without a look backwards.

Seconds later, Lindsey stepped hard on the pavement, still feeling the sizzle of anger as she walked towards her apartment. Only she wasn't sure if she was angrier with herself or with Greg. She had thoroughly screwed up any chance to get cooperation or information from him. If only she had controlled her feelings until she had picked his brain. Instead, she turned winning the case into a more important issue to Greg than ever. Winning was now about his ego.

"Damn," she mumbled.

How was she going to tell Mark she'd played the wrong game, and lost?

The words on the page began to drift together, and Mark tossed his pen onto the desk. Rubbing his eyes with his fingers, he tried to clear his view and then glanced at his watch. Exhaling loudly, he realized it was nine o'clock. No wonder he couldn't see straight. Working was the only way he knew to keep his mind off Lindsey with Greg. Only it wasn't working. Looking at the clock, he double-checked the time. It couldn't be this damn late and he'd made so little progress with his work.

Swiveling the chair around to the window, he stared out, a full moon a huge light in the dark sky. Like Lindsey was too in the darkness of his blank mind. After last night, he would have thought Lindsey would be in his arms about now, snuggled to him, safe and warm. Instead, he felt like the walls between them were bigger, wider, and taller than ever.

Backing out of their deal wasn't an option. He was too involved. Besides, he cared about her too much to leave her with the mess she would inherit. Being a fool wasn't on his list either. Seeing her with Greg had made him downright furious. He'd been ready to walk. Now, a bit calmer, he thought distancing himself from Lindsey was the smart thing to do. He needed a clear head, and he most certainly didn't need to be thinking with the one in his pants.

He sighed. What was it about Lindsey that drove him to distraction? He walked with a perpetual hard-on. But it went beyond the physical attraction. His life in general had been put on hold for Lindsey. He'd dropped his business plans and ran back to Paxton to help her. He snorted. And she was off with some other man. Correction, off with her ex. That was even worse.

Pushing to his feet, he decided on a beer at his old stomping ground, the Tavern. Royce would be there, and he wouldn't mind bending his ear. If there was anyone he trusted, it was his pal Royce Walker. And then tomorrow he would make some phone calls and let the rest of the world know he was still alive. A drink with the guys would do him good. Anything to keep his mind off Lindsey.

He walked to his car, determination building in his mind. Distancing himself from Lindsey was necessary so he could get a grip on reality. No way was he letting this kind of control slip out of his fingers any longer.

Chapter Nine

Stepping to her apartment door, she could hear the ringing of her phone through the wood. Hoping it was Mark, she quickly rammed her key into the keyhole. Slamming the door behind her, she raced across the room and grabbed the phone. "Hello?"

Click.

"Damn," she muttered and slammed down the phone, wishing she had signed up for the caller ID she'd insisted she didn't need. If she knew it had been Mark, she would call him back. But she didn't, so she couldn't, and she wasn't even sure why.

Then her eye caught on her blinking message light and silently she cheered. Three messages, surely one of them was from Mark. She hit the playback button and leaned against the desk. The first two were hang-ups, making her frown. Would Mark hang up without leaving a message? The third was from her father.

Shuffling to her bedroom, she quickly stripped down and put on a T-shirt and boxers before settling on the bed. With a sigh of resignation, she dialed the hospital. Her father was full of cheer. "Lindsey, where the hell have you been?" he demanded.

"I work for a living, remember?" she shot back, feeling defensive.

"I tried the office," he stated.

She grunted and rolled her eyes. "Building a case is

often in the field, you know that. Do I now have a curfew, Daddy?"

He grunted and then paused. "Look, about today . . ." His voice trailed off. Lindsey knew how hard it was for him to apologize. That was as close as it got.

Lindsey softened. "I'm sorry, Daddy. I hope you will forgive me for talking to you like I did. I just need Mark's help."

"I'll let him stay, but I warn you he is not to be trusted," he retorted. "In fact, I wouldn't put it past him to try and bed you to get the firm."

"Daddy!" Lindsey gasped indignantly. Her father never spoke of such things. The fact that Mark had, in fact, already been in her bed only made the statement more raw and hard to swallow.

"He wanted the firm, and I'm sure he still does. He has a reputation for getting what he wants, no matter what it takes."

Trying to ignore the warning bells in her head, she defended Mark. "He told me he doesn't want the firm anymore."

"Of course he did. He has to play things just right to get me to cooperate."

She mulled over his words, her heart beating like a drum in her chest. "Look, Daddy, you thought a lot of Mark for a long time. Ease up on him," she pleaded, and then added, "please? We both need him right now."

He grunted. "Just be careful. I hate being stuck in the bed like some kind of invalid, not able to handle things."

"I know you do," she said with understanding in her voice. "I wish I could make things different for you. But you're tough and you'll make it through this. We both will."

"I will, and don't you forget it," he ordered.

Lindsey smiled into the phone. She had definitely gotten her stubbornness from her father. "I won't, Daddy; just make sure you don't. Now get some rest."

Lindsey's smile was gone the minute she hung up the phone. Sitting on the edge of her bed, unmoving she replayed the conversation. Was she blinded by her attraction to Mark? Maybe he really did want the firm and she had given him the perfect chance to take it.

It was hard to be objective. The things she felt for Mark . . . things. What things? She hardly knew the man. Yet she felt as if she had known him a lifetime. Their sexual chemistry was nothing shy of exceptional. An added plus for Mark if he really was just using her. Like getting his cake and eating it too. She squeezed her eyes shut. The thought of Mark using her hurt far more than she wanted it to.

She needed to get some distance from what she felt for him.

When she finally settled under the covers, sleep was impossible. Eyes open or shut, her mind danced with pictures of Mark. His betrayal would be the ultimate pain. She had spent years getting her life under an iron thumb. Control, it seemed, had flown straight out the window. Mark had taken it from her as easily as stealing candy from a baby.

Now she had to decide how much she was willing to risk of herself where Mark was concerned.

Mark tipped back a long neck beer, and took a long swallow. Royce sat beside him, a smart enough guy to let him brood a while before asking questions. They'd met on business. Mark had been defending a client falsely accused of international terrorism. Royce had been with the FBI then, and it had been he who finally made the prosecutors see the light—they had the wrong guy.

"I can't believe you're back at Paxton, man," Royce said, shaking his head. "Should I wait until you down another beer before I ask why?"

Mark smiled wearily. "I'd say two more beers, because I still need an answer myself."

"Sounds like you need yourself a nice little female distraction. Too much work and no play is bad for the heart." He nodded towards an attractive blond at a nearby table. "Chelsea is always asking about you, man, and I can tell you first-hand she has a very nice way offering comfort." He paused to take a drink of his beer and then added, "Commitment-free."

Mark looked at the voluptuous blond who once would have had him licking his lips, and realized with surprise he no longer wanted her. He turned away from her and flagged the bartender, ready for another beer. Maybe then Lindsey would stop messing with his head.

"What do you say?" Royce asked after Mark ordered them both another drink. "A little loving on your mind?"

"Nope. Not tonight."

Royce raised a brow. "Ah," he said with understanding. "I sense woman troubles. Want to talk?"

Mark shook his head from side to side. "I don't know where to begin."

Royce smiled. "Since I have the good fortune of remaining unattached, I have all night." He let his gaze linger on Mark a long moment. "Who is she, man?"

Mark sighed as he allowed his fingers to drum against the bar. "Paxton's daughter."

A scuffle erupted across the bar. Two drunks were shoving each other. Royce shoved his barstool back, and straightened to his full height of six foot four. Mark already knew what was coming, but he twisted in his seat to watch the show.

"Hey," Royce bellowed as he stormed towards the two men, who had no idea what was in store for them. No one caused trouble with Royce around. Mark smiled. Royce's broad shoulders were stiff with tension as he stopped in front of the two men.

"Hey," he blurted again. Both men stopped arguing and looked up at Royce. Up being the operative word, because neither of them was over five foot ten.

The looks on the two men's faces—as if they were about to be stomped by the Jolly Green Giant—launched Mark into a burst of laughter. Mark took a long slug of his beer and prepared to enjoy the show. Several minutes later, Royce returned to the bar, the general peace of the bar restored. He slid onto the barstool and offered Mark a grin. Mark shook his head in a combination of disbelief and amusement.

The bartender slid a cold beer in front of Royce as a reward for his actions. Royce tipped back the bottle. After making a sound of satisfaction, he fixed Mark in a watchful gaze. "Now, where were we?"

Mark sighed as reality slipped back into view. "Paxton's daughter."

Royce's eyes went huge. "Didn't expect that one, I must say. So what exactly are we talking about here?"

He spent the next hour telling Royce the entire story from the day Lindsey showed up on his doorstep. By the time he left the bar, he felt better for voicing his feelings, but no less confused. Avoidance seemed his only strategy. With Lindsey there could be nothing personal until Paxton was behind him. Then and only then could he and Lindsey look objectively at their feelings for one another. And although Royce had offered to help with their investigation,

Mark had declined his offer. Royce was as big a control freak as he was, and that on top of dealing with Lindsey, it was just too much to contemplate. No, he would deal with this on his own.

Lindsey woke the next morning in a dark mood.

After tossing and turning the entire night, she felt irritable, and more than a little edgy. Every time she'd managed to slip into sleep, the phone would ring. Three separate times she had received hang-up calls. It had gotten downright creepy.

The fact that she had woken not once but twice with the same horrid nightmare hadn't helped matters. Hazy memories of the dream filled her thoughts. Replaying it over and over in her head, she tried to make sense of the dark images. Just like before, someone had been chasing her, and she had been trying to get to Mark. She wondered at the significance of Mark in the dreams. Was it about the case, or about her life?

The new light of day brought with it uncertainty. She wasn't ready to face Mark again. She felt too much like a vulnerable, open book. She was afraid she had no ability to control her emotions where he was concerned. Some time away from him would give her a chance to build a defense, to get back to her normal steadfast independence. She'd go to Vegas and look for leads. Decision made, she handled her travel arrangements and packed. Once she was in a cab on her way to the airport, she called Maggie.

No way was she going to tell Mark where she was going. He could hear it through the grapevine.

Mark's nerves were as sharp as a knife. No matter how he tried to concentrate on other things, Lindsey with Greg popped into his head. Once he had left the bar, he'd paced his bedroom, trying to understand the strange enticement Lindsey held. Finally, around three o'clock that morning he admitted he was falling in love with her.

That admission opened up a whole new can of worms.

Concentration was impossible. It frustrated the hell out of him that a woman, even Lindsey, could impact his work. Hell, he'd even let her create the very work he was trying to get done. He was here at Paxton for Lindsey, and no other reason.

He needed to talk to her, to clear the air, and decide where they stood. He pushed to his feet, and dogmatically walked towards her office. They needed to get some sort of understanding in place. Defining their relationship might allow him to get some work done.

Finding her office dark, he felt an instant of fear. First, that she had been out late with Greg, but then immediately after, that something had happened to her. He knew Lindsey wouldn't come in late because of Greg. Forcing a slow breath, willing himself to calm, he walked towards Maggie's desk.

"Maggie, where's Lindsey?"

Maggie inspected him with a tilt of her head. "My, my, someone got up on the wrong side of the bed this morning."

Mark took a deep breath, trying to control his anger. "Where's Lindsey?" he repeated in a steady voice.

"You mean you really don't know?" she asked cautiously.

Of course he didn't know or he wouldn't be asking. Quelling his irritation, he asked, "Know what?"

Maggie spoke slowly, as if she were preparing for the storm ahead. "She headed to Vegas this morning."

"What?" His eyes went wide, and anger began to take over fear.

Maggie stuck her pencil behind her ear and folded her hands together in front of her. "Yes," she said with a disapproving tone. "I assumed you approved the trip, though I was a bit nervous about her going alone, this being a murder investigation and all." Then she let out a short laugh. "Of course, she is in law enforcement. I just can't stop thinking of her like a little girl."

Mark couldn't agree more. "Damn that woman," he mumbled under his breath as he paced the floor several times, and then stopped in front of Maggie again. "Book me on the next flight out. Get me her hotel information as well."

Maggie shook her head in approval. "Do you want me to book you a room?"

Mark turned towards his office and spoke over his shoulder. "No, I'll call on my way to the airport. Just make my flight reservations while I cancel some appointments."

An hour later, Mark arrived at the airport with hastily packed bag. Leave it to Lindsey to pull a stunt like this. He wanted to throttle the woman. They were going to have a long talk—that was for sure. If he didn't know better, he'd think she was running from him, not her past. Not that it mattered. He wasn't about to let her chase after leads alone. Not on a murder case where she fit the victims' profiles.

By the time Lindsey's plane screeched to a halt on the Vegas runway, she was feeling downright sick. She loved flying over the Grand Canyon, but had hardly glanced out the window, too absorbed in her own regret.

Mark was going to be pissed, and she couldn't blame him.

Her stomach felt like it had lead in it, and her emotions were getting the best of her. It would be easy to cry, which was something she rarely did. Plain and simple, she'd come to Vegas without Mark, in an effort to lash out at him. It had been stupid and childish. But now it was done.

After a lot of thinking, she had decided she had overreacted. She trusted Mark. He wasn't using her, and she kicked herself for letting her father get to her. The night before, being around Greg hadn't helped. It had given her an overdose of men who wanted to control her. And she had allowed herself to put Mark into that same category.

During the entire flight, she had tried to justify her actions, but it wasn't possible. As the plane pulled into the terminal, she contemplated calling Mark. Perhaps if she told him she was wrong. No, she dismissed that idea. She couldn't call. It would be impossible to explain what she was going through over the phone. She could only hope that her actions hadn't damaged the bond that had started to form between them. She didn't believe Mark was after her for the firm. There was never any real doubt in her mind about Mark's motives. If she was honest with herself, she was just looking for an excuse to run from him.

It was going to take time and patience for her to be fully comfortable in a relationship with Mark. And she wondered if he had the patience to deal with her internal battles. Maybe she'd already pushed him away. Not that there was much hope of a long-term relationship between them. There were just too many obstacles, like her life in Washington. Still, Mark made her want more than a passing fling, and that scared her to death. She didn't want to lose who she was as a person. Every relationship she had allowed to be a part of her life had taken a part of her and destroyed it.

An hour later, she entered her hotel room, sank onto the edge of the bed, and reached for her briefcase. No more self-pity allowed. She'd come here for a reason. Finding the number for the local detective in charge of the Nevada killings, she dialed. After a few minutes of conversation, they agreed to meet. Since it was already late, they set up lunch for the next day. She could already tell she wasn't going to like the man she was meeting. When she'd described herself, he'd made a smart remark about her looking like the victims.

As if it was funny. Looking like a serial killer's profile wasn't ever funny.

Pushing to her feet, Lindsey stretched right and then left, trying to revive her stiff body. Hours on a plane had left her ready for a nap, but she needed to get to a library and do some research. Archived material on the local homicides should be easy to come by. She wanted to arm herself with all the facts she could before the next day's meeting.

A few minutes later, she stood in the hallway, waiting for the elevator to arrive. Her gaze floated to the large window at the end of the hall. For the first time since she arrived, she enjoyed the spectacular view of the mountains, so much a part of the Vegas experience.

A ding signaled the arriving elevator and Lindsey stepped onto the car, only to find it occupied by a man and woman curled together in a lovers' embrace. Great. Just what she needed. Another happy couple to remind her how damn alone she was. Lindsey stared at the metal doors in front of her as the couple whispered to one another, making kissing noises to boot. Clenching her teeth, Lindsey managed to make it through the ride to the bottom floor with feigned indifference.

A flood of cool air and bustling noise washed over her as

she stepped into the main casino. Slot machines chanted loudly throughout the room, with occasional whoops and yells from players. Lindsey took a deep breath, soaking in the energy of the environment, hoping it was contagious. Following a carpeted path much like the yellow brick road, Lindsey made her way to the lobby. After receiving directions to the local library, she darted to the cab line.

Hours later, sitting in the library, flipping through archived news stories, she felt more confident than ever that the cases in Vegas were linked—not only to the Williams attacks, but to the Hudson victims as well. The similarities between attacks were uncanny and downright eerie. The more she studied, the more convinced she became, and in turn the hotter her temper flared. There was simply no way the Vegas attacks should have been discounted before charging Williams.

The girls all matched the physical profile, the marks on the arms were the same, they were all college students, and the timing of the attacks worked. Yet the Vegas cases would have proven Williams wasn't guilty, and put someone's head in a noose for the unsolved crimes. Now, she knew, someone wanted a fall guy and Williams had been the unlucky candidate.

Greg, Lindsey thought. He had been pining for political office, and he needed the conviction. Damn.

Shoving a strand of hair behind her ear, Lindsey yanked open her calendar and started charting dates. When she was done, she sat back and scanned her work. Just as she suspected, a single perp could have been responsible for all of the attacks. The timelines fit and the aggressiveness of the attacks, if reviewed from the first Hudson rape, had progressively gotten more violent. It was typical for a repeat offender. They tended to get more confident with performance and therefore more aggressive. Squeezing her eyes shut, Lindsey fought the suffocating feeling, fear-based, threatening to consume her.

The real perp was still at large.

Hours later Lindsey arrived back at her dark, empty hotel room with heavy thoughts. As she flipped on the light, her eyes darted hopefully to the message button on her phone. Disappointment settled hard in her stomach. Mark hadn't called. Dropping her face into her hands, she fought the urge to scream and throw things. Or cry. She really, really needed a good cry.

Why did life have to be so complicated?

After a good thirty minutes of pacing, Lindsey decided she had to get out of the room. She'd go crazy alone in her room, lost in her negative thoughts. And she did love roulette. It would be good for a few hours of escape. A mere thirty minutes later, dressed in a black, slim-fitting dress, she stepped into the casino.

Scanning the tables, she looked for a roulette table that felt lucky. She might not trust her instincts in a criminal investigation as readily as in the past, but she had a sixth sense for roulette. An empty table called out her name, drawing her to its side. She took the middle seat, giving her full access to all numbers. To complete her escape, she ordered a Screwdriver.

The roulette dealer was a good-looking guy in his late twenties with a military-style buzz haircut. "So, what's your name?" he asked with a look in his eyes that said he wanted to gobble her up.

"Lindsey," she responded lightly, trying to ignore his flirtatious stares.

He nodded. "I'm Greg." He pointed to his badge and offered up a bright, white smile as he waved a hand across the wheel. "No more bets," he said to the players.

Lindsey wrinkled her nose as she watched the little white ball spinning on the wheel. "Greg?" She flicked him a quick glance and then returned her attention to the slowing white ball. "That's a bad luck name for me. I might have to change tables."

The ball bounced into the number eight peg, and the dealer dropped the marker onto one of Lindsey's chips. "It's not bad luck tonight. You just won."

Lindsey clapped and gifted him with a happy smile.

He laughed in return. "Why is Greg bad luck for you? Ex-boyfriend or something?"

She raised her brows and gave a quick nod. "Yeah, something like that."

His eyes narrowed, but he didn't press the subject. Lindsey busied herself placing chips on the table as he kept talking. "Where are you from?"

"New York," she said and then corrected herself, "I mean Washington." She groaned. "I think I need another drink."

"Maybe you don't if you can't remember where you are from," he teased, but flagged a waitress.

Lindsey dropped a five-dollar chip resolutely. She was ready for the spin. A quick nod to Greg and the ball was bouncing. "So are you here with this Greg guy?"

Lindsey laughed a little too loudly. Alcohol on an empty stomach was making her a little over the top. She waved a dismissive hand. "Oh, please, no way. I'm alone."

"Alone?" he said, with a satisfied gleam in his eye. "Well, that is the most interesting thing I've heard all night."

Lindsey was saved from responding when two older gentlemen joined the table. The excitement around the wheel escalated and more players joined the table. Soon there was a crowd, and Lindsey was smack in the middle of the play and loving it. She ordered several drinks, and focused on gambling, determined to keep her demons at bay, if only for a short window of time.

Tomorrow there would be plenty of time for worry.

Tired, irritable, and completely out of patience, Mark handed his bags over to a bellman and then plodded through the hotel lobby. The flight had been turbulent from start to finish, literally tossing passengers from side to side. Any hope of sleeping had been thrown out the window, leaving him with nothing to do but think about his troubles with Lindsey. Sitting still while his mind raced had been a difficult task that resembled torture.

Over and over in his mind, he'd contemplated her reaction to his arrival. It wouldn't surprise him if she yelled. His unannounced arrival would most certainly piss her off; he really didn't care. He'd spent the past several hours dealing with every possible angle she could throw at him. Ready for battle was an understatement. He was a bull ready to charge. It was time he and Lindsey set some rules.

He had no intention of going to any room but Lindsey's. Stepping to the check-in desk, Mark informed the desk clerk he needed a key for Lindsey's room. As expected, he was informed he'd need Lindsey's approval before receiving a key. Giving the man a sly, knowing look, he discreetly slipped him a hundred-dollar bill. Without further ado, Mark was handed a key.

Standing in the elevator, his body pounded and pulsed with the anticipation of holding Lindsey, touching her. He almost laughed out loud as he thought of his previous night's declaration of being hands-off until their business was complete. What a joke, he thought. Depriving himself of Lindsey was like taking a bottle from a baby.

Impossible.

He was so hooked, he should be scared shitless. But he wasn't. Not at all. And that little fact said it all. He was falling in love for the first time in his life. The old cliché "head over heels" finally meant something to him.

Loving Lindsey was complicated, and he knew it. She came with emotional luggage galore. Simply proclaiming his love wouldn't work with her; in fact, it might drive her away. No, with Lindsey he'd allow her time to get used to the two of them together.

Arriving at her door, Mark knocked lightly. When no answer came, he slipped the key through the slot and entered. The room smelled soft and feminine, like Lindsey. Her scent wrapped around him like a soft glove, making him groan at her absence. Marching to the window, he stood in frozen silence. Lights twinkled beyond the glass, but he didn't pay them any mind.

He was too absorbed with his next step. Why couldn't she have just been in her room? "Damn," he muttered, shoving a hand through his hair. Well, one thing certain, he couldn't just sit in the room and wait for her. He had to at least attempt to find her. If she was in the hotel, he would track her down. If not, he would end up back in the room. The thought made him grimace and head for the door with added determination.

Finding her on the slots would be near impossible, so he made a beeline for the tables. To his relief he spotted her almost immediately. She stood at a roulette table full of men. The flimsy black tank top of her dress revealed the creamy white skin of her back and shoulders. Skin he longed to touch. There was no doubt a few of the men around the table had the same desire.

He watched as Lindsey reached across the table to stack chips on her bets. The action made one of her breasts skim the man's shoulder next to her. Mark's spine stiffened as he zoomed in on the man's eyes: hungry, lustful, and far too potent. He all but licked his lips. A deep growl rose in Mark's throat as a wave of jealousy stabbed at him.

Mumbling a curse under his breath, Mark charged forward, fighting a caveman-like urge to scream, *Mine, mine, mine.* He stopped only when he was directly behind Lindsey. Watching her, he saw her stack a huge pile of chips on the number eight. Digging in his pocket, he found a hundred-dollar bill. Resting his hand on the softness of her bare arm, he was shocked when she didn't jump. Leaning forward, he put the money on the table.

"Put it on eight," he said to the dealer.

The dealer gave him an assessing look, then said, "Black inside," over his shoulder to the pit boss.

Lindsey knew it was Mark who touched her even before she heard his deep, sexy voice. When his hand came down on her arm, her skin sizzled with awareness. Pleasure, sexual awareness, need—you name it, she felt a surge of it.

Her senses raced with his presence, making her spare no time in turning around to face him. The sweet realization that he cared for her danced in her head, making her body's reaction all the more intense. No man would hop on a plane, and push everything else aside, to track down a woman for simple lust. Mark cared on a deeper level, and her alcohol haze made the fear that realization might otherwise evoke simply nonexistent.

She saw the surprise in his face as she turned and leaned into him, pressing her body into his, thinking of the rippling beauty beneath his shirt. Mark made her want him on a primal, deep level she wasn't sure she would ever quite understand. It was so instant, so powerful.

"Mark, you're here," she said in a voice that cracked with a combination of surprise, emotion, and pure, hot desire.

His arms tightened around her waist as he looked down at her with potent, dark eyes. "Yes, I'm here. I—"

She touched her fingers to his lips. "I'm sorry," she whispered and then pushed onto her tiptoes and replaced her fingers with her lips. It was a soft caress of a kiss that she longed to make more. But not here.

"You shouldn't have come here alone." It was a reprimand that lacked conviction. His eyes, his voice, his very demeanor suggested he too wanted their kiss to last longer.

"I know, I shouldn't have left. I—" Lindsey lost her words as the dealer called out the winning number.

"Black eight."

She digested the dealer's call in stunned silence. Machines clattered around her, and someone's happy scream ripped through the air. Turning to face the table, she confirmed where the marker was. Her body twisted back to face Mark, excitement in her voice, "Oh my God, Mark! We won! You won a lot!" Covering her mouth with her hand, she mentally calculated Mark's winnings. "More than a lot!"

He stepped towards her, realigning their bodies, his hand settling on her hip. "Because you're lucky for me, Lindsey," he whispered into her ear and felt her shiver in response.

Lindsey looked up at Mark, his words touching her like a soft caress. It felt like a dream to have him by her side. "Mark," she whispered softly.

Her message was clear. That one word, his name, held so much meaning. For a long moment they stood there, gazes locked, blocking out everything else. The silent message they exchanged was full of mutual longing and sexually-charged hunger. They wanted each other, and there was no doubt how sweet the night to come would prove. But there was more than pure lust between them. The impact of those feelings raced between them, making them both spellbound.

Recognizing how near losing control he was, Mark forcibly pulled them both back to reality. If he didn't, he would have kissed her, and it wouldn't have been the kind of kiss that should be made public. With the throbbing awareness in his lower body now making him immensely uncomfortable, it would have been the kind of kiss that would have gotten them thrown out of the casino.

Taking Lindsey's hand in his, he looked directly at the dealer. "Cash us both out."

There was no mistaking the disappointment in the other man's eyes. He had hoped to gain Lindsey's interest. Too damn bad. He shoved aside his caveman-like feelings and brought Lindsey's hand to his mouth. She leaned into him, resting her head on his shoulder as she let out a sexy, satisfied sigh.

When the dealer slid a five-hundred-dollar chip her way, her head popped up, surprise in her eyes. "It's more than I thought," she said, reaching for it, and then smiling at Mark. "I swear, I love winning." The dealer slid Mark two thousand-dollar chips. She stared at the chips as Mark reached for them. "Two thousand dollars in one hand. That's amazing. What a high."

Mark tossed a chip in the air and caught it. "Not bad for five minutes," he said and winked at her. But money was the last thing on his mind. "Come on, let's get out of here."

Lindsey gave him a hot look. "Yeah, let's get out of here."

Draping his arm around the soft curve of her bare shoulder, he anchored her body to his side as they began walking. Once they were near the restrooms, Mark flattened Lindsey against a wall and planted his hands on either side of her head. Her arms immediately slid to his waist. "You have no idea how mad I was at you." Unable to resist, he ran his tongue across the sensitive flesh of her earlobe.

Lindsey wet her lips, her eyes searching his, her voice hopeful. "Was?"

"Mmmm, still am," he said, in a voice that came out a hoarse whisper that echoed how much he wanted to get her alone and naked. Gently grabbing her chin in his thumb and finger, he locked her in a challenging stare. "What are you going to do about it?"

Lindsey swallowed and blinked, a moment of indecision flashing in her eyes. Then her fingers were in his hair, and she pressed to her toes, so that her lips could reach his. He took her invitation, his hands going to her cheeks, and his tongue past her teeth, kissing her with slow, sensual absorption.

He groaned into her mouth, feeling his body harden with the roar of demand. There was so much shared longing in the kiss, so much passion. When their lips parted, she looked up at him, her arms having found their way around his neck. A slow smile turned up the corners of her lips. "Let's go to my room, and I'll show you how I plan to make up with you."

He arched one brow, surprised she wasn't at least going to fight a little. After all, Lindsey ran from what was between them by coming here. He knew it and so did she. "No resistance tonight? No angry words because I followed you?"

She shook her head from side to side. "Did that feel like resistance?" She didn't give him time to respond. "You already wore me down." She paused, and then shocked him by adding, "Why do you think I put distance between us?"

Mark could only stare at her, taken aback by her words. Hearing her admission was more than he had begun to hope for. "Lindsey—"

She stopped him as she had before, putting two fingers on his lips. "Wait," she whispered. "One more thing first. I need to say this." Mark nodded, and she removed her fingers. "As for being mad that you followed me," she averted her gaze, looking at his chest, "I should be. With anyone else I would be." Her eyes lifted, and her voice dropped a notch. "With you, I'm not mad at all."

There was so much to discuss. But right now all he really wanted to do was take her back to the room and make slow love to her. Fighting the haze of his desire, he reasoned with himself. He needed to take advantage of her state of mind and settle some things between them once and for all. If they went straight to the room, there wasn't going to be any talking. Hell, he could barely think at present.

He needed to get them someplace where they could cool off and talk. "Have you eaten?" he asked, considering her with an intent stare.

Her eyes narrowed, a frown filling her face. "No, but—"

"Then let's get some food. Spago's is right around the corner. We can talk there. It's quiet."

She stared at him, her expression showing her confusion. Her look said food was the last thing on her mind. "No," she said stubbornly. "Let's go upstairs."

Mark raised an eyebrow in amusement. That she was so quick to admit her desire was an accomplishment. Brushing a strand of loose hair from her eyes, he said, "I want that very much Lindsey, but we need to talk." He nuzzled her ear. "We both know we won't do that in the room."

She leaned back to look at him, her eyes wide. "We'll talk," she said quietly. "I promise. Just not now." She grabbed his shirt in her fist and leaned against the wall, tugging until he flattened against her. "At this moment I just really need you to hold me."

Mark was only human and damn if he could resist a request from Lindsey that was seductively laced with need. Not to mention the fact that he was so damn hard his zipper was about to bust. A low growl escaped his throat as his hands settled on her waist. He could feel her soft curves pressing into his body.

Unbidden, a thought came to mind. Greg. He needed to know exactly where she stood with him before this went any further. "What about Greg, Lindsey?"

She frowned as she met his gaze. Reaching up with one hand, she palmed his cheek. "Greg is nothing to me. Not now, not in the past, not ever."

He wanted to believe her, but he had to be certain he could. "Then why did you go with him the other night?"

A fretful look crossed her face. "He promised to tell me the inside scoop on Williams. I didn't think I could pass on a chance to help the case just because of my own selfish desire to avoid him."

Mark digested and accepted her words as truth. He knew Greg well enough to know he was a manipulator. For him to use the case to get to Lindsey was easy to believe. "What are we waiting for?" he whispered. "Let's go to the room."

Chapter Ten

Standing in the back of the elevator, Mark pulled Lindsey in front of him, wrapping his arms around her stomach. People flooded into the compartment until they were crammed together in a tight shuffle of bodies.

Lindsey leaned back into him, not shy about molding her backside to his hips. It was a tease of a moment. "Stop," he murmured, near her ear.

She glanced up at him over her shoulder and touched his cheek with her fingers as she ground her hips a little firmer. "What?" she asked in feigned innocence.

Then she let her head fall back against his chest, giving him a view of her creamy white neck, making him envision her dropping her head just like that in a moment of passion. Unable to resist, he moved his hand to her neck and watched as her eyes fluttered shut, her full lips parting.

Glancing at the elevator lights, he felt the impatience of his desire to get her alone. Payback was coming Lindsey's way and she could bet on it. When the elevator reached their floor, Mark was forced to follow her out of the car, but he grabbed her hand in the process. Surveying the hallway, he found them alone and took advantage of the moment. In a quick movement, he had her in his arms, his mouth claiming hers in a possessive kiss, deep and passion-filled.

He wanted her to taste just how aroused he was.

His hand slid to the side of her breast and squeezed it gently, rubbing his thumb over her nipple. She shivered, and moaned into his mouth. Knowing he had pressed them both too far for the hallway, he forced himself to draw back. "Come," he said, taking her hand again and pulling her with him.

As he struggled with the key, for the first time in his life, Mark felt unsteady. Burning up with pure animal need, he couldn't seem to get the key in the door. Success came far too slow, and when they were finally in the room, he shoved the door shut. Before he knew what hit him, Lindsey became the aggressor. She pushed his back against the wall, her palms flat against his chest. He knew his surprise was in his face, but he couldn't help it. Her unexpected aggressiveness was not only a shock—it was a downright turn-on.

He reached for her, but she braced her knees around his, pushing his hands to his sides. "No, not yet." There was a forceful order to her voice.

Her hips pressed into his, soft curves framing his aroused, more than ready body. They rested thigh to thigh, hip to hip, perfectly molded together as one. He was so hot, it felt like he might explode. Harder, and hotter by the minute, he wanted to act, to touch her, and taste her, and yes, find his way inside her.

But he could see the intent in her eyes. She was in control. Palms on his chest again, she moved so that her eyes met his. "I can't believe you are here." It was a husky whisper.

Everything about her, about the moment, was so damn sexy, he could hardly keep from ripping off her clothes and burying himself inside her. He was glad the curtains were open, so he had the night light to see her by. He'd have hated to miss the gorgeous sight she made. Her hair was a wild, blond mass of silk flowing over her shoulders, her eyes glossy with passion and emotion, her lips swollen from his kisses.

"How could you think I wouldn't come for you?" he asked, his voice alive with his desire, low and a bit rough.

"Why'd you come?"

He had the feeling this was a test. Mark wasn't sure she was ready to hear the real truth about his feelings for her . . . but deep down he thought she knew. He reached up and wrapped a silky strand of her hair around his finger. "Are you sure you want an answer to that question?"

Her lips trembled, confusion flashing in her eyes. "What I want," she said softly, "is to forget everything but you tonight. I want you, Mark." She traced his jaw with her fingers and then flattened the softness of her open palm on his cheek.

Mark absorbed her words, her touch, and her every move like liquid fire in his veins. To hear Lindsey openly admit she wanted him felt more than right. Maybe because he felt it as an admission beyond physical need. "I want you too, baby. You have no idea how completely crazy you make me." His hands went to her hips, and then her perfect, round ass, caressing, and molding her even tighter against his hips.

She began unbuttoning his shirt, her hands moving impatiently to the bare skin. He wanted to kiss her, but she seemed intent on her task. Taking control from Lindsey was not something he wanted to do. Okay, so maybe he did, but he wouldn't.

"God, I love your body," she told him as her hands and mouth moved across the taut, rippling muscles now exposed.

Shoving aside the shirt, her tongue flicked his nipple. The impact was white lightning in his blood. He sucked in a breath, struggling to remain still and allow her to lead. "You like?" she asked, her fingernails lightly scraping both of his nipples at once.

His eyes fixed on hers. "Your hands and mouth on my body?" he asked. "The only thing better is my hands and mouth on yours."

And that was the end of his restraint. He had to kiss her. His fingers entwined in her hair, as he pulled her mouth to his, hungrily kissing her, tasting her as if she was sweet nectar, perfect and addictive. He couldn't get enough of her flavor, her mouth, her smell. Ah, her smell . . . soft, floral, and something more primal. There was something addictive about her, something that set him on fire, and made him burn with a need so intense, so potent, it consumed.

"Ah, Lindsey, you are amazing. I can't get enough of you. I don't think I can ever get enough of you." He murmured the words against her lips even as his hands moved to cup her breast.

She made a little sound of pleasure and her hands began a slow slide up and down his thighs. Her fingers spread, moving so close to his groin, he almost came undone. And just when he thought she would continue to tease him, she cupped his erection. She nipped at his bottom lip, even as her fingers stroked and teased.

With no warning she stepped backwards, out of his reach. He looked at her, his eyes full of questions. She gave him a seductive smile in return. Slowly, she unzipped her dress and then let it slide to the floor, stepping out of it and kicking it to the side.

Mark's eyes slid down her curvy, delicate body, taking in the provocative sight she made. Very small, very sheer black lace was all that covered her rosy, pebbled nipples. The panties were nothing but a swatch of lace that teased him with its perfect placement. His body was throbbing, hard with his desire. He couldn't remember ever having such a potent reaction to a visual. A woman's body turned him on, no doubt, but Lindsey downright made him burn.

"Come here," he ordered hoarsely, his hand raised towards her.

She slid into his arms, no hesitation, as if she too, could wait no longer. He buried his face in her hair, soaking in her fragrance and how amazing she felt in his arms. As much as his body raged, he had a sudden need to savor the feel of holding her.

He found her mouth, needing to taste her. His lips brushed hers, and he could have sworn hers trembled. Once, twice, three times he tasted those full, sweet things, before his tongue slid along hers in a long stroke. A slow, perfect kiss, he took his time, making love to her with his mouth. But as she moaned, her hands roaming his body, he grew more urgent, unable to hold back.

And then he was devouring her mouth with his, tasting her like a starving man would food. Even as he lost himself to the moment, to Lindsey, his mind registered the uniqueness of his need. Never before had he wanted so completely, in such an all-consuming way.

Lindsey was on fire, burning with sensations that only Mark could make her feel. Her need for him scared her yet made her feel whole in a way she wasn't certain she had ever felt in her entire life. She wanted to make him feel as good as he made her feel. She wanted to make love to him. Sinking to her knees, she quickly found the hard ripples of his stomach and began laying soft butterfly kisses on his warm skin. As her mouth distracted him, her hands worked to unbutton and unzip his pants.

Reaching for his belt hoops, she dipped her tongue into his belly button as she slid his pants, and then his briefs, down his legs, freeing his erection. Lindsey's eyes widened, her mouth going dry. How she didn't know, but she had forgotten how big he was, and just how perfect.

Mark stared down at her, and she could see the question in his eyes. Intentionally, she teased him, leaning down, and unlacing his shoes. She could almost feel the tension in his body. He wanted to tell her to leave his shoes alone. A hidden smile on her face, she finished her task, enjoying the tease as she drew it out.

She tugged at one of his shoes and pulled it off his foot, throwing it across the room. Then the other. Her hands slid under his pant legs, around his calves, greedily explored his muscular legs. Mark dropped his head against the door, his palms flattening against the wooden surface. She loved what that meant . . . that he had caved to submission.

Her hands moved to his waist, to his belt hoop. That got his attention. He raised his head, giving her a heavy-lidded stare. "Can I," she asked, wanting his clothes gone.

Mark groaned. "You can do anything you want to me, sweetheart."

She smiled, and then pulled his pants down, making sure his underwear came too. Her hand closed around his erection as she pushed to her feet. He moaned, and she smiled. She loved the power she had over him. Seeing this gorgeous, always-in-control man at her mercy was the ultimate high.

They stared at one another, her hand so intimately touching him, stroking him. "I want—"

He cut her words off with his actions, his hands going into her hair, his mouth claiming hers. Their bodies pressed together, his erection nestled between her thighs. It was a slow, sexy kiss that had them clinging to one another, their tongues caressing and loving.

He palmed her breasts, kneading with delicate, perfect

pressure. She was falling into a sensual haze. Her bra fell loose around her body. She never even knew he unhooked it. And his hands were on her bare breasts, fingers rolling and pinching her nipples. His hands moved to her butt, and he lifted her. She wrapped her legs around his waist, holding him, wanting him.

He sat her on the edge of the mattress, dropping to his knees in front of her. "God, you're gorgeous," he said, a gravelly quality to his voice.

She slid her hands to the side of his face. "You're gorgeous." And she meant it. He was perfect.

"Ah, Lindsey," he whispered, emotion in his voice.

She pressed her lips to his forehead, to his temple, to his cheek. He moved so that his mouth found hers, kissing her, tasting her. His mouth moved down her jaw, her neck, and then to her breast. Inch by inch he kissed, touched, and teased until his mouth closed over her nipples.

Hands in his hair, she arched into the sensation, her body burning with the feel of his lips, teeth, and tongue. "I want you, Mark."

"I want you too, baby," he said, but his teasing continued, his mouth nipping, licking, tasting until she thought she would die from pleasure.

And then he stood, urging her to her back, and then raising one of her legs. He kissed her ankle, her calf, her inner thigh, his lips and teeth making her squirm with heat. And when he was oh-so-close to her panties he switched legs and started all over. This time when he reached the lace, his mouth moved over it, the heat of his breath burning through the lace.

His hands went to her hips, and he leaned back to pull her panties off. The final barrier gone. His hands settled on her waist, moving her higher on the bed as he settled above her. His erection slid along her core, sending a rush of desire through her body.

His mouth covered hers, his tongue sliding along hers, even as he eased his body inside hers. Purposely slow, he inched his way to her core until their bodies were molded as one.

For long moments, they kissed, her breasts pressed into his chest, her hips one with his, hands exploring each other. It was as if she was having an out-of-body experience. Every touch was like sensual gold, awakening another nerve ending, making her need on a new level.

Together, as if they had the need at the same time, they began a slow rhythm, slow strokes, in and out, back and forth. She sighed into his mouth, moaned, whispered his name. His fingers touched her nipples, her lips, her hips.

With each touch, she wanted to be closer to him. Wanted more. And somehow, together once again, they became more urgent. Stroke by stroke, they pressed their bodies together with more power, more force. They kissed as if they were thirsting for the very breath of the other. As if they had to have the other to survive.

It was a powerful, amazing feeling that had her moving with him in a way she had never experienced. This wasn't sex. This was something more. Something as potent as a flame flaring to great heights, burning out of control.

Consuming.

And suddenly, the moment of ultimate pleasure was near. She fought it, not wanting to tumble over into satisfaction. Then this would be over. No. She didn't want it to be over. This was too good to end.

But it was too late. Her body was not her own. She shattered, tensing as the first spasm of orgasm took hold. So intense was her release, she could only call his name in her head. And as her body closed around his, she heard him moan and say her name. And then he shattered, hips pressing into hers, face buried in her neck.

Moments later, they lay pressed together, limp with the impact of their releases. Reality slipped into place, hitting Lindsey with a rush of emotion. The magnitude of what they had shared was so powerful, it was hard to digest.

Never, ever, had she felt so totally possessed and pleased by a man. The burn of tears in the back of her eyes took her off guard. A wave of panic took hold. Was she falling in love? She didn't want to be in love. That meant giving up too much. She'd worked hard to find herself. She didn't want to get lost again.

Turning her face to the side, she tried to hide her tears. Mark kissed her temple and rolled to her side, giving her an opportunity to escape his scrutiny. She sat up, feeling a second rush of emotions, taking a deep breath, willing the tears to go away. But a flood was coming, and she couldn't stop it.

There was no way to hide her sobs from Mark.

Mark's arms closed around her from behind. "What's wrong? Did I hurt you?" he asked in a tender voice full of concern that only made her cry harder.

Wiping at her face, she tried to gain control. "No, nothing like that. I'm sorry. I swear I'm not like this."

Mark stroked her hair. "I know, and that's what's got me the most worried."

"I'm," she sniffed, "fine."

Mark tugged her into his lap and then moved to rest his back against the headboard. Lindsey gave into the need for more tears and buried her face in his neck and let them roll. So potent was her release, it was as if years of tears had somehow been released. All she could do was cling to Mark, and let them flow.

And he was wonderful, whispering comforting words, and rocking her.

Long minutes later, she accepted a tissue from Mark, feeling calmer, but her eyes hurt and she was exhausted.

"Do you want to talk?" Mark asked, his hand running down the back of her hair.

"I guess a lot things hit me at once," she explained. "It's been a pretty emotional month."

Mark knew there was more to it and he needed to understand. "What was it about our making love that made it all cave in?"

Lindsey ran her hand through his hair. "You scare the hell out of me."

He knew that, but he didn't see any reason to say so. Instead, he wanted to understand her feelings fully. "Why?"

"Well," she said in a shaky voice, "I think I'm beginning to get used to having you around."

Mark studied her. "And that's bad because . . . ?"

"Because every time I have ever gotten involved with a man, I've felt like the relationship took over my identity. I can't do that again." She shook her head and shut her eyes. "I can't."

He brushed his lips across hers. "I'm crazy about you. I like your independence, and even how hard-headed you are." He smiled. "I don't want you to change. I just want to enjoy who you really are."

She blinked. "You make it seem so simple."

"No," he said. "I don't think it's simple at all. The truth is—I'm scared too." She looked at him with surprise. "I wasn't looking for this anymore than you."

Lindsey seemed to digest his words with acceptance. "Thanks, Mark."

His eyes narrowed. "For what?"

"For understanding. For not pushing me." She blew out a breath. "For being you."

Mark pulled her close, his chin resting on her head. "Don't thank me," he told her. "Just don't stop being you." He kissed her head. "All I want is a chance to see where we are going." He pulled back, and looked at her. "Is that fair?"

She smiled. "I'd like that too."

Mark laid down, pulling her into his arms, hoping this was one of many nights he fell asleep holding her.

It was dark, and she was alone. Fear laced her thoughts, made her hands sweat, and her body shake. The shadows danced menacingly around the room, a flash by the window—a shadow that moved. Oh my God . . . a man. It was the outline of a man, and she shoved aside her blankets, frantically kicking them away with her feet as she reached for her gun. But she couldn't find it.

Where was her gun? She grabbed her purse, feeling frantic, dumping the contents on the bed, searching.

Then suddenly, Mark was there, climbing through the window, going after the shadow of a man. Lindsey panicked and dug harder for her gun, reaching in drawers, under pillows. Giving up, she flung her purse to the ground and ran towards the window, not bothering with a robe. She had to get to Mark.

The window was open and she crawled through, desperation taking hold as she screamed Mark's name. But he was nowhere in sight. She moved to the fire escape, taking each step with urgency until she jumped into the alley. Still she couldn't see him. She started running as fast as she could, needing to catch up to him. Her breathing was harsh, labored, and tears were streaming down her face. Where was he? Where was Mark?

"Lindsey." She heard her name but she didn't see anyone. "Lindsey, baby, wake up." Her eyes fluttered. "Lindsey, you're having a nightmare. Wake up."

She jerked straight up into a sitting position, her skin damp, and she was wheezing, needing air. Her eyes went to his face. "Mark?"

She felt his arms wrap around her. "Yeah, I'm right here, baby."

Reality started to return with the sound of his voice. She turned and touched his face, his chest, and his shoulders, needing to know he was here. He was real. A deep sigh of relief escaped her lips. "Oh, God. You're here. You're okay."

Mark grabbed one of her hands and pressed his lips against her palm. "I'm right here. Everything is fine now."

He pulled her into his arms. "Lie down with me," he urged gently. Slowly he lowered them both against the sheets. Sinking into his hold, she allowed the safety of his arms to soothe her mind, slowly feeling her breathing return back to normal. After a few minutes, she leaned up and kissed his cheek, so very thankful he was okay, so very appreciative for his comfort.

She wasn't alone.

"Want to talk about it?" Mark asked, his hand smoothing her hair.

Lindsey rested her head on his shoulder. This time the nightmare had been more vivid, more frightening. And yes, she did want to talk, to tell Mark about it. "I keep having this same nightmare, over and over."

"You were screaming my name. Why?" he asked, his hand now drawing circles on her arm.

She strained, trying to force her mind to recreate her nightmare. Mark had been there, in the middle of the dread, but not a part of the darkness. "There's always a stranger trying to get to me, and then you're there, and I am trying to get to you."

Mark felt as if he had been punched in the gut. Was this some sort of premonition? They hadn't known each other long. "When did they start?"

Lindsey's thoughts raced. "I'm not sure. I think before I met you. But then, how can that be? You're in them."

"Maybe you had them before and now that I'm around, I became a part of them." It seemed logical enough.

She sighed. "Maybe."

"Rest, baby," he said kissing her head. "It's the middle of the night."

She snuggled closer to him, one of her legs entwining with his. Damn, she felt good in his arms. Within a few minutes, she drifted off to sleep. He lay there, holding her, his mind on everything from the nightmare to the murders. Lindsey made him feel protective from the first moment he met her. With each passing moment, the feeling grew more intense. Her nightmare felt like some kind of premonition. The very thought had him silently cursing himself. Hell, now he was sounding like Lindsey, with all of her instinct and gut-reaction crap. Besides, her nightmares were probably a product of her struggles with the past. Lindsey had torn herself up over Hudson for years.

He stared down at her, nestled by his side . . . so perfect, so needing someone to take care of her. She didn't think so, but he did. Everyone needed someone, and she was no different. No matter how much she tried to convince herself and the world differently.

He wasn't going to let her deal with life alone anymore.

Chapter Eleven

Mark woke up to the soft floral scent of Lindsey.

He smiled as he ran his hand down her hair. He was so glad he'd followed her to Vegas. He had always considered himself conservative, the type who would date a woman for a long time before deciding she was the one. Apparently, love didn't happen that way. It took even the most reserved by storm.

Because Mark knew no matter how many days, weeks, even months passed, Lindsey was the woman for him. It was crazy in terms of how long they had known each other, but it was no less true. No way was he letting her go back to Washington. But she was like a scared deer in the headlights, ready to bolt. One wrong move and she could get spooked.

He could lose her forever.

Lindsey raised her head and peered down at him, her eyes soft from sleep, her voice sultry and hoarse. "Morning, Counselor."

Their lips pressed together for a quick kiss. "Morning. How'd you sleep?"

"After the nightmare," she said, "wonderful. I love sleeping with you."

"Yeah?" he asked, but he didn't wait for an answer. "I love sleeping with you too. I was just thinking I could get used to having you in my bed."

She laughed and smiled widely, obviously pleased at his words. "You were, were you?"

Mark shook his head. "Sure was."

"Well, I'm glad you weren't thinking about how to get me out of your bed." She poked his chest playfully.

"Never," he said, his voice serious now.

Lindsey smiled and rested her head on his shoulder, fingers resting in his chest hair. Abruptly, she raised her head, a question in her expression. "Did you bring luggage?"

"It's downstairs. I need to call the bell desk. I'll do that and order us some coffee and breakfast."

Lindsey sat up, freeing him to move, blankets pulled to her shoulders. "Sounds good, but I'm supposed to meet up with a couple detectives for lunch at eleven-thirty. Make it a light breakfast for me, please."

Mark shot her a quick look. "I'm coming with you."

Lindsey pushed herself off the bed, letting the blanket drop. She walked towards the bathroom, oblivious of her nakedness. She peeked over her shoulder at Mark. "I know," she said and then smiled.

Mark laughed, pleased with her response. He was still smiling when he heard the bellman on the other end of the phone. Shoving his feet in his pants, he dialed room service. He'd barely finished his tasks when Lindsey exited the bathroom wearing the hotel robe, with wet hair falling over her shoulders.

He could so get used to her like this, comfortable and happy and, most importantly, by his side.

Lindsey took a quick shower, finding herself eager to join Mark.

It was an odd feeling, considering how used to being alone she was. She found him sitting on the bed, a room service tray in front of him. "That was fast," she said, surprised that the food had already arrived, but thankful for the blessing of caffeine. "Coffee, please."

"I made it worth their while," he said as he reached for the coffee pot and filled a cup for her. Then he patted the bed beside him. "Come sit with me."

She picked up her cup and let her nostrils flare with the scent. "I love the smell of hot coffee," she said, then took a sip of the steaming beverage. "I can't believe I'm not hung over this morning."

Mark chuckled. "You were tipsy, not sloppy drunk."

Lindsey surveyed the selection of fresh, plump strawberries, bagels, and cream cheese with approval. "This is perfect," she said and plucked a juicy strawberry from the tray and bit into it.

Juice dripped down her chin, and before she could get to a napkin, Mark leaned forward and licked it off. "And deliciously messy," he finished for her, and then leaned back into his former position and picked up his cup.

As if nothing had happened. Lindsey was completely speechless. The intimacy of his action had floored her. He drove her crazy, this man. She eyed him, looking for the source of his power over her. His hair was early morning rumpled, his very nice, defined chest bare for her viewing. He looked casual and comfortable, and too damn sexy to be legal.

Mark looked at her. "What?"

"You're a very bad boy, Mark," she said, enunciating every word in a teasing taunt. "You know very well what you just did."

He met her gaze with wicked mischief dancing in his eyes. "And you're a very bad girl. We both know how you teased me last night."

She wrinkled her nose at him and laughed. "Turnaround isn't fair play in my book."

"Is that right?" he asked. "I'll try and keep that in mind." He smiled and reached for the newspaper. "Want to share?"

She accepted, feeling the odd sense of comfort doing so brought to her. She drank her coffee and finished off her strawberry, sitting beside him, feeling his presence as if it was gold. Lindsey curled her legs under her body and smiled to herself. She'd never felt like this with Greg or any other man. Just being together, even without conversation, felt perfect.

A warm, safe feeling wrapped around her.

Unable to help herself, her gaze kept drifting to his profile. Mark looked up, as if he felt her eyes on him, but she didn't look away. The paper had dropped to her lap as she had abandoned her covert inspection for a more open one. He offered her a sexy smile. "Now, what are you looking at?"

"You," she said pointedly.

He grabbed her and pulled her over to his side, wrapping his arm around her waist. He planted a firm kiss on her lips and she smiled with satisfaction. Then she rubbed her hands on his cheek, feeling the morning stubble beneath her soft palms. "You don't like me like this?" he asked as he touched his own face.

She laughed at the ridiculous idea. "Actually I like you like this. Very much."

He grinned devilishly. "Oh yeah, how much? Show me."

"Gladly," she said as she wrapped her hand around his neck and pulled his lips to hers. Her tongue slid between his teeth, and she heard him moan.

Would she ever get enough of the flavor so uniquely Mark Reeves?

★ ★ ★ ★ ★

In the back of a cab, Mark beside her, Lindsey knew it was time to make a few confessions. "Mark, about Greg."

His gaze moved to hers, sharpness to his expression and tone. "What about him?"

Lindsey grabbed his hand. "Hey, take it easy," she said in a low voice. "I just want to tell you what he said about the case."

His eyes searched hers a minute, and then he relaxed, shoulders easing, expression less tense. Then, and only then, did she continue. "Well," she said, "here's the thing. I don't think it was such a good idea that I met with him."

Mark's eyes darkened. "What does that mean exactly?"

Lindsey looked out of the window as the cab screeched to a halt. "We're here," she said. "That was quick."

Mark paid the driver as Lindsey stepped onto the sidewalk. The sun was so hot, perspiration instantly beaded on her lip. She started to walk towards the restaurant, eager to find air conditioning, when Mark's hand closed around her arm, stopping her forward motion. She turned to him. Damn, she didn't want to finish this now. It was stupid to start such a conversation before this meeting.

She frowned at him. "What are you doing?"

"Finish," he demanded.

Lindsey sighed in resignation. "I ticked him off. He brought up the past," she paused, "as in him and me, telling me he loved me, and crap like that."

Mark's tension was palpable. "And?"

"I screwed up. I threw his words back in his face, so he lashed out. He offered life with no parole. I declined and told him we would beat him in court. I doubt he'll negotiate."

Mark stared at her a long moment without showing any

emotion, then abruptly he broke out in laughter, shaking his head from side to side.

Lindsey gaped at him in amazement. She had expected him to be angry. "I can't believe you are laughing," she blurted. "I thought you'd be furious."

To her amazement, he pulled her into his arms, and planted a kiss on her forehead. Then he looked down at her, understanding in his eyes. "It wasn't your smartest move ever, but I don't think he left you many options. He tried to manipulate you personally with business, and he got socked in the gut. He deserved it."

"Really?" she asked in disbelief. She hadn't realized it, but Mark was right. Greg was manipulating her, or trying to, as he always had in the past.

"Yes," he said, with amusement in his voice. "Really. Now, let's get the heck out of this heat, and get this meeting over with."

Lindsey grabbed his arm, deciding his good mood needed to be utilized to the fullest degree. He turned back and looked at her in surprise. "Since you are taking things so well and all," she said with a pause, "there is this tiny other thing."

Mark shook his head. "I'm afraid to ask."

"I interviewed Elizabeth's boyfriend."

Mark's eyes went wide. "What? On your own?" She nodded. "Do you know how dangerous that was?"

Lindsey cringed at his tone. "I will say, as much as I hate to admit it, the owner of the Pink Panther was pretty creepy."

"You went to the Pink Panther?" he asked incredulously. She nodded.

Throwing his hands up in the air, he said, "I give up." Then he grabbed her hand. "Tell me about it later. We need to get this meeting over with."

Lindsey and Mark stepped into the Carrow's lobby at exactly eleven-thirty. Two men moved towards them. The one who seemed in charge was stocky, with brown hair and eyes. He also lacked good manners. Not bothering with hello, he eyed Lindsey and said, "Damn if you don't look just like the victims."

Mark bit back a harsh retort. He might be paranoid, but Lindsey's resemblance to the victims bugged the hell out of him. Mark watched the man's face as Lindsey responded to him. "Yeah, well, it's coincidence." But it bothered her, he could tell. Her face was etched with tension, her body stiff.

The man snorted and shoved his hands into his worn jeans pockets. "A damn spooky coincidence."

Lindsey's voice held irritation, thick and unhidden. "I won't introduce myself, since clearly you've figured out who I am." She waved a hand towards Mark. "Kevin Woods meet Mark Reeves, an associate of mine."

Mark shook hands with the man, who then motioned towards his partner, a tall, lanky man with curly black hair who appeared nearer forty than thirty. "This is my partner, John Conner."

A few minutes later, greetings aside, they sat at a table, a round of coffee ordered, but no food. Once the waitress filled everyone's cups, Kevin narrowed his gaze on Lindsey. "I did some checking on you, Lindsey. You're that attorney who handled the Hudson case." His tone was accusing.

Lindsey leaned forward and rested her elbows on the table, her face cool and composed. "I didn't know Hudson was known in Nevada."

Mark didn't care how they knew about the case. "What's the point?"

John interjected, "His point is that we did some digging.

There are similarities in the victim profiles of Hudson, your new client, and our perp. We are all about solving this case, but we also want to know who we're dealing with and what their motives are."

Kevin made a face. "A connection is unlikely. You wouldn't be here if you weren't trying to make one. Hudson was convicted with DNA evidence. Are you trying to save your name here, Lindsey, or catch a perp?"

Mark felt the heat of anger, quick and hard. He kept his tone low, but it reeked of his frustrations. "That's out of line. We're trying to save lives here. Are you going to help us or not?"

"I care about saving lives, not my name," Lindsey said, as if Mark hadn't spoken. "And just in case you don't get how the legal world works—I won my case, and that makes me look damn good. What the guy did or didn't do after doesn't impact that job." Kevin stared at her, his face flushed with the heat of anger. Lindsey continued, determination in her voice. No way was anyone speaking until she was done. "And that's exactly why I joined the FBI." She paused and let the words sink in. "I'm here to catch a murderer, plain and simple. If you want to do the same, then let's get down to business. If not, let's stop wasting each other's time."

Kevin's temper had noticeably declined. "I'm just trying to make sure we all have the same agenda. Nobody wants this guy more than me. I saw the bodies with my own eyes. I know what he's like, what he does to his victims."

Lindsey's eyes filled with shadows. "You're wrong. I want more." Something about the way she said the words silenced the table. For long moments, no one so much as blinked.

Kevin broke the silence, shifting in his chair as if he

couldn't take it anymore. "You're pretty certain they're all connected, aren't you? That your Hudson guy is innocent?"

Lindsey met his gaze with a direct stare. "As you said, there's DNA evidence against Hudson. That's hard to beat." She paused, and then added, "Unless it was planted."

Mark looked at her with surprise. This was the first time he'd heard this theory, though he thought it made damn good sense. John set his cup down, leaning forward as if he had already considered her theory. "It could have been planted. I was thinking that on the way over here. I had a case last year . . ." He waved off the words. "Bottom line, it could be a plant. What was the DNA source?"

"I don't know," she said, and exchanged a knowing look with Mark, as if she wanted his silent approval.

"There's no way you could," Mark reminded her.

She nodded. "I know." She refocused on the other two men, explaining, "I dropped out after Hudson was charged with the final attack. I never saw the DNA evidence."

John reached for his cup. "Find out if it was hair, because it's damn easy to plant. If it is, then it's a whole new ballgame as far as I'm concerned." He took a drink. "Okay, let's backtrack. If the cases are connected, then our perp is now in Manhattan, or at least was recently, right?"

Mark nodded. "Yes, but if it's the same guy, he's smart. Williams was picked up, and he dropped out of sight."

Lindsey cleared her throat. "I did a calendar tracking of all of the attacks yesterday. The timelines support one attacker."

"That's all the more reason why we need to play connect-the-dots with you guys," Mark said deliberately, pleased with Lindsey's sharp actions.

John turned his attention towards Mark. "I know who

you are too. You've gotten a lot of creeps put back on the street."

"Not this again," Lindsey said. "I thought we established we are all on the same team here?"

Her eyes met Mark's and he could see her apprehension. But she didn't have anything to worry about. He didn't let guys like these get to him. Mark shrugged. "You know the saying—don't throw stones if you live in a glass house." He paused for effect. "I inherited a lot of bad field work and I'm obligated to do my job." Mark's meaning sliced through the air, though his tone was nonthreatening. He was reminding them that police errors set a lot of bad guys free. "I hate what we have to do for the system sometimes as much as anyone else, but I respect what the principles are built on. Just as I am sure you do."

Lindsey looked at Mark, appreciation in her eyes, before she switched her attention to the entire table. "I believe we can help each other, but we need to be on the same team. Is that possible?"

A waitress appeared and started filling cups. Kevin took a drink of his, and then said, "We all want the same things."

Mark could tell from Lindsey's face she wasn't happy with his response. After a long pause, Lindsey asked, "All of your victims went to the University of Las Vegas, right?"

Kevin nodded. "Right."

"Any common classes or professors?" Mark asked.

"No, none," Kevin said, setting his cup on the table.

"What time of day were the bodies found?" Lindsey asked.

"All late night, early morning," Kevin said.

"Alcohol in their blood?" Mark asked.

"Yes." Kevin frowned. "Explain that question."

"Just wondering if a bar could be the connection," Lindsey explained. "We think it might be in New York."

Kevin's brows sunk as if he was afraid they had missed something. "We never found that kind of connection."

"What about boyfriends?" Mark asked.

"Nope," Kevin responded. "No steady ones, at least."

Lindsey had pulled out a notepad and was going down a list. "Evidence on the bodies?"

John spoke up. "Yes, same pattern on all. Rope burns on the arms, a few other similarities between victims."

Lindsey stared at the tablecloth in deep thought. All eyes were on her strained face. Mark sensed some transition in her mood. She was bothered by something. He decided to save her a response. He cleared his throat, and responded for her. "That sounds like our guy's pattern."

"Got pictures?" Kevin asked.

"Yes, we do," Mark commented, but didn't reach for them. "What I don't understand is why the Williams cases weren't linked through the national system."

Kevin and John eyed each other. Mark noted the exchange with interest. They knew something. After a pause Kevin said, "We think the same thing. Look, why don't we finish up our coffee and go back to the station? We can compare notes."

Mark and Lindsey looked at one another and then nodded their agreement.

They rode to the station with the detectives, which left Mark with no feasible opportunity to pry into Lindsey's head and figure out what she was fretting about. Once there, they were taken to a room holding a couple of folding tables and a wall of whiteboards.

As soon as they were alone, Mark exhaled, relieved to finally get a minute with Lindsey. He walked to her, his hands going to her arms. "What's up, sweetheart?"

She glanced at him, eyes guarded. "What do you mean?"

Mark winced inwardly. She had already shut him out again. What in the hell was it going to take to get by her walls? "You know what I mean," he said deliberately. "You clammed up at the restaurant and have stayed that way ever since. What's bothering you?"

She shrugged her shoulders, diverting her eyes to the floor. "Nothing."

"That's crap and we both know it, Lindsey," he said in a low voice. "Don't shut me out."

The door opened, effectively silencing their conversation. "Here we go." Kevin held up a stack of pictures and then walked to the whiteboard and began taping them up. Lindsey opened her files and pulled out two stacks of pictures, and without a word stood and started to tape them up as well. She put the Hudson pictures on one row—even though only one of his victims was dead—and the Williams pictures on another.

When everything was in place, they all stood, in utter silence, staring at the horrific sight. It was as if evil had visited the room and was now alive and well. Lindsey wrapped her arms around her body, hugging herself as if she was cold. And as he let his gaze move back to the pictures, he couldn't blame her. The sight before them was gruesome, the images showing obvious torture and violence. This guy had made these women suffer.

Kevin cleared his throat. "Damn," he said. "I'm afraid this is bigger than we thought. What a sick bastard." Then he exchanged a look with his partner. "Better get Bill."

Mark tore his eyes away from the pictures and looked at Kevin. "I take it Bill's your boss?"

He nodded. "He'll want to see this," Kevin said, looking

back at the pictures as if still astounded by the magnitude of the scene.

Mark gave Kevin a steady look. "Tell me again how these attacks were dismissed as unrelated."

Kevin leaned against the wall and crossed his arms in front of his body. "Well, now, that does seem to be the million-dollar question, doesn't it?"

Lindsey made a frustrated sound that drew their attention. "Yes, it is. Who's going to answer it?"

Mark glanced at Lindsey with concern. Anger had returned some of the color to her cheeks, but it was clear she was a ball of nerves. He wanted to grab her, and comfort her. But he knew he couldn't. Not here, not now.

Best to focus on catching a killer.

Stepping into the hotel, Mark by her side, Lindsey couldn't shake her thoughts of Greg. No, that wasn't completely true. Something else was bothering her. It seemed when it came to Hudson, she was damned if she did, and damned if she didn't.

Had she just believed in herself, and him, in the past . . . well, a lot more than one woman was now dead because of her mistakes. She had been so freaked over the woman she thought Hudson had killed that she allowed herself to get off track. Now many more women were dead.

Her biggest failure had been to doubt her instincts.

But she couldn't go back, and that was hard to swallow. All she could hope for was to save the victims of the future.

Mark unlocked the hotel door. "What an afternoon," he said.

"It didn't surprise me the local guys blame the missed connections on the New York officials and vice-versa," Lindsey said.

Mark shoved open the door, and motioned Lindsey forward. "I doubt we'll ever know the truth." Entering the room, a burst of cool air washed over her skin, making her sigh with the sweet relief of being out of the heat. Lindsey couldn't shake the feeling that Greg had somehow been behind it all.

She made a direct path to the bed, falling onto the mattress with a bounce. "I am so exhausted, it's painful."

Mark toed off his shoes, and walked over to Lindsey and took hers off. "Yes, but we accomplished a lot."

Lindsey leaned up on her elbows. "Do you think we made the right decision, agreeing to keep this quiet?" She studied him, her voice full of concern. "Shouldn't the public know there might be a serial killer on the loose?"

He spread out on the bed, and turned to face her, resting on one elbow. "I do," he said, meaning it. "He's in hiding right now, and we can't risk letting him know we're onto him."

Lindsey's put her hands under her head, staring up at the ceiling. "I suppose that's true."

Mark's eyes narrowed. "What happened today? Why did you get upset?"

She rolled to her side, facing him, fingers fiddling with the buttons on his shirt. "Nothing, I'm just tired."

He shut his eyes and took a deep breath before refocusing on her face. "As I said," he paused a beat, "we both know better."

Mark slid closer so that his thighs brushed her leg. Watching her distress, he traced her bottom lip with his index finger. "What's wrong?"

Her lashes fluttered to her cheeks. "I don't think I can talk about it right now."

He was silent a long moment, his hand slowly moving to

rest on her hip. "I won't press you," he said, and then he did just what he said he wouldn't do. He pressed. "I'd like to think you'd trust me enough to share what's bothering you."

Lindsey wet her dry lips, and cleared her throat. It was hard talking about her feelings. She wasn't used to it. But she found herself wanting to find the courage to tell him. Her voice cracked, but the words made it past her lips. "So many women are dead."

Mark pulled her closer. "Please, don't do this to yourself," he said. "You've beat yourself up enough."

Even though she knew he was right, she couldn't quit blaming herself. The pictures of the victims wouldn't leave her mind. "Why didn't I think of the DNA being planted back then?"

His voice was a soft echo of reason. "It was a tough call. You were ready to be out. Besides, you handed over the case."

She squeezed her eyes together. The images just wouldn't go away. "I might have stopped so many women from dying."

Mark leaned down and pressed his lips to her eyelids, one at a time. "A big maybe, Lindsey. Stop doing this to yourself."

A large teardrop rolled down her cheek, and Mark wiped it away with his thumb. "I would have dropped Hudson, too."

Her eyes popped open. "You would have?"

"Hell yes," he said. "In two flat seconds. No hesitation. And I wouldn't have questioned his guilt after that final victim was killed. I would have assumed it."

She touched his cheek. "Thanks for saying that."

"Don't thank me for telling you the truth."

She swallowed hard. "I have to catch this guy."

"Catching the killer is not your job," he pointed out in a tight voice. "Giving Williams the best defense possible is." His expression was tense, his tone demanding. "You're too close to this."

Lindsey didn't want to argue with Mark, but she also wasn't going to agree to do his bidding. "And that can't be changed."

"Lindsey—"

Her hand cupped his jaw, cutting off his words with her action. She didn't want to fight. She knew he was worried about her, but if he kept pushing, she was going to fight back. "Let's drop this for now." Then, in a lower voice, "Please."

Lindsey turned and fell onto her back. "I can't believe we have such an early flight in the morning."

"We could take a later one," he offered, his palm flattening on her stomach. "Better yet, let's stay an entire extra day and just forget everything but you and me." He closed the distance her move had put between them, his mouth near her ear. "What do you think?"

Lindsey laughed as he nuzzled her neck. "We shouldn't."

"No," he agreed, and then pressed a kiss on her lips. "We shouldn't, but ask me if I give a damn."

Lindsey couldn't stop from smiling. "What about the case?"

His knuckles brushed her cheek. "It'll be there when we get back. It's one day, baby. But it will be one hell of a good day, I promise."

She crinkled her nose. "I swear, you make me lose my good sense."

Mark smiled. "Is that a yes?"

"I don't know. It's tempting but—"

"No buts. You need some play time," he said decisively. "And we need some time together. We'll be more effective when we get back."

"Objection," she said in her best attorney voice. "Use of closing argument tactics in the bedroom considered out of line."

Mark laughed. "That obvious, huh?" Lindsey nodded. Mark laughed, but then turned serious. "Look," he said, staring at her with big, puppy-dog brown eyes. "I just want you to myself for a day. Is that so bad?"

Lindsey stared at him a moment, caught off guard by the raw emotion she saw in his eyes. God, what this man did to her. She would never say yes to something like this in the middle of a case. But then, she'd never experienced anything like what Mark made her feel.

Slowly, she nodded her approval of his plan.

"That's a yes," he confirmed. "Right?"

Lindsey smiled and nodded again.

Mark slid on top of her, his weight on his elbows. "Say it."

"Ye—" But she never finished, because he kissed her.

Lindsey walked beside Mark, her arm linked with his, a soft smile playing on her lips. The day had been nothing short of perfect. Mark had proven he was far more than some stiff-necked attorney. He had also made her remember a side of herself she had long ago forgotten.

A sudden breeze gushed around them, cooling the air and Lindsey's skin. But it also brought with it some rather menacing-looking clouds. "Looks like it's about to storm," she said. "Maybe we should head back to the hotel." But she hated to see the day end. It had been such a good time.

They'd started the day out at Starbucks, which they both loved. For hours they had sat and talked. The time had flown by so quickly, when she had looked at the clock she'd been shocked. From there they had taken the day minute by minute, one adventure at a time. Four times, they had ridden the roller coaster at New York, New York hotel.

Mark had caught the attention of a certain alien female with big ears at the Star Trek ride. Lindsey had threatened to elope with the guy dressed as a Klingon.

"Afraid of a little water or what?" Mark asked, giving her a challenging look. "It feels good out here. The temperature must have dropped a good fifteen degrees."

Lindsey conceded, more than happy to drag out their time together. A part of her was afraid this perfection forming between them would go away when they returned home. That maybe it was vacation bliss and nothing more. It scared her. "Yeah, I suppose you're right. I guess if it starts raining we can dodge into a building."

No sooner than the words were out of her mouth, the sky opened up and the water came down in buckets. They laughed, and Mark grabbed her hand, pulling her with him as they ran for shelter, huge droplets of water hitting them in rapid succession.

The cold water hit her warm skin with icy results. She shivered against the impact, following in Mark's footsteps, but before they found shelter, he pulled her into his arms, her body pressed against his. She looked up at him, taking in his wet hair plastered to his face, and wondering if he ever looked bad. "What are you doing?" she asked, water getting in her mouth. "We're getting drenched."

"I know," he yelled over the pounding of the rain. "Isn't it great?" Mark bent down and claimed her mouth in a hot, passionate kiss, his tongue sliding against hers in long, sensual strokes that quickly made her forget the rain. When he raised his head, he wrapped his arms around her hips, latching his hands behind her. "You're sexy as hell dripping wet."

Lindsey's eyes darted to the wet T-shirt now plastered on Mark's well defined pecs. "You look pretty damn sexy yourself."

Mark picked Lindsey up and started twirling her around in circles, making her laugh, and then scream. "I'm getting dizzy. Stop!" She laughed some more. People were looking at them but she didn't care. "I'm soaked, Mark."

When he let her go, she was unsteady and tumbled into him. "See, my plan worked," he said with a devilish grin. "You're throwing yourself at me."

Fifteen minutes later they stepped into their hotel lobby and paused, dripping wet. Lindsey giggled like a schoolgirl as people turned to look at them. When was the last time she had felt so carefree? Mark tugged her close to his side, wrapping his arm around her. The hotel air conditioning only added to her shivers. She was glad to share his body heat.

Mark's eyes drifted to her chest. Her eyes followed his. Her nipples were dark and perky beneath her thin shirt. "Oh, um, not good." She crossed her arms in front of her body.

"No," he agreed. "We need to get to the room."

By the time they stepped onto the elevator, her teeth were chattering. Mark pulled her close and ran his hands up and down her arms trying to get rid of her goose bumps. "Any better?"

"Hmm, not really, but don't stop," she said, teeth making a chattering sound, voice shaky. Mark smiled and planted a kiss on her forehead. "How about a hot bath and a bottle of wine?"

"Purrrrfect," she said with a chill tinting her voice.

A few minutes later, Lindsey rushed from the hotel bathroom—wearing only a towel—to the bedroom, in search of her wine glass. "Hurry up," Mark ordered. "The water feels great."

Lindsey spotted her glass on the dresser, but her eyes caught on the blinking message light on the phone. Her stomach lurched. "Did you tell anyone we were staying an extra day?" Lindsey called to Mark.

"No, why?"

"We have a message." She sat down next to the phone, on the edge of the bed, wine forgotten. She'd only told Steve.

"Probably a courtesy customer service thing. Leave it. Come join me."

"I told Steve," she called back. "Maybe it's important." She heard Mark moan as she punched the retrieve button. A recorded voice said, "You have four messages." She looked towards the bathroom, and opened her mouth to tell Mark, but for some reason, shut it again.

The first call was a hang-up. She frowned as the second call played. It was a hang-up. And so were the next two. Her hands fisted tight around the receiver. Like the calls she had gotten at her apartment in the middle of the night.

"Who was it?" Mark yelled.

She debated . . . tell him—don't tell him. He was already too protective. If this was nothing, he'd make her life hell and what purpose would it serve? This was a private hotel room. No one could get to her here. She set the receiver down.

"Lindsey?"

She pushed to her feet and walked towards her wine. "You were right. Courtesy call."

Chapter Twelve

The plane ride was bumpy.

Just as Mark was certain his path to Lindsey's heart would be. He looked down at Lindsey, curled under his arm, hand on his chest, and a smile played on his lips. Slowly, her walls were coming down. He wasn't kidding himself, though. There was still a long way to go. She was a loose cannon in some ways, ready to explode and jump to conclusions. He needed to get rid of her past skeletons to ensure a future with her. To do that, he was afraid she would need to get Hudson behind her. That could mean catching the killer, a task that might not prove easy, and could, in fact, prove dangerous.

The plane jerked, the turbulence getting heavier. Over the intercom, the pilot announced a seatbelt warning and asked the flight attendants to sit down. Lindsey lifted her head, confusion in her eyes. "I hate when it gets bumpy," she admitted as she gripped the arms of her seat, knuckles going white.

Mark gave her a comforting smile. "Ah, now, you know that planes are tough. They can take more than people would ever imagine possible." He slid his hand on her knee and gave it a light squeeze. She swallowed hard, nodding. The plane jerked a couple of times in a row, and her face was etched with unspoken fear. "Talk to me and keep your mind off the plane," he told her.

Her lips were thin, her jaw tense. "About what?"

He wanted to know about the place she called home. "Tell me about Washington."

She shrugged and then grimaced as a heavy bump shook the plane. "There's not much to tell."

"Have you ever met the President?"

"Yeah, I've met him."

"And?" he asked, surprised she hadn't said more.

"Nothing to tell," she said. "I was on a special task force that got up close and personal. It was a once-in-a-lifetime kind of opportunity."

Mark looked at her, searching her face, praying he wasn't going to lose her to her job in Washington. "You like your job there?" he asked but almost didn't want to hear the answer.

"If you would have asked me that a month ago I would have said yes, but—"

"But what, baby?" he asked, quietly encouraging her.

She gnawed her bottom lip. "I don't know what I want anymore," she admitted, seeming to fight a bit of confusion. "Did you ever doubt your decision to leave Paxton?"

The plane jerked and Lindsey jumped, letting a little yelp escape her lips. Mark couldn't hold back a small chuckle. She glared at him. "Don't laugh at me, damn it. I hate this."

He held his hands up in mock surrender. "I'm not, I swear. You're just cute like this."

Lindsey shot him an angry look. "Like this?" she asked in question. "Like what?"

A slight smile played on his lips. "I think it's adorable that you are afraid of flying."

Lindsey rolled her eyes. "I am not afraid of flying," she said between her teeth. "I simply don't like turbulence."

The plane jerked again and Lindsey grabbed her seat arms, shooting Mark a warning look. "There's a big difference."

Mark smirked. "If you say so, sweetheart."

"Ohhhhhh," she growled. "Anyway, you didn't answer my question. Did you know you wanted to leave Paxton with absolute certainty?"

Mark's expression grew serious as he thought about her question. It was time to tell her about the past. "I didn't want to leave, Lindsey. Your father gave me no option."

Her eyes filled with a million questions. "I offered to buy your father out." Mark held up a hand. "Nothing hostile about it, I promise." He paused to see her reaction. When she nodded her understanding, he continued, "We agreed on the financial aspect of things, but when it came to other things, it got hairy."

"What other things?"

"He wanted certain partners guaranteed certain things," Mark said grimly. "I couldn't do it. The partners in question were ones I didn't even want to keep around."

Lindsey understood. "So what happened? Did you pull out or did he?"

Mark put two fingers to his temple. "I did. We argued. It got nasty, and I just finally had enough."

"I see," Lindsey said. "So you wanted Paxton."

Mark eyed her, trying to understand what motivated her words. "I thought I did, but when I left—it felt right." He paused, thinking back on the past. "When it came down to it, I decided Paxton wasn't supposed to be a part of my future. When you showed up on my doorstep, it was hard to fathom returning."

"And now?" she asked.

Her short questions were making him nervous. How was she feeling about him and the past? Had Edward planted

ideas in her head? "All I know is how important you've become to me, Lindsey." He took her hand. "I came back for
you and no other reason. I want you to know that with certainty. I need to know you believe me."

Lindsey looked into his eyes, and he saw her soften, yet
she didn't reach out to him. "I know. I believe you."

He'd hoped she'd say more. He stared at her, searching
for any underlying feelings. Finally, he said, "Good."
Forcing himself to sit back in his seat, to not press her, he
closed his eyes. Her walls were still there, and as many
times as he had promised himself he'd be patient, he wasn't
feeling it at that very moment.

An hour later, air laced with a tension that had seemed
to sprout out of nowhere, they were in his car, heading towards his apartment. "Mark, where are we going?"

He stared at the road as he answered. "To my place."

She cleared her throat. "Aren't you forgetting to take me
home?"

He peered at her from the corner of his eye. "No, I'm
not. I have no intention of taking you home."

She slapped her hands in her lap. "Mark, I have no
clothes. I need to go home."

His response was immediate and clipped. "We'll go by in
the morning."

"I don't want to have to deal with it in the morning."
Her voice was sharp.

He wanted to insist, to bully her, to do anything possible
to get her to do things his way. He counted in his head,
willing himself to calm. This was Lindsey. Pushing would
get him further away from her. They pulled to a stoplight,
and he turned to her, a soft plea in his voice. "I don't want
to give you up for the night, Lindsey."

He watched her expression go from anger to understanding. "I need clothes," she said softly.

"We can either go get your stuff and take it to my place or I can stay at yours."

Lindsey smiled, laughing with her defeat, but clearly not unhappy about it. "Fine, your place. Mine doesn't have much since it's temporary."

Her words took a bit of his satisfaction. He didn't want New York to be anything but permanent for her. "It's settled then. We will get your clothes and you will come home with me."

"Okay."

Mark took her hand and raised it to his lips, kissing it softly. "Thank you." And then he added, "I would never have done your father wrong."

She looked at him, her eyes wide. "I know that."

"But yet you've barely spoken to me since I told you about the firm."

"I'm sorry," she said. "It's not you. I just hate the way things are with my father. He's on my mind."

Mark reached over and took her hand. "He'll be okay."

"I hope so."

He knew there was something else. "What is it, Lindsey?"

She looked at her lap. "Just trying to figure out what to do with the firm. That's now clear as day."

"It'll work out," he said, because it was better than nothing.

He didn't know what to say to her. Yes, he did.

Stay.

The minute Lindsey walked into her apartment she knew someone had been in it. She stopped dead in her tracks just inside the foyer, making Mark run into the back of her.

"Hey, what are you doing?" His hands went to her shoulders to keep from knocking her down.

"Someone has been in here." The phone calls were back in her mind. Was it the same person who had been in her house? Worse, could it . . . She cut off the thought, afraid to even think it in her head. No. It wasn't. This was New York. Anyone could have broken into her place.

"What?" he asked in amazement. "How can you know?"

Lindsey shot him a look. "I make my living knowing things like this."

Mark held his hands up. "Sorry," he said. "Let me re-phrase." But he didn't. "How do you know?"

"One, I smell cologne." She shivered. The thought of someone being in her apartment made her hair stand on end. She moved to the table a few steps away and pulled out the drawer, removing her gun, which she had left behind. She hadn't wanted to deal with it at the airport.

"Shit," Mark said. "What are you doing?" he asked.

"Checking it out," she said shooting him a reproachful look.

"Give me the damn gun and stand outside," he ordered.

"No, Mark—"

He glared at her. She glared at him. "This is not up for discussion, Lindsey. Give me the damn gun, and don't you dare ask if I know how to use it."

Lindsey stared at him and then finally handed him the gun. She didn't doubt he could handle the weapon. She just didn't like having to let him. If he had been anyone else, she wouldn't have. "I'm not happy about this."

Mark took the gun. "I'll be back. Don't move."

"You're two seconds from me taking the gun back."

He turned without saying another word, walking towards the other room. Lindsey could barely stand waiting on him, and was about a second from going after him, when he returned. "Well?"

"It's all clear," he said, "but you're right, someone was in your bedroom. Better call the police."

Lindsey stared at him. "What does that mean?" He looked like he didn't want to tell her, appearing to stall as he handed her back her gun. She put it in her purse. Something told her she wanted it near. "Mark? Are you going to answer me?"

He let out a loud breath. "Your sheets are rumpled and lingerie is flung everywhere."

Lindsey could feel the color drain out of her cheeks. "What?" she gasped.

Mark's tone was grim. "You said you smelled cologne? Is it familiar?"

Lindsey nodded, still trying to make this all seem real in her mind. "But I can't place it."

Mark put his hand on her back and urged her to step into the apartment. "Call Steve and have him come over." Then he had a better thought. "Why don't I call him and you sit down and get your bearings back."

"I'm fine really. This doesn't seem real." On second thought, "But yeah, okay, you call Steve."

She followed Mark into the living room and sat down. She was thankful she had let Mark search her place. Finding the bed a mess firsthand might have been too much. Something inside her was certain this wasn't some freak break-in. This was about the phone calls. . . . and about Hudson.

She knew it was him, the killer, the rapist: the crazy man who had invaded her life in far too many ways.

The realization hit her like a two by four. Her insides felt like they started to shake, and she felt a coldness creep into her limbs, taking over her mind. She hardly remembered giving Mark the number to call Steve. The deep rumble of Mark's voice as he spoke to Steve barely registered.

"He's on his way." Lindsey heard the words, but somehow they seemed to be in a tunnel, muffled and far away. Mark's hand was on her leg, warm and comforting. "Lindsey?"

Jarring herself back to reality she blinked twice and then cleared her throat. "Ye . . ." She couldn't quite get her voice back. "Yes?"

"Why do I know you're not telling me something?" He was searching her face, his eyes probing.

Her mouth and lips were dry. She swallowed. "It's just a feeling I have."

"Talk to me. What feeling?"

She could barely get the words out. "It's him."

His response was to sit down beside her and pull her close. He held her, not saying a word, and she was so glad. Talking wouldn't have helped right now. She needed to calm down first. They sat there for several long minutes before Mark spoke. "It's not safe for you to stay alone."

Lindsey looked up at him. "I was going home with you anyway."

He looked down at her with concern etched in his every feature. His brown eyes burned with emotions so intense Lindsey could feel them like a touch of his hand. "Yes, but you can't stay here alone until this guy is caught."

Painfully, she accepted the truth. She was going to be under lock and key until this guy was caught. Between Mark and Steve, they would watch her like hawks. "I know."

He took her hand in his and pressed her palm against his mouth. "I know how difficult this is for you. I want you to stay with me where I know I can keep you safe. On the other hand, I don't want you to feel pressured—but you have to stay somewhere safe."

Lindsey forced a smile. There was no question she wanted to be with him. "I'll stay with you."

A knock on the door had Mark pushing to his feet. Lindsey followed, eager to see Steve and start solving this. Just moving, getting into action, was helping her get herself pulled back together again.

Lindsey answered the door while Mark hung back a little. Steve greeted her with a strong hug that almost squeezed the air out of her chest. He was worried. With him was his partner Garth, and Lindsey waved to him over Steve's shoulder.

"Hi Garth." He had soft gray eyes, understanding and calm. She liked that about Garth. He was a good match for Steve. Both were good guys but with opposite demeanors. Garth tended to take things in, silent for the most part. Steve on the other hand was a jump-in and make-a-splash kind of guy. Not as extreme as Lindsey, but enough so that even when he complained about her off-the-wall tactics, he didn't refuse to go along for the ride.

Steve pulled back. "You okay?"

Nodding, Lindsey said, "I'm fine."

Mark had moved to stand directly behind Lindsey. He quickly introduced himself to Steve and Garth, sparing no time before getting down to business, filling them in on what he'd found. Within half an hour, Lindsey's apartment had turned into a madhouse of activity.

Lindsey stood back, watching as items were dusted for prints and bagged.

Watching had her on edge. She felt as if her life was one big whirlwind she couldn't control. When Steve and Mark asked her to go have coffee with them, she agreed. They needed to talk, and it would be easier someplace else. Garth was more than capable of seeing things through at her place.

Once they were at the coffee shop, she settled into a chair between Mark and Steve. Funny how Steve had once been the only man she trusted. Now she included Mark on her trust list.

"I just got assigned the Williams case," Steve said, resting his foot on his knee. "The FBI was called in some time back, but it was considered a slam-dunk. The agent involved is heavy into another case right now. I asked some questions, got permission to look at the case a bit closer. So let's compare notes."

Lindsey told them about her field visits. "I think the owner of the Pink Panther is a good suspect."

"Not the boyfriend?" Steve asked.

"Ex-boyfriend," Lindsey amended, "and I'm not ruling him out. At this point, how can we rule anyone out?" She had an idea. "Seems to me we are in a position of power."

Both men perked up. "How so?" Mark asked.

"I'm the trump card," she said. "The perfect bait."

Mark and Steve chimed in at the same time. "Oh, no."

"No way," Mark insisted. "Not even considering this option."

"It makes sense," Lindsey said firmly, refusing to have her idea dismissed. "I can't sit around and wait to be attacked." She glared at both men. "Correction, I won't."

Mark took a deep breath, his tension evident. "No way, Lindsey. We are not using you as bait."

Steve cleared his throat. "Both of you, please, hear me out." Dropping his leg off his knee to the floor, Steve leaned forward. "I called and spoke to a profiler on my way over here. I figured we are dealing with different circumstances than what we thought in the past. So I thought maybe some new insight was needed. The guy I talked to didn't know the case, so I explained the general points." Steve sighed. "He gave me his off-the-record opinion." He hesitated, as if he wasn't sure he should continue.

"Well?" Lindsey prodded, suddenly feeling more anxious than before.

Steve's face was grim. "He called this guy a 'lust killer.'"

Lindsey wasn't getting the point. "We knew that. He kills for the sexual high."

"Right," Steve said, "but you didn't think that fit Hudson. At the time he wasn't a killer."

Lindsey nodded. "True."

"The profiler said lust killers start out small, like Hudson raped and didn't murder, but once they crossed the line, they get off on the thrill of the kill and can't stop."

"Which fits if we are dealing with one man," Mark offered.

"We are," Lindsey said with confidence.

"Okay, here's where this gets sticky," Steve said, eyeing Lindsey. "I asked about this fixation on you."

"I wouldn't call it a fixation," she argued.

"It is," Steve said, dismissing her words. "The profiler said it is common for the killer to want to get involved with one of the investigators, often even giving them tips."

"Because deep down they want to get caught, right?" Mark asked.

"Exactly," Steve agreed. "The fact that Lindsey resembles the victims complicates matters. He may actually be confused about what he wants from her, using her as his link to the investigation and hunting her at the same time."

"Hunting . . . do you have to use that word?" Lindsey asked.

"Candy-coating isn't going to get us anywhere. I think you're a target."

Steve looked at Mark. "You won't like this, but as I talk this through, I think using Lindsey as bait is an option. She's already a walking, talking victim. Better to take this bull by the horns."

"There has to be another way," Mark said, his face etched with stress.

"Mark, this is a great opportunity to catch this guy before he kills again. God, every time I think about this thing being pushed under the rug and an innocent man being jailed, I get more and more livid."

Steve eyed Lindsey. "You think it was Greg's famous hunt for the U.S. District Attorney's seat?"

"Oh, yeah," Lindsey said firmly. "To think I almost married the man."

Steve sighed. "Figures. Anyone who cares about his political career more than catching a killer has a dark side himself."

Her apartment had smelled like her, all soft and sweet. He'd needed to feel close to her. But it just hadn't been enough. He needed more. He needed her. He couldn't wait much longer. It had been far too long, this time they had spent apart.

She was the only perfect one. Her ivory skin, her green eyes. Ah, her eyes. He couldn't wait to stare into them, and see her respond to him. And respond she would. She would be the only one who saw him for what he was. Who knew he was special. Because she was his everything.

No. He couldn't wait. The darkness was too intense, too

consuming. He had to have her. She would make him better. Right. Even alive.

It was time.

It had been a long, sleepless night.

Lindsey stepped into her office dressed in a black skirt and a sheer floral pink shirt with a matching pink belt. Far more casual than usual, she didn't have many options considering most of her clothes were dirty, and crammed in her suitcase. Work attire was out of the question since she hadn't taken any professional clothes with her to Vegas.

Mark had meetings all morning, and Lindsey resigned herself to do phone work rather than her preferred method of hitting the pavement. Midmorning Steve called and confirmed her suspicions. The Hudson DNA had indeed been hair.

Hanging up with Steve, she struggled with a deep feeling of anger. So many dead women. Two innocent men punished for horrendous crimes they didn't commit. Publicly these men had been annihilated, labeled as killers. Shoving her chair back, she pushed to her feet. She was going to see Greg, damn him and all of his political agendas. In her book, he was a killer himself. People died because of his greed.

Grabbing her purse, she rushed through her door and bumped smack into Maggie. "Oh, sorry," Lindsey said. "I didn't see you."

"I'm fine, dear." She glanced at Lindsey's purse.

Lindsey followed her gaze. "I'm going out for a while."

Maggie's expression filled with a combination of surprise and concern. "Is that wise?"

Lindsey rolled her eyes. Mark had been wagging his

tongue. "I'll be fine. If Mark asks, tell him I went to see Greg."

Not giving her time to say another word, Lindsey made fast tracks to the elevator. Once she was in the lobby, she waited impatiently for a taxi. The doorman was struggling. Fearful Mark might come chasing after her, Lindsey took off on foot, with her destination the subway. Once there, she found herself more nervous than she wanted to be. She sat in a corner, searching the other riders' faces, looking for signs they might be the killer. She couldn't shake the feeling of being watched.

"Damn it," she mumbled under her breath. Mark was making her crazy. He was so damn nervous, he had her on edge. She'd end up afraid of her own shadow if she wasn't careful. She'd dealt with plenty of criminals.

The car screeched to a halt, and Lindsey hopped to her feet, eager to escape confinement. She walked through the subway station, refusing to give into the urge to glance over her shoulder. Pausing as she stepped onto the street, she let out a sigh of relief. The sun was bright, blinding in fact, but its warmth signaled wide open space, and her escape from below.

Determination in her steps, she walked towards Greg's office. She wanted the truth and she intended to get it.

Mark ran a hand through his already-tousled hair as he approached Maggie's desk and handed her the documents he'd edited. "I'm sorry, Maggie, but I made more changes."

Maggie smiled with her normal good nature. "Not a problem."

Mark gave her a half smile, stress etched in his features. Being away for several days had loaded him down. But it was well worth it. "Thanks, Maggie. You're a doll." He started to turn away.

"Mark," Maggie said, her voice a bit hesitant.

Mark registered the oddness of her voice and turned to face her again. She was wringing her hands together, looking everywhere but in his eyes. "What is it, Maggie?" he encouraged gently. "You know you can tell me anything."

She nodded. "I know. I just hate to get in the middle of things. Lindsey—"

Mark stiffened. "Lindsey what?"

She let out a long breath. "She went out—"

"What?" Mark demanded, suddenly so tense he thought he might explode.

She gulped. "Yes, and she told me to tell you if you asked, but I didn't think I should wait."

"Where?"

"To see Greg."

Mark said a choice curse word under his breath. It took him several seconds to calm down enough to think straight. Damn, he didn't have time to chase her all over town. But she could be in danger. He cursed again and focused on Maggie, his mind made up. "Cancel my appointments."

Maggie sighed. "I'll do it. Sorry, Mark."

Mark grimaced. "You did the right thing by telling me."

Chapter Thirteen

Lindsey stood silently in Greg's door.

Greg was sitting at his desk, head tilted down as he studied a file.

Lindsey stood silently at his door, assessing him. He was a handsome man, there was no question. His sense of style was classy, his body muscular, his shoulders broad. But there was something empty and cold about him.

Delicately she cleared her throat. His head jerked up and his eyes narrowed. She watched him closely. His expression went from calculating to welcoming. Funny how she never noticed his tactics before, yet they had to have been visible.

"Lindsey," he said, waving her forward. "What a surprise." He pushed to his feet and rounded the desk, his eyes making a quick perusal down her body.

He rested his hip on his desk as she moved, putting a chair between them. He was already too close for comfort.

His eyes were shrewd. He knew what she had done. "So, what do I owe the pleasure of the visit?"

Never one to mince words, Lindsey went for the jugular, just as she had in the courtroom. "I went to Vegas, Greg." She watched for his reaction.

He didn't even blink. "Oh?" he said. "I'm surprised you managed time for play while running the firm."

Lindsey shook her head from side to side, disgust lacing the action. "Please don't insult my intelligence by playing games, Greg. We both know what I found while I was in Vegas."

If it weren't for the muscle that jumped in his jaw, she would never have known how angry he was. The man was made for politics. "The only games I want to play with you, Lindsey, are between the sheets."

His words were meant to rattle her. A sorry method, low down and dirty. Lindsey almost laughed, despite the flashbacks to their past. "I can only be thankful those days are over." The words were out before she could stop them. She felt them with so much intensity they had simply spilled from her lips.

An evil smirk appeared on his lips. "I don't believe you. You liked it, and you know it." His eyes traveled down her legs in a slow, penetrating gaze that made her skin crawl. "I've always had a thing for leggy blondes, darling, and you certainly fit that bill."

His crudeness floored her. This was a new side of Greg. She ignored his comment. "You knew the Vegas murders were connected to the local cases."

"I knew no such thing," he said, but his arms crossed in front of his body. A defensive stance.

Her tone alone accused. Her words were like knives. "It didn't serve your political agenda, so you covered up the connection."

He laughed, but it sounded bitter. "You're barking up the wrong tree." He paused and narrowed his eyes at her. "Kind of like you did with Hudson."

Lindsey gave him a level gaze. "Nice try, but I know they're all connected. I was right about Hudson, and you know it as well as I do."

He pushed off the desk and took a step towards her. Lindsey automatically moved a little farther behind the chair. "You're getting a little too cocky for your own good, Lindsey."

She studied him, trying to read his words. "What does that mean, Greg?" she asked. "It sounds like a threat."

He took another step, but this time she forced herself to stand still. The door was open. She was safe. The thought hit her like a punch in the stomach. Why would Greg be dangerous? But her instincts said he was. As if to confirm the truth, he said, "You don't want to cross me."

Lindsey refused to back off. The victims and their families deserved justice. "You cost lives with your little oversight. I think the press would be very interested."

He moved swiftly, so swiftly that he was holding her arms before she knew what was happening. "Do it, and I can assure you the press will get an earful about Paxton. I'll be sure your daddy is ruined."

Shock and anger twisted in her gut. It was hard to believe she had ever been with this man. She responded in a low voice, through clenched teeth. "Get your hands off me."

He reached up and ran a finger down her cheek. "Aw, but you like my hands, now don't you, Lindsey?" He moved as if he might kiss her.

Lindsey turned her head to the side and tugged at her arm.

"Let her go."

Relief washed over Lindsey at the sound of Mark's voice. One look at his tense jaw, dark eyes, and tightly drawn body told her he was ready for a fight. Greg dropped her arm as if burned, turning to face Mark. His actions spoke of nervousness, but his voice was cool. "Well, well, the cavalry is here. Hot on her trail, are you, Mark?"

Mark's gaze settled on Greg's face in an unblinking

stare. "What exactly were you trying to prove, or do you make a habit of manhandling ladies?" he said through clenched teeth, not showing any emotions on his carefully masked face.

Greg's lips twitched. "I was simply renewing an old friendship."

Lindsey wanted to say something, but it was clear this had become a battle of wills between the two men. She walked to Mark's side, but he never took his eyes off Greg. She managed a voice that was remarkably steady. "Greg was warning me not to cross him or he would ruin Paxton."

Mark still had Greg locked in a cold stare. "Is that so?"

"Just a conversation between friends," he explained. "We were just saying how dangerous it could be to get into media wars. She made her point, and I demonstrated mine." He smiled with smug satisfaction. "Quite effectively I believe."

Mark was silent for a long moment, as if calculating his move or calming his temper. Lindsey wasn't sure which. "We all know what has gone down, so let's make this simple," Mark said, a bite to his tone. "Drop the charges against Williams and make this easy on us all."

Greg crossed his arms, back in his defensive posture. "Not gonna happen."

Mark inclined his head. "Then we'll see you in court."

Mark turned to leave, followed by Lindsey, and Greg spoke to his retreating back. "The media war won't be friendly. Keep that in mind."

Mark turned slowly. "No, you keep that in mind. Don't underestimate my ability to come out on top."

Lindsey followed Mark out the door, thinking of the ease at which his arrogant exterior slipped into place. It wasn't a show, though she knew he had a much softer side.

She'd witnessed it firsthand. He really believed he was better than most, and with a sigh of resignation, Lindsey thought he probably was. Not that she would ever tell him that.

Calming now, she started to process the events that had just played out. She stopped walking. Mark stopped with her as if he had been monitoring her footsteps. He looked at her expectantly.

"Why are you here?" she demanded.

He stared at her as if she had lost her mind. "This is not the time or place for this conversation."

Who made him the almighty deciding factor? "I think it is."

He reached for her arm but she jerked out of his grasp and pointed at him. "Don't."

He surprised her by moving so close their bodies were practically touching. "I will *not* apologize for being worried about you."

"I can take care of myself. I don't need a babysitter."

"Running off alone while a killer is stalking you says different."

She glared. "Go to hell, Mark." She started to walk.

His hand snaked out, catching her arm, and turning her towards him. "I am not letting you walk out of here alone. Either walk with me or I swear to God I will throw you over my shoulder and carry you out of here."

He meant to do as he said. As much as she didn't want to go with him, she didn't want to make a scene. Her lips thinned with barely contained fury. "Fine," she said through clenched teeth.

Together they walked to the front of the building. Lindsey toyed with the idea of darting once she was on the street but decided against it. Immaturity and misplaced anger wasn't going to get her anywhere. Instead, she let Mark hail a cab.

They rode in silence, both staring out the opposite windows. Her anger turned to thoughts about the case, her anger at Mark becoming secondary. "We should call Vegas."

Mark nodded, giving her a quick look. "Yes, they have a right to know they were duped."

She nodded. The pleasure of setting the two men free was clouded by the thought of a vicious killer still being on the prowl. "There is enough evidence to at least get Hudson a new trial, and probably free Williams."

Mark turned and met her gaze. "Let's think this through. We can't alert this creep that we are onto him."

Lindsey swallowed. As much as she hated the truth to his words, she had to agree. Hudson deserved his life back, but it was more important to ensure no one else became a victim.

"We need to call Steve," Mark added.

Lindsey nodded. "I'll call and see if he can come over as soon as we get to the office."

Mark slid across the seat, his finger going to her chin. His face was so close, his expression so dark, that Lindsey's breath caught in her throat. "Don't," he said in a dangerously soft voice, "pull a stunt like this one again." Lindsey opened her mouth to protest but he cut her off. "And don't get on your high horse," he added. "This is not a game, or even a power play. This is life," he paused for meaning, "and death."

His words cut like a knife and she shivered. He was right. Death was in the air.

A single white posy in a simple vase sat on the reception desk. Without asking, Lindsey knew who it was for. And who it was from.

Mark's hands settled on her shoulders and she leaned back against him, needing the source of strength he offered. Forgotten was the argument over Greg.

Judy reached for the vase. "More flowers."

"Don't touch that," Mark said sharply. Judy recoiled, looking wounded by his tone. Mark turned Lindsey to look at him. "You okay?"

Lindsey nodded automatically. "I need to call Steve." And she turned away from Mark, needing to get to her office. She mentally searched for her composure. By the time she called Steve, she was beginning to pull herself together. Her hand was remarkably steady as she hung up the receiver.

She squeezed her eyes shut, and inhaled and exhaled several times. Her head fell back on the chair, and she tried to relax her body. She jumped as Mark leaned over her, his hands on the arms of her chair. She could hardly believe she hadn't heard his approach. "Wow," he said in a calming voice. "It's just me."

"I can't believe I didn't hear you."

Mark kneeled down in front of her, his hands sliding to her knees. "The mind has a strange way of sensing danger. I'm not dangerous to you. You have good instincts. I'm sure, had I been someone else, you would have been alert well before you were."

His words didn't support what he had said to her in the past. "But you don't believe in instinct, remember?"

Mark gave her a reassuring smile. "Not in myself, but I've learned to trust yours."

"Don't," she said flatly. "I've done nothing but get us all in trouble."

His fingers tightened on her legs. "That's far from the truth. You were right all along. If people would have listened to you, things might have been solved a long time ago. People like Greg, who hid the facts for personal gain, caused this hell."

The intercom went off. "Steve is here," Judy stated.

"Send him in," Mark said, and then returned his focus to Lindsey. "Don't start doubting yourself. We need your instincts more than ever."

Lindsey smiled but didn't say anything. Mark straightened to his full height and with his normal grace moved to the office door and opened it. Steve stood there about to knock. Mark offered him his hand. "Glad you're here."

Steve stepped into the room, his eyes on Lindsey "You can't seem to get rid of this particular case, can you?"

Garth walked through the door directly behind Steve, and shook Mark's hand. He gave Lindsey a quick nod. She tried to smile, but couldn't. "What do you think, Steve?" she said, wanting to get on with finding answers.

"I have the flower being taken to the lab right now," he said walking towards her and sitting down in a chair.

"We won't find anything though," Garth added. "You know that. No florist tag, and Judy said the delivery person wasn't more than fifteen or sixteen. Probably grabbed off the street and paid to bring it up." Garth sat in the chair next to Steve.

"Did you read the card?" Steve asked.

Lindsey swallowed back the queasiness that was lifting to her throat. She could feel the eyes of the room watching her. Steve pulled a piece of paper and slid it on the desk in front of her. "I wrote down what it said. The lab will, of course, need the actual card."

She read it in silence, Mark walking behind her to lean over her shoulder.

Ring around the rosy
Pocket full of posies
Ashes, ashes they all fall down.
I knew you would come back. Tonight we celebrate.

Lindsey pressed her palms on the desk, trying to hide the way they shook. Mark squeezed her shoulder in silent support.

Steve reached for the piece of paper as if he was afraid Lindsey would read it again. "His fixation on you is confirmed."

Lindsey's hand closed down on the paper. "No. Do you understand what he is saying . . ." She looked around the room. *"Tonight we celebrate.* He plans to kill another woman."

"Tonight," Mark said.

"But not you," Garth said quietly.

Lindsey focused on Garth. "How do you know?"

"Instincts," he said. "You're not the only one who follows them. It's not you. He's toying with you."

Steve looked at Lindsey. "The words 'ashes to ashes' and the choice of the posy are both symbolic of death."

"What are the chances he will harm Lindsey?" Mark asked.

Garth responded again, "I don't think she's in immediate danger. Right now he appears to be enjoying the game."

"But," Steve interjected, "we can't take chances." He jabbed a finger at the note. "He could be talking about Lindsey."

"Either way," Lindsey said, "he plans to kill again tonight."

"Any evidence found at the apartment?" Mark asked.

Steve looked at Mark. "Nothing helpful, I'm afraid."

Lindsey's mind was racing. "He'll go to the Pink Panther to choose his victim. I'm sure of it."

"It fits," Steve said. "The question is, will he expect us to be there?"

Steve looked from Mark to Lindsey. "Will he, Lindsey?"

Lindsey thought a minute. "If he's been watching me, which we have to assume he has, then yes. He knows I have been there and that I know it's his place." She paused. "He knows I know."

Mark shook his head. "It's going to be impossible to catch the guy. He probably picked the victim weeks ago. I can't believe he will grab her at the Pink Panther."

Steve replied, "He might. These guys get bolder and bolder."

Lindsey tapped her fingers on the desk. "We need to throw him a curve ball."

The room fell silent while everyone seemed to consider her words. "Me," Lindsey said, unable to think of anything else. "I'm the curve ball. The last thing he will expect is for me to come walking into the Pink Panther. His attention will turn."

"Oh, no, forget it!" Mark declared, his face etched with tension. "You are not going to be the lure for some psychotic killer."

Lindsey bit back the nasty retort that formed on her lips. He was just worried. "Mark," she said. "We're talking about stopping this guy once and for all. I'm trained to deal with this kind of thing. That other woman he plans to kill isn't."

Garth's eyes were alert but he kept quiet. Steve exchanged a glance with him and then gave Mark a level stare. "Look, I know how worried you are, but Lindsey is a trained professional."

Mark started to protest, but Steve held his hands up stop-sign fashion. "Wait," he said. "Hear me out." Mark exhaled, his eyes hot with anger. Steve continued, "Lindsey is more to me than a job. She's a friend. I don't like this one bit, but it makes sense. We need to save lives."

Mark practically yelled his response. "She's a damn target for a serial killer." He walked to the window, giving them all his back. As if he needed distance to calm himself.

Lindsey and Steve stared at one another. "Why don't I go back to my office and give you two time to talk." Steve pushed to his feet, followed by Garth. "Call me when you make a decision, but we don't have much time."

Lindsey nodded. "We'll call you soon."

The two men left without another word, pulling the door shut behind them. Mark kept his back to the room. Lindsey approached him and wrapped her arms around his waist, laying her head on his back. "Thanks for worrying about me."

Mark turned to face her, his hands on her waist. "Please don't do this."

She cupped his face with her palm and he rubbed his jaw against her hand. "Mark—"

"You're going to, aren't you," he said, taking her hand in his.

She gave him an understanding look. "I have to. Other people could die if I don't."

"There has to be another way."

She tried to make him feel better. "I'm a trained professional, and if it will make you feel better, I will tell them if you aren't in the observation van I won't do it."

He nodded. "I definitely want to be with you."

Lindsey gave him an understanding smile. "We better go to Steve's office."

Mark cursed. "I have to be in court in an hour. It won't take long, but nevertheless, I have to go." He paused. "I don't like the idea of you going anywhere alone right now."

"Mark—"

He raised a staying hand. "I know," he said. "You can protect yourself. You're a trained professional."

"I'll meet you at Steve's. Call me when you get out of court."

As soon as Mark was gone, Lindsey grabbed her purse and headed out the door.

She needed to go by her apartment and grab a few things. It had been days since she had restocked. She needed clothes desperately. Digging her cell out of her purse, she dialed Steve's desk, figuring he was already back in his office. "Bryant here."

"Oh, Garth, hey. Is Steve around?"

"I'm not sure where he went. He was just here."

"Oh," she said. "Then will you tell him I am stopping by my apartment and then I'll be there. Mark is in court, so he may or may not join us."

"Not a problem. I'll pass things along. Be careful out there on your own."

Lindsey grunted. "Yeah, yeah, I know. I'm a trained professional, remember?"

He laughed. "Yeah, I know. We all know, but this guy is good at what he does too," he reminded her. "Just keep that in mind."

Seconds later she ended the call and the coddling which seemed to be coming at her from all directions. Deciding against a cab, she took off walking. It would clear her head and give her time to think. Mulling over the investigation made the walk go by quickly. Before she knew it, she was hitting the elevator button to her floor. A few minutes later she entered her apartment, tossed her purse on the entrance table, and headed to the refrigerator. No way was she going to think about *him* being here. She refused to be intimidated. A cool drink was in order after her brisk walk. Grabbing a bottle of water, she tipped her head back, letting the cool liquid soothe her throat and body.

Stepping into her bedroom, she began pulling items out of her drawer, her eyes avoiding the bed. Suddenly, this didn't seem like such a great idea. She wanted to get out of there and fast. She started to turn, eager to grab a suitcase and go.

All of a sudden she was off balance, pulled backwards as a large hand closed over her mouth. This was it, here and now; she was the next chosen victim. The note had been about her. Panic seized her, as she felt something slip over her head, covering her face, a sweater cap perhaps. She didn't want to die. She didn't. Willing herself to calm, to remember her training, she forced herself to take even breaths but the cloth over her face took all the air. The hot breath of her attacker was on her face, his mouth so near, his hands on her body.

Her skin crawled with his touch, her stomach twisting. He hadn't spoken . . . she wanted to hear his voice, to know if she knew this person. He tugged her against his body with such force, she grunted from the impact. A second later, she felt her back hit the mattress.

No! She squirmed, not wanting to be trapped, kicking and punching. But then he was on her, one of his long legs wrapped around her left leg, his hands holding her hands over her head. Before he could trap her second leg, she brought her knee up and rammed it into his groin. He gasped, and for a split second he let her hands go, and that was all the time she needed. She reached for the nightstand, grabbing the phone and smashing it into his head. He hollered out and she rolled off the bed, frantically yanking the cap off her head.

Her only thought was to get to her gun, no looking back, no worry about his identity. She needed her gun. She made it to the bedroom door before her feet came out from under her. His grip on her ankle so tight it made her cry out. But then she hit the floor, palms flat, her body feeling the jolt from head to toe. Twisting around, she intended to kick him in the face, but she momentarily froze.

It was Garth.

He laughed, clearly enjoying her shock, his hand inching up her leg. The pure evil in his eyes brought her back to reality. She kicked him in the face as hard as she could, high heels and all. "Bitch," he yelled, blood gushing from his forehead. He reached for her free foot, trying to get it before she kicked him again.

She reached for a corner lamp and pulled it on top of him, kicking at the same time. His hand slipped off her leg, and she scrambled forward in a crawl. But he was fast. He shoved the lamp aside, and grabbed hold of her shoulders. "I like it when you fight, Lindsey." She felt his body press into hers, his hips against her backside. She wanted to throw up. "We're going to have fun, you and I."

She shook her head, fighting her emotions, her fear. "Why? Why are you doing this?" she whispered through trembling lips.

"Because I want you," he said in a taunt, his lips by her ear. "And I am going to have you. I've waited forever for you. I even tried to replace you, but those other women just weren't good enough." He licked the side of her face. She was trembling, and she tried to stop. Something told her he got off on her fear.

"You're sick," she whispered.

"No, I'm smart. I kept you guessing. Admit it." His words were filled with pride so sickening Lindsey felt her head spinning. "You connected the murders, but never to me."

She wanted to know the truth. "Vegas? How did you manage those killings when you were here?"

He smiled. "Ah, but I wasn't. I took a leave of absence to care for my poor, sick grandma in Texas."

Lindsey shut her eyes tightly. "And Hudson, you planted the DNA evidence."

"Yep, nice inside track I have, don't you think?"

Her palms pressed into the floor. She had to get away. "You'll never get away with this."

"I have so far." He moved, rising to his feet, and she thanked the good lord to have him off her. He yanked her to her feet and pushed her back against the wall, hands over her head.

"I hope you burn in hell," she spat as she struggled against his legs, trying to keep hers free.

He laughed. "You wound me, Lindsey. I think you should kiss me and make me feel better."

No matter how hard she tried to fight the panic that was welling up inside, or the nausea at the thought of his lips on hers, she couldn't. She twisted her head to the side and he moved his hand into her hair and yanked her head backwards. "Uh-uh, I want my kiss."

Tears welled in her eyes as his mouth came towards her. She wanted to sink into the ground and disappear. Why hadn't she listened to Mark when he warned her about going out alone? And then his mouth was on hers, and her fighting instincts kicked in. The instant his tongue passed her teeth, she bit down as hard as she could.

"Ah!" he yelled, pulling back in shock as his hand went to his mouth. He backhanded her. "I'm bleeding, you bitch."

Taking advantage of one free hand, Lindsey hit him in the face and twisted to try and get away. He pulled her by the hair and then slapped her again. This time harder. "Stop fighting and make this easy on yourself."

Dragging her by her hair, he yanked her back to the bed. Lindsey cried out, feeling as if her hair was coming out by the roots. She kicked him, and he hit her again. Pain lashed through her cheek and eye, making her shake from head to foot. Or maybe it was from a combination of fear and adrenaline. Darkness threatened to take over as spots appeared in front of her eyes.

In her head, she yelled. No!

She wasn't ready to die.

Standing in front of the courthouse, sticky with perspiration, Mark dialed Lindsey's cell phone, trying to remain calm.

This was his third attempt with no answer. Pacing the sidewalk he felt tense, agitated, afraid. Where was she? Something was wrong, really wrong. He felt it in every inch of his body. Maggie had confirmed Lindsey had gone to Steve's but Steve hadn't seen her.

He dialed Steve again. "She's not answering her phone, home or cell. I've got a bad feeling about this."

Steve cursed into the phone. "I'm going to head to her apartment since it's only a few blocks from where I'm at. But then—"

"Just go, and I'll meet you there. Just be careful. I'll be

about ten minutes behind you."

Mark hung up and started to run down the street, feeling his pulse pounding in his temple. Wherever Lindsey was, she needed him, he could feel it. It felt like forever, though it was only minutes, before he arrived at her apartment. He took the stairs two at a time, not bothering with the elevator.

Standing in front of her door, he raised his hand to knock, but then dropped it. Instead, he tested the doorknob. When it turned, he knew it wasn't good. He fought the urge to run through the door, and yell Lindsey's name. Pushing the door open, he tried to see what he could hear.

Then Lindsey screamed.

Mark took off running, headed towards her voice, desperate to get to her. Red-hot rage exploded inside when he saw the man on top of her. Lunging forward, he reached for the man's shirt, yanking him off of her body. "You son of a bitch!" he screamed as he flung him to the ground.

Mark's breathing was erratic as he took in Lindsey's bruised face, pain wrenching at his heart.

A low growl from the attacker drew his attention. Realization hit with a bitter sting. "Garth?"

The other man let out a burst of harsh laughter, pushing to his feet and lunging at Mark all in one move. His arms wrapped around Mark's waist, as he sent him stumbling backwards. Mark managed to get his arms under the other man's, and pry him off. Garth countered by throwing a punch, but Mark managed to block it.

Pure adrenaline powered Lindsey now. Her mind went back to her options. Gun. In purse by door. Had to get to her gun. She kept repeating her objective in her head, afraid the fog would take over. Stumbling, fighting dizziness, she managed to make it through the room and into the hall. She stumbled, falling to her knees, tears streaming down her cheeks. Crawling the rest of the way, she found her purse and dumped it.

The front door burst open, and then Steve was there, squatting down beside her. "Oh, God," he said. "Are you okay?"

She nodded, swallowing a sob as she grabbed his arm. "Help Mark. It's Garth, Steve. It's Garth."

Steve frowned, but he acted without haste as his training dictated, pulling his gun and rounding the corner with stealth-like speed. Steve holstered his gun as he took in the two men going hand to hand. He might shoot Mark. He had no option but to do this the physical way.

He moved forward, yanking Garth from behind just as Mark jabbed him with a right hook to the face. Garth toppled over on Steve, knocking him to the ground. In a split second, Garth flipped around and yanked Steve's gun from his holster.

Pointing the gun at Steve, he laughed, "Too slow," he spat. "Get up." Cutting a sideways glance at Mark, he added, "One wrong move and he's dead."

"Drop the gun, Garth," Lindsey said from the doorway, her gun pointed at him.

She felt Mark's eyes. "Lindsey—"

"I'm fine Mark." But she wasn't and she knew it.

Garth sneered at her. "No you're not, darling. You're bleeding. Why don't you just hand over that gun and sit your pretty little ass down. Poppa will be right over to kiss it all better."

Mark took a step towards Garth. "You son of—"

"Call off your dog, Lindsey," Garth warned. "Or Steve's a dead man." He jabbed the gun to Steve's temple.

Mark stopped dead in his tracks. "Garth," Lindsey said stepping forward. "This little game is over. Drop the weapon."

"Or what, darling?"

"I'll shoot you."

"I doubt that."

"If you think for a minute I will hesitate, you're dead wrong."

He laughed again, the sound making Lindsey shiver. "Let's find out. How about a little game of chicken?" He shoved Steve. "Get over there beside Mark."

Lindsey kept her gun aimed at Garth. "I bet I can shoot one of them before you can manage to put me down." He smiled. "You choose which one will live and which one will die."

Garth waved the gun between Steve and Mark. Lindsey kept her gun aimed at Garth. She didn't doubt he would shoot one of them. Maybe both. He was crazy. She should shoot him before he could shoot them. But. . . . she was foggy. It was hard to think. Should she?

"Game's up, Lindsey," Steve said quietly.

Lindsey heard his words, and absorbed their meaning. He was telling her what to do. She pulled the trigger, no hesitation. A second later, Garth crumpled to the floor.

Lindsey had shot him.

Steve's words washed over Mark. He had reminded her of her training, of her only option. She had to shoot first. And Steve knew she wouldn't wilt under pressure.

Mark's eyes darted from Garth to Lindsey as he watched her lean against the wall and then slip down to the floor. Mark ran to her side, pulling her into his arms. The courage she had shown amazed him, but most of all it made him proud. She was amazing, such a combination of vulnerability and strength. She was the woman he loved and he was thankful she was alive. Losing her would have been a nightmare. Stroking her hair, he rocked her, whispering comforting words.

"He's dead," Steve said.

It was over.

Finally, after hours at the hospital, Mark carried Lindsey through his front door, her head resting on his shoulder. He had taken her to the emergency room as soon as Steve's back-up arrived. She had a concussion and a lot of bumps and scrapes. More than anything, she had the trauma of the experience.

Lindsey had turned over her weapon to the authorities, and would now be subjected to an internal investigation. Standard procedure, even though she was on leave. Still, he hated it. He didn't want this to get dragged out any longer than it had to. She deserved to put this behind her.

Ever so carefully he set her on the bed. Lindsey's eyes fluttering open. "Where are we?" she asked.

"We're home, baby," he said as he bent down and kissed her forehead.

She blinked and looked at him through swollen eyes. "I hurt all over."

"I know. You're due some more pain medicine," he told her. "Let me get you something to drink to take it with and then we'll get you undressed."

She nodded. He started to turn. "Mark?" He gave her a questioning look. "You saved my life."

He sat down on the edge of the bed. "And you returned the favor, if I remember correctly."

Her lips trembled. "I should have listened to you."

He kissed her hand, afraid of hurting her if he kissed her

anywhere else. "It's done and over. I'm just glad I didn't lose you." Emotion lodged in his throat. "Rest. I'll get your pain medicine."

"Thank you," she whispered, her eyelashes fluttering to her cheeks. "I'm so tired. So very, very tired."

"Hey, Maggie, have you seen Mark?"

"He went out for a bit, but I don't know where." She studied Lindsey's face. "That black eye is really looking better now."

Lindsey touched the spot under her left eye. "Yes, finally. Now it sorta looks like a bad birthmark."

"Gives the rest of us females a chance for once," Maggie said with a playful smile.

Lindsey snorted. "Right. You too funny."

Mark rounded the corner. "What trouble are you two cooking?"

Lindsey laughed. "That's for us to know and you to find out."

Mark moved forward, aware that his pulse was beating rapidly, tension lacing his body. He had something important to tell Lindsey. "Come to my office, and let me try and pry it out of you."

Lindsey laughed and followed Mark. Once they were in his office, Mark pushed the door shut and pulled her into his arms. "I have ways to make you talk."

Lindsey unbuttoned his jacket and dipped her hands beneath it. "Please, make me talk."

"Actually, there is something I need to talk to you about." He took a step backwards, taking her hand in his. "Come sit with me."

Mark pulled the chairs around so that he could face her. He'd taken a big step. One meant to help Lindsey let go of the past. He could only pray it was the right move. He loved her. He had no question he wanted to spend the rest of his life with her.

Lindsey touched his cheek. "What's up?"

He let out a breath. "I've given a lot of thought to you and me, and to the firm." Her eyes widened. "I know you don't want to run Paxton, and I came back on a limited timeline."

Lindsey nodded. "I know, and I appreciate what you have done for me."

Mark smiled, thinking of how things had changed between them. He wanted her to let go of the past. To choose to be with him out of desire, not pressure to run Paxton. "You have a job waiting for you in Washington."

Her voice was almost a whisper. "Yes, but you have a consulting business to get back on track."

"If I leave, it'll force you to take over, and then you'll resent me. I can't deal with that." And he couldn't. It would destroy any hope they had of a future.

Her eyes clouded. "But it's not fair for you to stay and miss out on your own business. I understand if you need to leave."

He rubbed the back of her hand with his thumb. Better to just get it all on the table. "I made an offer to buy Paxton, and this time your father accepted."

Lindsey blinked, her expression dumbfounded. "What?"

He nodded. "I don't want you to leave, but deep down I know you don't want to stay. To have you practice law here at Paxton, by my side, would make me very happy. But it would be selfish. I care enough about you to want you to be happy."

Lindsey stood up and walked to the window, placing her back to Mark. "So this is goodbye," she said without turning.

It took every ounce of willpower he possessed not to go to her. "I hope not. I want you to stay. But I can't kid myself. You left this place once, and when you returned you never intended to stay. I can't win either way things go."

Lindsey stared out, her voice shaky as she spoke. "You should have talked to me."

"Maybe," he admitted, "but I have thought about this until it felt I might go nuts. This was the only way I could make the choice yours. Now you have options. Stay or go, but follow your heart."

He heard her draw in a breath before turning around to face him. "I don't know what to say."

"Say what you feel."

"You're a good man, Mark."

Mark tried to smile, but failed. Her eyes were distant, her body stiff. His heart felt like it was being shattered into pieces. A good man. Not good enough, it seemed. He'd so hoped she would come to him. That she would choose a life with him. "You're a free woman, Lindsey."

Then afraid of what he might say next, he pushed to his feet, and strode out of the room. He had never needed air as badly as he did at that moment.

Chapter Fourteen

Three Months Later

Lindsey slipped through the doors of the elegant New Yorker Museum feeling apprehension from the top of her head clear down to her freshly manicured toes.

Already her father's retirement party was in full swing. The dance floor was filled, the tables packed. He'd made an amazing recovery, her father, nothing shy of a miracle. And Lindsey had been talking with him on the phone a lot. He'd even made amends with Mark, often talking about the great things he was doing with the firm. His turnaround was baffling, but welcome. As daughter and father, they were on the mend, and for that she was thankful.

But there was still one person she needed to connect with.

Mark.

She'd spent three long months in Washington, away from him, missing him every minute. Every day she hoped he would call. But he didn't. She'd dialed his number too many times to count, and then hung up at the last minute.

Her nightmares hadn't gone away. The dark images still woke her in the night, leaving her shaken and scared. But now she understood them. They'd never been about the murders. They were about her fear. About losing herself, her life, and her love . . . Mark.

Lindsey handed her coat to a checkperson, and eyed the

room, looking for Mark as discreetly as she could. Her hand smoothed her black satin slip dress, nervous about looking her best. She'd dressed with care, taking extra time to fix herself, wanting to look her best.

She'd come to a life-altering decision. She could only hope it wasn't coming too late. Mark was the love of her life, and she wanted to be with him. Nerves were jangling through her entire body as if she were a schoolgirl with a crush.

Taking several deep breaths, she took a moment to take in her surroundings. She had always loved the Museum, and a moment to explore its beauty would help take her outside of her anxiety. Lindsey had spent hours on the phone with Maggie planning the party. It was exciting to see how beautifully it all had come together. Surveying the room with pride, Lindsey took in the high ceilings and the dim lighting. The setting was elegant, the music soft and soothing, the tables of food delectable, even from a distance.

She sucked in a deep breath, and willed herself to step forward. She'd barely taken two steps when Maggie found her. "Lindsey," she said with a warm smile and big hug. "We've missed you."

Lindsey hugged her back, feeling the words with more emotion than expected. "It's good to be missed."

Maggie pulled back. "Have you seen Mark yet?"

Lindsey nodded apprehensively. Maggie, angel that she was, had made a point of filling her in on Mark on a regular basis. Lindsey never asked, but she darn sure listened. And Maggie was no fool. She knew Lindsey hung on every word.

"No, not yet. I just got here."

Maggie surveyed Lindsey, stepping back and inspecting her appearance. "His eyes will pop out when he sees you in that dress, sweetie."

Lindsey tried to smile, but she didn't quite make it. "We'll see," she said, and changed the subject. She was getting more nervous by the minute. "The party's lovely. You did a wonderful job."

"We did a wonderful job," she corrected. "Come," she said with a nod of her head. "Let's go see your father."

Together they maneuvered through the crowd, making their way across the room. Lindsey kept an eye out for Mark, but to her disappointment, he was nowhere in sight. Her father's table was near the front of the room. Lindsey saw him before he saw her, which gave her a moment to digest his incredible transition. He'd put on a good fifteen pounds, and his color was healthy, his smile happy.

The minute he spotted Lindsey, his eyes lit up and he pushed to his feet. Maggie grabbed Lindsey's arm to gain her attention. "I better circulate. Catch up to you in a few."

Lindsey nodded and moved towards her father. The minute she was within his reach, he pulled her into a bear hug, holding her tightly and rocking. "I missed you," he said softly.

Lindsey looked up at him, fighting back tears. She couldn't believe how good he looked. "I missed you too, Daddy."

"I want you to meet Elizabeth," he said, motioning towards a short, dark-haired woman, who pushed to her feet and smiled.

She looked familiar . . . oh my. Lindsey remembered. "Aren't you one of the nurses from the treatment center?"

She nodded and laughed, her eyes friendly and happy. "Yes, I'm the only one who would put up with your father."

Lindsey laughed, feeling herself relax ever so slightly. "Well, that makes you a saint, doesn't it?"

Edward laughed with the two women. "Lindsey, Elizabeth has agreed to be my wife."

The words hit her with such surprise she sank down into a chair. "W . . . wife?"

Elizabeth reached out and patted Lindsey's hand as Edward sat down. "Yes, but I know I can never replace your mother nor would I try. I love your father very much, and I promise to be good to him."

Lindsey looked at Elizabeth and then at her father. He had changed, and she would venture to say this woman had a lot to do with those changes. Lindsey smiled. "I'm very happy for you both." She paused. "I mean that."

"Good, because we're happy together," Edward said, as he looked at Elizabeth and smiled.

Lindsey watched the two of them, a smile turning the corners of her mouth up. No doubt, these two were in love. Her mother would want them to be happy. A rush of emotion threatened. What she shared with Mark had been special. She'd allowed fear to take it from them. "If you two will excuse me, there is something I need to do."

Edward's hand reached out and grabbed her wrist. "The last time I saw him, he was at the bar."

Lindsey swallowed and nodded. She didn't ask how he knew who she was looking for. No doubt Maggie had told him. "Thanks, Daddy," she said softly.

Standing at the bar, Mark made like a hermit. Socializing was the last thing on his mind. If it wouldn't have been downright rude, he would have passed on the party.

Shit. That was a damn lie. No way would he have passed on seeing Lindsey. It tore him up to know she was in town, but she hadn't even called him. She'd blown him off like a bad day, and it hurt like hell. He'd actually thought he might be getting over her until he heard she was coming to town. All those tucked-away emotions had roared to life, and refused to be put away.

How he was going to see her, and act unaffected, he hadn't a clue.

Why he had ever thought getting involved with Lindsey was a good idea, he didn't know. Tipping back his drink, he finished it off. Like he'd had any option. She'd had him by the balls the moment he set eyes on her. He was pitiful. There'd never been an inkling of hope for his heart. On that note, he ordered another drink. Though he wasn't a big drinker, tonight was an exception. Anything to ease the pain of the knife she had planted in his chest and kept twisting. His entire situation was ironic—no, a joke, a bad joke on him. Paxton was thriving, and he was even getting along with Edward. Hell, he'd even become great friends with Steve. A shared near-death experience tended to build friendship. Even Greg had high-tailed out of town. Everything had come together, but still he wasn't happy.

Because he missed Lindsey.

He was standing alone, looking incredibly sexy in his tuxedo. And she knew her fascination with him, her need to be with him, hadn't been imagined. Passion, hot and fierce, raced through her veins. But it was so much more than that.

She needed him in every way possible.

Her mouth grew dry, and her pulse raced dangerously fast. Nerves flip-flopped her stomach. God, how she had missed him. As if he felt her gaze, his head lifted, and their eyes locked. Oh, those eyes. They enticed her with their shrewdness—so assessing, so amazingly seductive. One look from him had always been enough to make her knees rattle. His gaze slipped down her body in a slow inspection that was hot and intimate.

For the briefest of moments, emotions flashed in his eyes, maybe even anger, but then they were gone. He pulled the shutters down, blocking what was inside from her view. Completely still, he just watched her: no smile, no welcome home. Of course, what had she expected? She'd pushed him away time and time again. She would have to go to him. It was her turn to expose herself, to risk being denied.

But he was worth it.

Slowly she stepped forward, never taking her eyes from his, not stopping until she was directly in front of him. "Hi," she whispered a bit breathlessly. Heat sizzled in the air between them despite the uncertainty of their relationship.

His eyes darkened, and for a split second, she really thought he might reject her. Silence filled the air for what felt like a lifetime. She had forgotten just how big he was, tall and broad, and incredibly masculine. Finally he spoke, "Hi, yourself." His voice was soulfully deep, a velvet perfection that gave her goose bumps.

She wanted to touch him—no, she needed to touch him. There was no option—it was a physical need, so real it was like hunger. Lindsey reached out and ran her hand down his lapel, the touch making her burn for more. "You look very handsome." And sexy as sin.

He reached up and put his hand over hers, his eyes loaded with unspoken meaning, with desire. His touch warmed her body, and made her ache. "And you look like pure temptation," he said in a voice as soft as a caress.

A slight trickle of relief filtered into her mind. At least he wasn't denying he wanted her physically. It was the encouragement she needed to step closer to him. Grasping both his lapels with her hands, she said, "Yeah?"

His voice was husky as his hands settled on her waist. "Oh, yeah."

She swallowed and wet her dry lips. His gaze dropped to her mouth, and she knew he wanted to kiss her. And, oh, how she wanted him to. It felt like forever since she had felt those sultry, warm lips on hers. "I've missed you, Mark." Her voice cracked with emotion.

Mark looked down at her, so beautiful, so everything he wanted in his life. But when would she leave him again, get scared and tuck her tail and run? Was he convenient for the night, a chance to ease her loneliness while in town? *She missed him.* The words rang in his head over and over. She had been gone for months, not one phone call, and now she suddenly missed him.

He had suffered enough heartache to last a lifetime over Lindsey. No way could he watch her walk away again. As much as he wanted to drag her off and make wild, passionate love to her, it was best to keep his distance. When she left, and surely she would, he would be screwed over again. The thought made him drop his hands to his sides.

His voice was icy. "You have a funny way of showing it."

"Mark—" Lindsey started to plead her case when the loudspeaker came on.

Maggie's voice filtered through the room. "It's time for a special tribute. If you could all gather around." She paused and there was a shuffle in the room. "Lindsey and Mark, can I get you both up here?"

Lindsey pulled her bottom lip into her teeth. Her eyes flashed with something that resembled desperation. "No," she said, surprising him as she flattened her hands on his chest. "Promise me you'll hear me out before the night is over." He stared at her, trying to get a grip on what he was feeling.

Maggie called for them again. Lindsey's eyes held a plea. "Please, Mark."

He'd never seen Lindsey seem so willing to lay herself on the line. Something in her voice, and in her actions, touched him deep inside. It wouldn't hurt to at least hear her out. Decision made, he didn't say a word, but he took her hand in his, loving the feel of her soft skin against his rough palm. He nodded towards the stage and pulled her behind him, moving quickly towards Maggie.

Lindsey couldn't breathe or think. The only thing that kept her slightly composed was the possessiveness of his hand over hers. His touch gave her comfort and hope, and she clung to it as a source of strength.

An hour later, she stepped down from the podium with Mark by her side. To her relief, he reached for her hand again. "Come dance with me," he said softly.

Lindsey didn't want to dance; she wanted to leave with him, now. She stopped walking, tugging on his hand. He turned and looked down at her, a question in his eyes. "Let's leave," she said, and then added more firmly, "now."

Slowly, a sexy grin slid onto his face as he tugged her up close and personal. "You can't run out on your father's party. Let's dance a few dances first."

Lindsey swallowed. "And then we'll leave?"

He reached out and ran his hand through her hair, a gentle caress that made her ache to feel him closer. "Yes," he said. "Then we'll leave."

"Together?" she asked, needing the confirmation as much as her next breath.

Mark chuckled. "Yes, together."

Lindsey let out a sigh and her shoulders visibly relaxed. "Okay then. Let's dance."

He led her to the dance floor, and she melted into his arms, needing his warmth, his nearness. He buried his face in her hair. "You smell good," he whispered by her ear.

Lindsey wrapped her arms around Mark's neck and pressed her body against his, wanting to be as close as their public setting would allow. "You do too," she said softly, meaning it, wishing she could get lost in everything that was Mark and forget about the party.

Their eyes locked and held. For the first time, she wasn't shaken by how easily he got to her. A simple look and he had her on fire. She wanted all he was, and all they could be together, no matter how much risk that came with. His hands slid over her hips, his touch setting her on fire, making her forget where they were.

"When are you leaving?" he asked, breaking her out of the sensual fog the music and his touch had formed.

She wet her lips, looking up at him, trying to decide how to answer. This wasn't the right place or time. She reached up and ever so gently traced his jaw line with her fingers. "Mark—"

Lindsey's father appeared by their side. "Can I have this dance?"

She looked at Mark, a desperate question in her eyes. He gave her a reassuring smile. "I'm not going anywhere. Dance with your father."

She opened her mouth to speak, and Mark rested his finger on her mouth. "I'm not going anywhere."

She nodded, trying to take comfort in his words, offering a bright smile to her father, and slipping into his arms. "You look very handsome, Daddy."

He watched her closely. "I didn't want to interrupt you and Mark. I know you have some things to work through, but I wanted to make sure I cleared the air." He paused. "He's a good man, Lindsey. I was a stubborn old man who gave him a bum rap."

Lindsey laughed. "Yes," she said. "You were."

"I just wanted to make sure none of those things I said impact how you deal with Mark."

His concern touched her deeply. Lindsey smiled. "Thank you, Daddy. This means a lot to me. More than you know." She paused, wondering what she should share. "I may be too late to resolve things. I'm not sure."

"He's crazy about you," he assured her.

She hoped he knew something she didn't. "But that doesn't make him willing to become involved with me again."

He pushed a piece of hair behind her ear. "Do you love him?"

Her expression softened. "Oh yes, I love him very much."

Edward stopped dancing. "Then go tell him. Get him away from here. Go someplace private, and make him believe it."

Pushing to her tiptoes Lindsey kissed his cheek. "Thank you, Daddy." She looked at him, amazed at the changes Elizabeth had made in him. He had been lonely, much like she had. Love had made him a new person. "Wish me luck."

She turned into the crowd, but she didn't see Mark. Panic started to build. With each passing second, her heart pounded harder against her chest. But then he was there, pulling her into a dark hallway. Mark. The man she loved. Seconds later, his mouth was covering hers, and he was kissing her with such passion, such emotion, she thought she might go up in flames. Their tongues and hands explored as they molded their bodies together in wild abandonment.

He pulled away too soon and she stared up at him, her breathing erratic.

"I want you," he admitted hoarsely.

She already knew he wanted her, but did he love her? Closing her eyes, she reached for courage. Her lashes lifted, and she looked into his eyes. "You asked me a question," she said. His gaze sharpened but he didn't say anything. "You asked when I was leaving." She paused, trying to assess his expression, but all she saw was smoldering heat and a hint of anticipation. "I used to think home was in Washington, but now I know home is where you are."

He leaned against the wall and let his head fall back, his eyes rolling shut. Fear wrapped around her heart. He didn't want her. His sudden retreat made her feel like she had been slapped. Of course, she deserved rejection, but she so didn't want it to be reality. Feeling the tingling of tears, the rush of painful emotions, she turned to leave.

Mark's hand snaked out and grabbed her wrist. When she turned, he was looking at her with an emotionless mask. "Why now?" he demanded in a low voice that seemed almost angry.

Jerking her arm away was the first thought she had, but she couldn't find the strength. She needed to be alone to think and cry. "Let me go," she whispered.

His face filled with harsh determination. "Oh, no, sweetheart. You're not getting off that easy," he said as he tugged her against his body. Lindsey refused to look up at him, choosing to stare at his chest. "Look at me, Lindsey," he demanded.

"No," she said stubbornly. "Just let me go."

"Is that what you want?" he asked harshly, but then softened his voice. "Tell me, Lindsey."

She dropped her head to his chest as the first tear streamed down her cheek. Angry at her lack of control, she swiped at it. "No," she whispered with her face buried in his shirt. Then she forced her gaze up to his. "That's not what I want, but obviously it's what you want. I told you I wanted to be with you, and you went cold on me." She wiped another tear away with a rough swipe of her hand. "I put it all on the line, as hard as that was for me, and you—"

"You put it all on the line?" he demanded. "How about me? You're the one who walked out on us, Lindsey." His eyes were dark and turbulent. "I don't want to count on you—correction—I won't count on you again and then have you turn your back on me. I can't do this again. Not like before."

And then she understood. He was afraid she was still undecided. She hadn't convinced him how serious she was. Quietly, she asked, "Remember my nightmares?" He nodded slowly, his eyes holding a question. "They weren't about the murders. I've been having them every night since I went back to Washington. At first I thought we hadn't gotten the right guy, that my subconscious mind was warning me there was still a murderer loose." She looked down and tried to calm her shaky voice by inhaling and exhaling. When she felt able, she looked back up at him and continued, "And they really were warning me, but not about what I thought. All along they were about you and me. About me being afraid of you leaving me."

He let out a heavy breath. "What are you saying, sweetheart, because I need you to be real clear with me. No guessing games and no maybes."

Her lips trembled as she spoke her heart. "I'm saying, I love you, Mark Reeves. I love you so much it hurts every minute I'm not with you."

Mark's hands cupped her cheeks. "There is no in-between this time. Are you sure?"

Tears streamed down her face. "I love you, Mark. And I want to be with you every day of my life. I even want to work by your side, if you'll let me. You were right, you know? I'm an attorney. It's what I have always wanted to be, but it took you to help me see it."

He kissed her then, so tenderly, so perfectly full of love that Lindsey felt dizzy. Before he said the words, she knew. She had known a long time, but she had been afraid. He raised his head, his knuckles softly caressing her cheek, his eyes potent with emotion as they met hers. "I love you, Lindsey Paxton."

She smiled through her tears. "You have no idea how glad I am to hear you say those words. I was so afraid I waited too long. I was such a fool, Mark." She grabbed his hand and kissed it. "I'm sorry."

"I know how you can make it up to me," he teased.

She laughed through her tears, loving how easily he made her smile. "Well, I hope it's with hot sex."

"That is the best offer of apology I've ever heard." Mark wrapped his arms around her waist, his eyes dark with emotion. "Marry me, Lindsey," he said tenderly. "Spend the rest of your life with me, and make me the happiest man alive."

Lindsey wrapped her arms around his neck. "I would be honored."

He kissed her again, a long kiss that sealed their future. "Let's elope, tonight. We'll go back to Vegas."

Lindsey stared up at him, surprised. A slow smile filled her face. "I like Vegas, and I love you, so let's do it."

About the Author

Lisa owned and operated a temporary staffing agency for over ten years, earning numerous awards. Of these achievements, the one she is most proud of is being recognized by *Entrepreneurial* magazine on the top ten growing women-owned businesses list in 1998.

The corporate world offered only limited opportunity to explore her creative side, so she began writing romantic suspense. Since starting her career, she has placed in numerous contests, including winning the *Romantic Times* Aspiring Writers Contest for her romantic suspense novel, *Hidden Instincts*.

A mother of two, she lives in Austin, Texas, where she writes on a daily basis, eagerly working on her next plot, and discovering new depths to her writing.